THE IMMERSION BOOK OF STEAMPUNK

Edited by

Gareth D. Jones

and

Carmelo Rafala

Immersion Press

Sussex, England, UK

THE IMMERSION BOOK OF STEAMPUNK

ISBN 978-0-9563924-4-2

Published in Great Britain by Immersion Press, 2011

www.immersionpress.com

Cover art by Charles Harbour

IMMERSION PRESS

Sussex, England UK

www.immersionpress.com

TABLE OF CONTENTS

Introduction

Like many of the speculative genres, a definition of steampunk is difficult to pin down. As you're reading this volume I'm guessing you ready have an idea of what it is. Before I ever became aware of the steampunk phenomenon, I loved original Victorian SF – Jules Verne, Arthur Conan Doyle et al. The chance to return to that era is irresistible. In this volume I wanted to explore the entire spectrum of what steampunk represents and to capture its essence in a selection of stories by authors with a variety of backgrounds.

I think I've succeeded in that aim. The authors we have on board range from long-time professionals to relative newcomers, published novelists, well-known names from the steampunk community, and from three continents. Their varied backgrounds shine through in the styles and settings of their tales. We have stories that contain elements of science fiction, fantasy, adventure, espionage, comedy, romance, fable, and all the while spending most of our time in the good old Victorian heartland.

Prepare to be immersed in the world of steampunk.

—Gareth D Jones

I love the way people seem to want to announce to the world—on a fairly regular basis—the death of science fiction, fantasy or any other genre that falls under the speculative umbrella. How many times have I heard such reports? Far too many to count. And each time the doomsayers have been proven wrong. Sales figures may rise and fall, but in no way is that a sign things are not well in the land of the imagination.

Take steampunk for instance. As a genre of speculative fiction, steampunk has had its shares of ups and downs. However, it is seeing a resurgence at this moment the likes not seen since cyberpunk hit the market. In fact, I will dare to say steampunk's popularity has surpassed cyberpunk in its heyday—something I am sure no one could have anticipated.

Really? someone asks. Aren't steampunk stories simply cute little tales about parasols and pistol carrying adventurers in airships, right?

Well, no. You see, steampunk is so much more than that. It has taken the most interesting time in western history—and problematic on many levels—played with it, changed it about, and asked, "What if?" What if Victorian society moved ahead with the times and did not die with the centuries, but rather *changed* the centuries to suit itself, adapting new ideas on everything from social structures to gender relations to spiritual contemplation in to its structure along the way? In many ways, steampunk is the ultimate in alternative world storytelling. I mean, as writers have the whole of human history and its possible outcomes to contemplate and draw inspiration from, it doesn't take much to see how that statement could ring true. (Well, it is *possible*, isn't it?)

So when someone cries out about the death of science fiction or fantasy or steampunk, cover your ears. Walk away. Better yet, denounce them as lunatics. Yes, dear reader, steampunk, like her other speculative siblings, is here to stay. And that suits me down to the ground.

—Carmelo Rafala

THE IMMERSION BOOK OF STEAMPUNK

Follow That Cathedral!

Gareth Owens

...and with that, Pixie dived from the open door of the Zeppelin, the air around her suddenly becoming liquid, rushing over the smooth leather of her helmet and bringing tears to her eyes.

"Always some bloody thing!" she grinned into the gale, falling headlong towards the welcoming embraces of Mother Earth and Mother Russia below.

Siberian night enveloped her, storm filled frozen darkness, cloud shrouded full moon, and below, the steam powered lightning of *The Iron Czar*. A hissing, glowing, monster of a train, three storeys high, and even longer than the leviathan *Fourteen Bags of Mischief* hanging above.

Pixie saw the orange furnaces erupting sparks through the twin stacks, as if Hephaestus himself stoked on the imperial railways.

Kirby wires between Pixie and the nose of the airship took up the slack, her harness tightened, squeezing the breath from her as she slid down the gradient gravity prescribes for a pendulum. Spreading her arms out wide, she released the winglets of her full-length leather drop-coat, ankle wings for trim springing from her boots. Suddenly the harness became her trapeze and she somersaulted with creak of leather, freed into the hundred-knot headwind.

Orange fire below and frozen storm above, these were the moments Pixie lived for. Card tricks in the dark. A moment of genius for her own consumption and not for the sharing. She flew alone, arms wide, graceful as an angel dancer sweeping over a darkened stage. The first swing reached

2

the peak of gravity assistance and Pixie saw the roof of the train below her slow in comparison, stopping for a second just past the midpoint of her pendulum arc, then once more seeming to gather pace against her, leaving her trailing as she fell back.

"There have got to be easier ways for a pirate girl to catch a train," she said.

With an emphatic flick, she opened her drop-coat out wide, catching the full blast of the wind, whipping her back up the arc of swing like a human kite. Then, pulling her arms into her sides, she rocketed forwards again, a bullet through the air, streamlining, catching the train once more but this time lower as Jeti tried to match the altitude of the dirigible.

Eyes wide, Pixie saw the end of the last carriage, a black wall lit with a single dim red eye of a lamp. A sudden graunch through the cable, the winch bit, dragging her six feet further up in the air. Her speed increased as the cable shortened. She flew far too close and far too fast, sweeping up, only just carrying over the edge of the roof, arms held out backwards like the *Spirit of Ecstasy*. The bitter smelling pitch of the Russian rustproof coating mere inches below her nose. She lifted at the end of the swing, snapping upright, and with a perfect matching of momentum; she stood, placing her boots down and solid on Imperial rolling stock.

A single twist to the circular brass locking clasp and she shrugged free of the harness and drop-coat, before it could pull her over backwards. Jingling cable fading away into the storm as her crew winched it back. Pixie's knee length mini-crini sprang back into shape, like a chrysanthemum released from a fist.

She wore the dark red corset, all the rage in St Petersburg Jeti assured her, but always with that twinkle in her eye. Pixie never knew whether her second-in-command was joking at her expense or not.

Pixie set off at the run towards the storming volcano of the armour-plated engine. She knew she should put Jeti off at the next port, but she just couldn't do it to her. Dear, sweet Jeti van Borkel, the girl might not have been the best steersman this side of the Roaring Forties, but she did have such a cute popo, particularly in those Oxford bags she wore.

Momentarily distracted, Pixie nearly tripped over a spinning onion dome of an air-vent sticking eight inches up from the curved roof.

The smokestacks ahead towered above the train, roaring out a roman candle of sparks and smuts into the steaming night. She unholstered the Tatham and Egg matched pistols. There might have been newer guns across the Unfallen Empire, but few could make a hole in a person as big as the mighty Tatham and Egg. And one thing Pixie had learned, in this man's world a little girl better carry a great big gun. She smiled at their familiar weight, the original flintlocks long ago replaced. It helped she enjoyed the use thereof.

She reached a gap between carriages and leapt out across the space without consideration. Certain things in her line of business definitely went better if one only thought about them afterwards.

Her information said the package would be in the Royal Pullman, two carriages back from the engine. She put her head down and ran faster, the vast pistons of *The Iron Czar* rocking the roof below her with a rhythm alien and strange.

Since the Unfallen Empire swept to the edges of the Russian Imperium twenty years before, the Romanov defence had been to lay a network of these new rails. Twice the gauge of the old European iron roads, with huge metal-made dark demons like *The Iron Czar* to pull the trains. Each wheel below Pixie stood fully twenty feet tall, and flat out, downhill, all sails set and the wind behind, this Iron Czar could deploy troops anywhere in the empire at near enough three-hundred steam-driven miles per hour.

Pixie reached another gap between carriages and once again leapt out into darkness. The cars beneath her clattering boot heels only carried cargo and materiel for the Grand Imperial Zeppelin Armada being assembled at Archangel. Fabric, Duralumin alloy for skeleton, Gold Beater's Skin for the gas bags, and lastly, all the doings of a Lane Process hydrogen factory. Nothing worth nicking, so no guards and no concern for stealth. She tried to run a bit faster but she was already panting and her legs burned from the sudden exertion.

Pixie had started her run three minutes after *The Iron Czar* left Tsaryovokokshaysk Station after a stop for sand and water. Distant enough to avoid the Maxim guns of the garrison, and close enough so *The Iron Czar* had not yet reached full steam.

Pixie judged she had about thirty seconds left before the great train reached a ton-and-a-half, a speed she knew from experience marked the point she could no longer hold her footing. Lightning speared down from the furious heavens opening the endless steppe, the huge shadow of *Mischief* fading into the roiling darkness of the storm.

Another leap, another carriage, the wind now becoming a wall. Pixie looked at the length of the roof ahead and reckoned this to be as far as she could hurl her seven-and-a-half stone into the mounting headwind.

Step by step she walked hard, making the end of the carriage before swinging down the ladder, standing panting by the connecting door. She took a few moments to get her breath back. Here, in the dead air between compartments, she felt the skin of her face glow, her frozen cheekbones focusing the burning cold.

Pixie holstered her right-hand gun under her arm and tried the door handle. It turned and opened, easy and oft oiled. Left hand first Pixie entered the carriage.

Plain wooden floor of planks, smelling of sawdust and new glue on pine. She took a moment to remove her gloves and flying helmet, then once again drew her second gun and holding the pair out before her, straight armed, she strode off confidently down the middle of the car.

The freight space stretched wide, filled with tall crates, each marked Fragile and Explosive in picture glyphs, so even the surfs that loaded the cargo could understand the simple concept of "You drop this, it go boom and so do you."

Against the far wall Pixie spotted a crowbar where it had been casually thrown onto a pile of the bright clean straw. She took it and wrenched open a corner of one of the crates. The wood broke a bit, but she could see inside enough to recognise a low pressure hydrogen Dewar flask.

"Gas glass?" she said aloud. Tsar Nicolai obviously had more hurry for his aerial force than the Admiralty thought; clearly so, if he was prepared to risk transporting gaseous dihydrogen.

Pixie took up her guns again and opened the connecting door between the last of the freight and the Imperial Pullman car. She cast an approving eye over the opulence of the fittings. The Romanovs seemed not to be short of a shillin', despite all this outlay on a gasbag navy. The Pullman had been done out as a dacha on rails. Ornate Russian woodwork, stained glass windows, rich dark icons interspersed with the crest of the double-headed eagle. Even the door had been painted as an oversized Palekh miniature, gold leaf on black lacquer, intricate and fabulous.

Pixie turned the concealed handle and entered. The interior of the dacha, no less lavish. Warm air greeted her, along with the sharp smell of recent death. A piled log fire in the central hearth, backdrop of flames and silhouetted like shadow puppets against a living background, the slumped, blood drenched, throat-slit corpse of Grigori, Exarch of Tartaria, and next to his wilting meat, the elegant shape of Anastasia Tsoilikiskya, Trotsky's scalpel.

Pixie caught the sparkle, a single ruby of blood dripping from the end of a two foot gleaming blade.

"Still using that Japanese bread-knife then Ana you old whore."

"Pixie, dahling." Ana's voice Russian velvet. Contralto, sweet and familiar as first love remembered, dangerous as pay-day in Limehouse. "Late as usual."

"I didn't expect the Trots to be playing." Pixie cocked both pistols.

"No dahling, you never do."

"Did he tell you where it is?" Pixie indicated the dead bishop with a brief wave of one of her pistols.

"Oh yes... of course he did." Ana purred. "Are you going to shoot me now?"

"After Lisbon? I really should." Pixie seemed to be contemplating. "But to be honest I'd rather take a couple of days over it... maybe next time. So, how were you planning on getting off the train? I suppose what I'm actually asking is, where's Felix. Unlike you, I don't want him dead, and if he was to leap out at me and I had to kill him, it would be a cause of some regret, for a day or two anyway."

"You're such a sentimentalist Pixie dahling. But you needn't worry. Right now Felix should be diverting the points about fifty miles down the line. Why leave the train, when I can take it with me?" Ana paused and walked around the front of the body, draping herself on a *chaise longue* admiring her work with the bishop.

"How's Jeti?"

Pixie moved further into the room; the flames caught but could not warm Ana's perfect blue eyes.

"The chest is under the fire," she spoke without taking her eyes from her kill. "The bell-pull by the stairs operates it if you pull three times, like an 'S'."

Pixie indicated for Ana to get up with the flick of a pistol.

"Call me over cautious Ana, my old doll, but I think it might go better if you do the tugging."

"Oh very well." Ana sighed. She stood and Pixie saw the deep red of the ankle length skirt Ana wore. She posed, so slim, all whalebone and straight lines. Pixie bit her lip; Lisbon came back to mind, bitter and still burning.

"Jeti's fine, thanks for asking."

"I'm glad, really." Ana walked past the fire roasting ecclesiastic corpse and bent down briefly. She lifted the flap of his jacket to pinch her sword clean on the rich green silk of the Exarch's *podryasnik*. As she did, Pixie caught a flash of white paper sticking up. Ana saw it too and without interest she pulled it from the dead man's pocket and tossed it towards Pixie; then continued to wipe her blade.

"It's an offer from Buckingham Palace," she said over her shoulder. "Princess Alice in marriage to the Tsarevich. Cement relations between the two great empires. Peace in our Time. The usual weak-minded posturing from desperate carrion feeders trying to hold on to their illegitimate power over the proletariat."

"That almost sounded like you meant that, my duck," Pixie said. "But there'll be no revolution for you. Not with British boots marching on Minsk, and Lenin cold in a Swiss grave, an unjacketed round in his bonce."

"Ah yes," Ana flashed her eyes wide with sour humour. "How does the saying go? 'If you step on a nail, an Englishman put it there'." Standing straight she turned to face Pixie. "But this peace would be a good thing for the Russian people," she said. "Without the distraction of a foreign empire on our sacred soil, there would be nothing to take attention away from the Tsar's corruption and incompetence. He wouldn't last the first winter. Finally, Russia could be free of the German taint. And what concerns us all will be decided by all of us."

With the metal cleaned she replaced the blade in the short scabbard nestling between her shoulders, hidden once more by her tumbling black tresses. Pixie indicated the bell-pull, and Ana glided across the luxurious deep rugs covering the floor. Pixie stooped and retrieved the letter. The mark of the Royal Standard clearly visible, even from across the room.

Ana stood by the bell-pull like a scolded child, waiting. Pixie looked up briefly from the envelope and waved Ana to get on with it, while she opened the paper. Ana yanked three times on the green velvet of the cord and the burning logs rolled to one side.

Under the centre of the fire box a circular and intricately etched metal plate, cracked open like the iris of a cat's eye. Worm gears rotated and the plate ticked and clicked breaking into smaller parts which swung out and away like petals of a mechanical flower. Beneath the plate was a hexagonal space containing a tall rosewood box inlaid with gold. The box rotated, rising up on some unseen piston coming to a halt two feet above the floor.

"So what is it? Actually?" Pixie said.

"They didn't tell you?"

"Indulge me."

"Pixie, dahling, Who controls the world's only supply of naturally occurring Helium?"

"I'm not in the mood for a game, you murdering old tart."

"You're no fun anymore." Ana pouted. "Alright, The American helium embargo means the European air-fleets are reliant on the hydrogen economy, even the Unfallen Empire, even you dahling and your stolen airship, all have to use dear old but rather combustible hydrogen. Yet there is one thing lighter even than hydrogen."

Pixie snorted, but the aim of her pistols did not even slightly waver.

"Nothing's lighter than hydrogen, dozy mare."

"Oh, so you do know, then."

Ana produced a small golden key from her décolleté and unlocked the box. The rosewood split from top to bottom and Ana fanned the sections out to reveal the contents.

"Oh, that's pretty." Pixie crouched down beside her to get a better look at the package.

"Fabergé. The Uspenski Cathedral egg." Ana spoke as if introducing unacquainted guests at one of her soirées.

A white base of alabaster, and resting on it a perfect little cathedral, with a clock and the imperial coat of arms, and cradled between the tops of the green tipped towers, a white pearlescent egg looking for all the world as if a balloon hung between the spires. This crown to the piece had the top section of the egg made from a golden dome surmounted by the three armed cross of the orthodox church of the east.

"It's very nice and all..." Pixie sounded puzzled. "But *Fourteen Bags of Mischief* are a bit expensive to hire for a touch of common-or-garden housebreaking."

Ana reached forward suddenly, but came up short when the she found the muzzle of one of Pixie's Tatham and Eggs pushed hard into her elegant, soft white throat.

"I don't like any quick moves, petal."

Ana looked down at the blue metal of the barrel.

"Quite." she reached forwards again, but slowly and smoothly, keeping furious eye contact with Pixie the entire time.

She found a hidden catch on the back of the dome of the egg, flipping it to reveal what looked like a dark red Baltic amber inkwell inside. Ana twisted the inkwell around once and a low hum began.

"You might want to move back a bit." Ana smiled and winked, pulling up and backing away. Pixie stood, and took two steps back, keeping about the same distance as Ana from the humming cathedral. Ana stood directly on the other side of the fire place.

The Alabaster base jumped as if knocked. Pixie gave a little start at the sudden noise, her eyes snapping to the close focus of someone as just spotted a snake. The little cathedral lifted up from the rosewood box and drifted free from the floor.

It floated, carried on some delicate breeze, drifting at about waist height. Flying... properly flying... without wing or bag.

"This has come as a gift to the Tsar from our American friends."

Something odd seemed to be happening to Ana. Pixie could see her edges blurring, as if she stood behind a badly made glass door. "The Romanovs loaned the Uspenski Egg to the Carnegie Museum, and this is what came back. A gift from the American government and some Serbian émigré called Tesla."

"How is it doing that?" Pixie stood transfixed. Stone made mantle-clocks did not leap into the air of their own accord."

"You are quite correct when you say nothing is lighter than hydrogen. So if you could get a big enough bag and fill it with nothing, it would have more buoyancy than the same volume of hydrogen, and none of the usual explosive side effects in case of accident. But creating a vacuum has always needed machinery far heavier than the buoyancy of the amount of nothing they could make. Mr Tesla has solved the problem. His machine weighs less than the amount of nothing its little engine can produce, so it floats. Brilliant isn't it?

"You don't need to build Zeppelins any more, just affix enough of these little wonders to a real ship and you can make an ironclad flying dreadnought. If this gets to Archangel, in two years the entire Russian navy will be sitting in the skies over London, unopposed."

Pixie blinked as the cathedral floated, peaceful and charming and toy-like. She had no thoughts, merely an unthinking mood of surprise.

On the other side of the fireplace Ana slowly and plainly reached behind her neck, and smiled at Pixie with the ravenous blood desire that lit her soul as she drew the dark blade from its scabbard. Pixie shook her head as if trying to refocus, and then fired her left hand gun. The modern lock on the venerable pistol clicked, and one of the huge self propelled shells Pixie had specially made by Imperial Ordnance fired up inside the barrel and rocketed across the space. Ana should have been nothing but a blood spattered shadow across the beautifully decorated fittings and the memory of her smile.

"Oh, Pixie." Ana sounded as if someone desirable had stroked her thigh. From the other side of the room a book case exploded. Vellum and pages and ornaments and plants and black soil from the flowerpots, an impromptu blizzard. Pixie took a step back and levelled the other pistol. She'd missed. She *never* missed!

Ana walked up to the still floating model cathedral and, with her short sword in one hand, she pushed the Fabergé Egg in front of her as if it were a trolley.

"What this *Tesla* Johnny has made the bag to hold his nothing out of," Ana said, "is a sort of invisible wall. To be strong enough to hold the nothing, the invisible stuff coincidentally is strong enough to stop quite big bullets as well."

Pixie backed up another couple of steps. Ana using the bag of nothing as a shield as she stalked across the rug strewn floor. Pixie held herself back. She wanted to squeeze the trigger, but she had already seen a shot go around Ana, deflected by the invisible 'not gas'. But, Pixie thought, if that Trot bitch wanted to slice her up, she'd have to step out from behind Tesla's un-balloon, and then Pixie'd give her a face-full of Tatham's finest.

"О Боже мой! Pixie, you have no idea how long I've wanted to do this."

No fear showed on Pixie's face, only fury. The look a swordsman has when waiting for a gap in their opponent's defence. Animal and intense, the two professionals danced; each looking for the right distance, the perfect angle. Silent now, the time for words gone, only the wire of the fight and predatory electrification fired their nerves like living lightning.

Ana closed in and Pixie felt the invisible gas bag press against her, solid as leather. The contact unexpected, rocked her back on her heels and Ana struck, catching Pixie across the top of her arm.

Razor thin trickle of red rising on her pale skin, a line drawn on her in life. The depth of the sudden cut shocked, and Pixie pushed back against the Uspenski Cathedral. Ana stumbled a half step backwards. She regained her footing and began the dance again.

Pixie looked down at the little floating Fabergé curiosity. The invisible bag had only taken to the air once Ana opened the top. Maybe the bag went upwards, like a proper balloon. Pixie dropped the aim of the gun and fired into the floor at Ana's feet.

The shell exploded, destroying a foot wide circle of the unseasoned pine, showing through to the hurtling rails beneath the carriage.

Ana fell backwards away from the impact, losing her grip on Tesla's proof of concept. Pixie turned her pistols around in her hand so they became solid war clubs, wood with a diamond of metal right at the skull smashing point of the butt. She could still feel the warmth of the barrel across her palm.

The door at the engine end of the carriage swung open and the dead Exarch's bodyguard came piling into the room, summoned by Pixie's gunfire. Ana reached up from where she lay and twisted the inkwell of the Tesla bag and the Uspenski Cathedral fell deadweight into Ana's lap. She rolled up onto her feet and tucking the egg under her left arm while dancing through the baffled Cossacks of the body guard.

They looked at the scene, trying to parse the situation. Fifteen minutes earlier the Exarch had hustled them all out from the carriage so he could be alone with the velvet filly, redemption through sin. Now their charge lay dead and a new strange woman dressed like some insane circus acrobat fought with the bishop's first whore. The clarity of Cossack logic shone through.

"Kill them both!" The officer shouted.

He died quite quickly. The expression of surprise froze on his face as he looked down at the point of Ana's sword erupting from his chest, having already sliced through the close packed muscle-meat of his heart. The five remaining men, all battle hardened veterans, lasted little more than ten seconds. Pixie whirled around in a high spinning kick.

"Little Dragon Whips its Tail!" she shouted, as the four inches of razor steel lining the heel of her boot caught the closest Cossack across the throat. He went down coughing and gurgling. She cart wheeled out, regaining her feet behind the corpse of the bishop. Ana, using the body of the officer as a shield moved back into the room, while two of the Cossack lifted their rifles and fired point-blank into the chest of their erstwhile commander. She jolted her left hand down and a little spring-loaded Derringer jumped into her palm. With two quick spasms of shot, she put a small bullet through each of the two men.

Two guards left standing, and Pixie hooked the nearest rifle barrel with the butt of one of her pistols, pulling it aside enough so she stepped inside the man's reach, bringing a fearsome knee up through his groin, his testicles finishing somewhere near his lungs. Pixie finished him off with a couple of skull shattering blows with the butt end of her pistols.

The last guard having seen the rest of his unit go down like a bunch of conscripts, threw his rifle to the ground and put his hands in the air. Ana slit his throat. Seemed to be her thing at the moment.

"I'm sorry, what were you saying?" Ana asked, pushing her hair back from her face. "Oh yes, I remember."

With that she turned reclaimed the Uspenski Egg from where it had fallen on the floor, and ran through the door.

"Oi, you trollop, that's my bloody cathedral!"

Pixie broke her guns and reloaded with her own heavy ordnance. Thus

10

rearmed she moved to the door. Muzzle first, she emerged.

The Iron Czar now roared through the Siberian night at over two hundred and fifty miles per hour. Pixie experienced the noise of the steam-driven monster as a vast rushing, punctuated with hammer blows from Vulcan's forge as the great wheels clanged over the joins in the rails. The wind streaming past the train rendered climbing up on to the roof a simple impossibility, therefore Pixie reasoned that the Trot tart must have gone forwards through the last remaining carriage.

She stood to one side; then kicked the door open. The blast of a shotgun tore from the darkness in a way that would have made a fair sized hole in a girl as small as Pixie. She leaned in quickly and fired a speculative shot down the middle. The gun clicked; then kicked a little. The bullet found its mark with a deep masculine grunt and the shell exploded. Pixie reloaded in cover, then slipped into the car as quickly as she could, not wanting to throw a classic "door-silhouette target practice" moment to Ana.

Ana had killed the lights and the darkness of the bodyguards' carriage slowed Pixie. She closed her eyes and put her senses out: the howl of the passing air, the odd rhythm of the oversized wheels, the space too wide. She tried to hear anything that seemed out of place in the soundscape, but nothing. The door at the other end of the carriage swung open, and for half a second Pixie caught a glimpse of Ana as she rolled through towards the engine. Pixie leapt to her feet and ran after the fleeing Trot, only to trip full-face, starman, on the blood spattered carpet, over the corpse of the engine driver, the origin of the shotgun round. Tatham and Egg had made a real mess of him.

Pixie had a moment. If the driver was here, then…?

She got up in a rush and ran for the door, hurling herself through in time to see Ana working furiously at the coupling. Ana shrieked with frustration at the sight of Pixie. The coupling mechanism on these huge trains had been built by men, for men. A great black iron lever operated the steam driven teeth biting the chains of the train together. Ana had tried to shift it, but even with arms and legs all straining together she had not been able to move the lever one imperial inch.

"See? There is a down side to being so skinny, bitch!" Pixie levelled the gun at Ana's face. She had never seen her looking so dishevelled. Hair loose around her face, her skin flushed and red, the ankle length red velvet slashed now to the waist, stocking tops in the snow. Between them lay their prize. Ana had placed the Uspenski Cathedral Egg on the running platform.

The coal tender, lying between them and the engine, had a path cut through the middle of the twin stacks of coal piled on either side. The exposed mechanism of automaton stokers, swinging grab buckets and taking great bites of the black fuel and delivering it straight to the maw of the Hell furnace powering *The Iron Czar*.

Pixie had caught Ana in an uncharacteristically vulnerable position.

11

She's gone for an all-or-nothing bet with the coupling, and come up snake eyes.

"So, Ana." Pixie knew the rule, shooting or talking…always a binary choice. "It's been a blast working with you again, but I think it's time we went our separate ways, don't you my duck?"

She leaned down and placed the end of a barrel against Ana's lips. If she moved even a fraction Pixie would feel it through the gun. With the other hand she pulled the Uspenski Cathedral egg towards her, grabbing it by one of the towers.

She leaned in close to Ana's neck, almost as if to bite it.

"*Dahling*," she mimicked, "you are a work of art; a simple bullet would be a waste. I will sculpt your death into something magnificent, a structure of begging and screams, but today we part with a promise: I will come back for you, my duck. Give my regards to Felix."

Pixie pulled back the gun and with a beautifully judged stroke laid it across Ana's skull just behind her ear. She bent down and picked up the unconscious revolutionary and with two arms she carried her, placing her so she lay face down in the coal. Then she returned to the gap between the carriages and with one hand she took hold of the tall lever and gave it a sudden sharp yank. The teeth biting down onto the connecting couplings released their grip and Ana and *The Iron Czar* steamed on into the storm; Pixie and the rest of the train began to glide into entropic friction.

Pixie eased an incendiary round out from her belt and chambered it. An almost post-coital Zen-like stillness fell over her as she watched Ana disappearing into the wind-whipped sleet.

She turned back into the train and walked through, sauntering, almost skipping as she carried the cathedral, one handed. She could feel the rhythm of the rails slowing. She passed through the Imperial Pullman, retrieving the letter from Buckingham Palace.

From outside the train she heard the gathering heavy drone of the Maybach engines of the *Fourteen Bags of Mischief*. She headed back into the freight cars. She lined up and fired the incendiary round into the pile of straw at the end of the car. She watched it burn for a few seconds, making sure the flames took, a faraway smile in her eyes. Then she left through the back and climbed onto the roof of the burning carriage.

Overhead the great black shadow of *Fourteen Bags of Mischief* caught up with, and held station over where Pixie stood.

From the main gondola the supply lift came down on a cable, kept stable by a fair amount of ballast. The basket clonked onto the roof of the train, and Pixie stepped aboard, slipping the harness around her shoulders. The zeppelin put her nose up into a turning climb and headed back for the safety of the clouds. Pixie, winched up into the heavens, looked down as the carriages below her erupted into an orange fireball. Then the Tsar's cargo of hydrogen caught and a fast rising conflagration shot upwards into the sky.

Pixie smiled. She liked the idea of floating fire. The great Russian wheels rolled on through the Siberian night engulfed in British flames, just the way Pixie liked it.

The phone in the basket rang. It was Jeti.

"Well? How did it go?"

"Set course for London, Miss van Borkel, we have a princess to rescue, or kidnap... depending on your point of view."

As the cable winched her back towards her home in the clouds, Pixie looked down at the piece of paper in her hand.

"Peace in our time," she muttered, mulling over Ana's words. "Now, where's the fun in that?"

The Machines of the Nehphilim

James Targett

The spires of the xenopolis rose into the sky on Fitzroy's right as the electric phaeton carried him across Tower Bridge, as if they might pierce the heavens from which they had fallen.

Fitzroy found it impossible not to gaze at them. There was no longer any shelter of fog or smoke to shield him from their presence, the Nephilim had seen to that. The London sky, the very air he was breathing, was cleaner than at any time in living memory. His belief was that the aliens wanted the air to be clearer so that every Londoner could see the Nephilim colony rising above their city.

He dragged his eyes away, tracking an ornithopter's descent from the spires. It passed across the city in a westerly direction, falling earthwards against a backdrop of purple twilight.

Fitzroy wondered if the marvellous flying machine would be carrying one of the Nephilim to his meeting with Lyons, the ambitious man from the Home Office. Maybe not such a foolish thought: the aliens were turning up in all sorts of unexpected places these days. His considered opinion remained that Lyons's affairs would be unlikely to have anything to do with London's guests.

He settled back into the phaeton's seat. It was so much smoother than a Hackney cab, despite the quality of London's streets. No smell of horse or horseshit, either.

For an interlude Fitzroy forgot about the Nephilim.

*

As he was ushered into the offices on Eldon Street, Fitzroy realised what his considered opinion was worth. Lyons, replete in a dark grey three-piece suit

14

and royal blue cravat, sat on the lip of his wing-backed chair, interlocked hands dangling between his knees, as he earnestly engaged in discussion with the tall ascetic form of a Nephilim. A third vacant chair completed the group. Fitzroy could only assume that it was for him.

The Nephilim had the pallor of a corpse. Its neck, limbs, face and body were elongated beyond any human norm. Most of its frame was hidden behind a vibrant blue robe with the texture of silk (though the Nephilim had promised the merchants they traded with that all their fabrics were artificial). The creature's ears ended in generous lobes; while the silver irises of its eyes were of an acuity and colour not found among men.

Fitzroy hovered for a moment, the retreating footsteps of his usher falling softly into the background. Lyons looked up, his serious expression briefly replaced by a lighter smile of welcome.

"Fitzroy! So glad you could join us. Have a seat."

Fitzroy placed his hat and gloves on a side table. The other two did not speak until he was comfortably seated.

"Have you met Ezekiel?"

"I don't believe I have had the pleasure."

Of course Ezekiel was not the Nephilim's real name: that would be unpronounceable. Ezekiel would be the name that the creature had chosen for its dealings with Christian folk.

Fitzroy leaned forward and offered his hand. There was a moment's pause and then Ezekiel responded; it was obviously one of their ambassadors trained in human etiquette. Its hand was very dry, the bones very prominent. Fitzroy had to remember to keep his grip relaxed. One squeeze and Ezekiel's thin fingers would be crushed.

Ritual handshake completed, Fitzroy turned his attention on Lyons.

"You requested my presence, sir?"

"Yes."

Lyons glanced at Ezekiel who nodded in reply. Fitzroy's stomach squirmed with unease. Lyons should be the master here, not the deferential servant.

"There is a situation."

"Of course there is, sir. I am not the type of man who is called upon when events are going well. Now, if you could explain the problem in some detail?"

Lyons mouth tightened at the corners.

"Are you aware that there is a new colony in Moscow?"

It took half-a-dozen heartbeats for Fitzroy to understand Lyons's meaning. Involuntarily his gaze flicked across to Ezekiel.

"Another clan," Ezekiel said, and then uttered a name that was as fluid as syrup to Fitzroy's ears. "Which translates, crudely, as Nine Unwanted Daughters. The Daughters are unaffiliated with my own clan."

"The Children of Zero?"

Ezekiel blinked lazily. Fitzroy wasn't sure if that was a confirmation.

"It means, Fitzroy, that the Nine Unwanted Daughters have an alliance with the Tsar," said Lyons. "This could be problematical for the interests of the Empire."

"But that isn't the situation I have called you here to discuss, it is merely some additional information, which may prove relevant but is mostly for illustrative purposes. I am sure that you will read more about it in the newspapers of the coming weeks."

Lyons paused theatrically.

Fitzroy wasn't in the mood.

"Are you going to tell me what the problem is?"

Lyons retained his manner of sober bonhomie.

"There is a renegade," said Ezekiel. "From the Nine Daughters. An anarchist sympathiser. Having fled Russia and is bound for Great Britain. We are worried the renegade plans to contact Marxist elements within the Russian émigré community."

"And you want me to stop it?"

"Yes," replied Ezekiel.

"We believe that it will avoid trouble for our own country: you understand that we cannot have revolutionaries gaining access to Nephilim technology and engineering. Also, his capture and return to Moscow has the potential to generate political goodwill between us, and either the Tsar or the Nine Unwanted Daughters, possibly both."

"Or maybe one and not the other. Destabilising the new alliance,"

"I wouldn't spend too much of your valuable time airing opinions such as that. Likewise, it is my recommendation that you do not breathe a word of this conversation to anyone outside the room."

Fitzroy didn't bother to acknowledge Lyons' warning. If he didn't know when to keep his mouth shut and eyes open he wouldn't have got as far in this business as he had.

"Is there any other information?" he asked.

"The one you seek goes by the name Isaac. Your Empire's spies have information that he was last seen boarding a sea-ship bound for..." said Ezekiel, before it had to stop as he struggled on an unfamiliar word. The Nephilim gave up and looked at Lyons for help.

"The ship's destination was Whitby."

*

Fitzroy took the night train from King's Cross. Once it would have been the Night Sleeper to Edinburgh; now the engine was a streamlined Cyclops, with mighty pistons for limbs. The boiler was a new model, based on Nephilim designs. They would reach York in two hours, topping one hundred miles per hour on the way.

As they left London, he saw navvies working on the new lines for the electrical trains the Government were planning on officially unveiling to the public next year. The setting sun reflected off the parallel tracks; Fitzroy had to look away before the lines of fire burned his eyes.

That night he stayed in the Royal Station Hotel, having passed through the marvel of York's new train station with its long platforms and vaulted glass roof. The night porter at the hotel was mildly disconcerted by his late arrival and lack of reservation. The introduction of a small incentive quickly resolved any confusion on the part of the porter.

Fitzroy lay on his bed, fully dressed, studying the play of light on the patterned ceiling. He had to start in Whitby, if only to confirm that the ship had arrived. He feared that, if Isaac had made landfall, it would be hard to track him across the wilderness of the North York Moors.

At least the Nephilim would stand out amongst the locals. However, if the creature had allies…

Fitzroy brooded, wishing that Lyons had been more forthcoming with his information. There were too many factors that he was unaware of, and that bothered Fitzroy.

Eventually he slid off the bed and fetched his bag from the bureau. He had travelled light, without time to do any more than collect his ready bag before catching the train at King's Cross.

On top of his neatly folded essentials lay his gun. The revolver he had carried for years had been replaced with the new handheld; it came with a magazine of bullets that fed into the gun's handle. The extraneous curves of Nephilim design decorated the piece, making its heritage undeniable. The weapon was dissastifyingly lightweight, with a quality that left Fitzroy feeling queasy.

He had planned to clean the weapon. Instead he left it alone and removed the spare straight razor he kept in one of the ready bag's internal pockets. He opened the blade and admired the play of light on the sharp metal edge.

Fitzroy held the blade above the skin of his left hand. He let the blade touch his pale flesh. An ounce of pressure would be enough to draw blood. He lifted the razor away, right hand trembling. Closing the instrument, he abandoned it on the bureau top and strode to the window. Peaking past the edge of the curtains Fitzroy saw only darkness and night shadows.

It was going to be a long night. He decided to order a bottle of whisky from Room Service.

*

A tender that was purely human in design pulled the train from York to Whitby. The journey, despite the shorter distance, would take longer than the trip from London to York.

The conductor's shout was incomprehensible to Fitzroy, drowned out by the engine's boiler as it emitted a final set of hisses and sighs of steam. A carriage door slammed shut; the conductor blew a piercing blast on his whistle, echoed by the tender, and then the train lurched into motion.

A flicker in his peripheral vision caused Fitzroy to turn his head just in time to see a man dressed in a pale grey suit with a priest's dog collar enter the compartment.

"Father."

The priest placed his hat, overcoat and Gladstone bag on the luggage rack.

"I'm neither a Roman," he replied, with a quiet smile. "Nor an Anglican."

"Forgive me, Reverend. A Methodist then?"

The Reverend nodded and sat down.

"No need for forgiveness. Allow me to introduce myself: Reverend Thomas."

"Call me Fitzroy."

They shook hands.

Fitzroy sat back in his seat, letting his body relax into the rattle-shake of the train carriage. It did nothing to appease his headache. A cloud of gloom and bad temper settled over him like the weather. Perhaps it was a condition of being in Yorkshire. Already he was as sullen as the natives.

With each jerk of the train the new gun swung against Fitzroy's ribs, despite his tailored shoulder harness. It unbalanced him, confounding his attempts to reach equilibrium with the train. The weapon was a distasteful presence in the way that his old revolver had never been. On balance he was happy to carry the weapon, in case it did come to a fight with the rogue Nephilim. He could not imagine that Isaac would be unarmed or would go to his death willingly.

Another jerk, more savage than the others, and the laws of momentum caused the gun and harness to swing against his jacket. Fitzroy's hand moved reflexively and pulled the jacket back into place. It was too late though, Reverend Thomas had seen. The preacher's face was abruptly pale and tight-lipped.

Fitzroy settled back into his seat, the Reverend watching him.

"I hope a doctor joins us at Pickering."

"Why is that?"

"We'd have the start of a joke." Fitzroy grinned. He knew the smile was a mistake: it wasn't natural and contained too many teeth. He appeared feral instead of friendly. "A priest, a doctor, and an agent were riding in a train carriage, when out of the window they saw …"

He gestured with his left hand. Outside the sky was dirty grey, with an unhealthy yellow tinge; the landscape was rugged moorland, desolate and without the romanticism of the Brontë sisters' novels. Gusts of wind blew occasional drizzle hard against the windows of the train carriage.

Reverend Thomas's lips remained pursed.

"Don't worry Reverend. I'm not going to hurt you."

"I can see that sir," the Methodist minister replied. "With a weapon like that you can only be about Government business."

*

By the time that Fitzroy reached Whitby the weather had deteriorated even further. Steady rain had set in. The wind gusting from the sea frequently accelerated the rain into squall-like blasts, the rain mixing with salty spray.

The town was a melancholy place, slouched in the valley where the River Esk cut its way down from the North York Moors and out into the North Sea, There were a handful of ships in the harbour, spars and stays rattling with the wind. The silhouette of the ruined Abbey dominated the East Cliff; opposing it on the West Cliff was a cluster of upstart hotels.

Fitzroy carried his own bag off the train. His coat was buttoned to his throat and he held his hat in place with his spare hand. Fitzroy did not head immediately to a hotel. Instead he stalked down the quayside until he found the harbourmaster's office.

Any view from the outside was obfuscated by the condensation that misted the narrow windows. Fitzroy knocked once on the door and pushed it open. A man, in his sixties with white mutton chops, glanced up from his ledger. Beside his elbow a mug of tea was gently cooling. A wood stove threw out enough heat to cause Fitzroy's coat to steam.

"Can I help you?"

Fitzroy placed his bag on the floor and removed his hat.

"Yes. I wish to know if *The Spirit of Whitby* has made port? It is expected."

The whitebeard licked his finger and then flicked through the most recent pages of his logbook. His finger moved incredibly slowly as it traced a path across the page. Fitzroy wanted to rip the book from the old codger's hand and scan the entries himself. It would take a quarter of the time.

Finally the old man looked up.

"Not in the logbook." He shook his head. "No ship of that name has been here in the last three weeks."

"Very well."

Fitzroy placed his hat back on his head.

"You staying in town? I can have the boy send word when she arrives. Though could be some time, what with the weather an' all."

"Yes."

"A hotel?"

"I was thinking that first of all I would like a drink."

"Red Lion serves a good pint."

Fitzroy nodded.

"Send the boy to the Lion then."

*

The Red Lion was warm and welcoming enough. Fitzroy ordered a drink and a portion of the steak and kidney pie. He took a corner table and was happy to eat by himself, without any disturbance.

He was halfway through his first pint, his empty plate in front of him, when, with a polite cough, Reverend Thomas deposited himself in front of Fitzroy.

"You don't mind?" asked the minister.

"Not at all."

Fitzroy was so surprised to see a follower of John Wesley in a public house that he forgot to be abrasive.

"Forgive me if I were rude earlier. The sight of *that*—" Thomas nodded at Fitzroy's jacket— "rather startled me."

"You weren't meant to see anything."

"May I ask what Government business is it that brings you here?"

Fitzroy set his pint down on the table. Reverend Thomas watched the gesture. The other man waited until the minister's gaze tracked back to his face.

"First of all Reverend, the matter is confidential. Secondly, as you have both observed and hinted at, I am carrying a gun. Anybody who might be undertaking business for the Government, and who is armed, while out of any military or police uniform is not going to tell you why he is carrying a gun.

"Lastly, you only assume I'm on Government business; never ask anyone why they are carrying a gun if it is not obvious. The answers could be unpleasant."

Reverend Thomas could not summon a reply. Fitzroy smiled, enjoying baiting the priest as much as he had enjoyed being uncommonly direct with Lyons.

"Drink?" Fitzroy asked, standing up. "You do drink, don't you?"

"No sir. I have taken an oath of temperance."

"Pity. You can have tea then. Or water."

Reverend Thomas was still seated at the table when Fitzroy returned. The agent decided to continue his game, poking fun at the priest until something gave. The man was off-kilter, out-of-place, with the manners of a rabbit.

"So what brings you here? Missionary work?"

"I am on sabbatical."

"Well you couldn't have picked worse weather for it."

"I am on a trip to research the life of St Hilda. She founded the abbey you can see on the cliff top."

"A Saint, eh? Isn't that a bit Roman? Tell me, what miracles did she perform?"

"Apparently she drove the snakes from this area of Yorkshire. Turned them into stone. Here—" The Reverend reached into his pocket, produced a small circular stone and flicked it at him.

Fitzroy caught the item reflexively, astonished that the minister was taking charge of the conversation. The stone was the size of a large coin and had been expertly polished.

"It's a fossil," he said, recognising it from one of the exhibits at the British Museum.

"Yes. An ammonite."

"You told me that it was a petrified snake." Fitzroy placed the ammonite on the table.

"That's what St Hilda's followers thought. It all depends on your viewpoint."

"Faith is a viewpoint? That sounds strange, coming from the lips of a priest."

"Perhaps." The Reverend smiled. "Keep it. You can find hundreds up and down this coast. Buried in the same cliffs they dig Whitby jet from. Or even lying on the beaches hereabouts."

"I thought you'd all be for miracles and the divine, not science," Fitzroy replied, drink at his lips. "Aren't you taking some of the mystery away? Revealing the magic trick?"

Reverend Thomas eyed Fitzroy levelly. Any suggestion that he was a potential victim for Fitzroy's acerbic humour had vanished.

"God did not mean us to be ignorant. He left us this marvellous universe to decipher and understand." The Reverend stood up, smiling. "Don't waste your time on Earth with misdirection and magic tricks. Look for the truth."

"You're just peddling the same trite 'truths' as every other witch doctor and occultist," snapped Fitzroy, abruptly annoyed that his game with the Reverend was over before it had properly begun. He felt like he was being talked down to, given Sunday School parables to muse over.

"I cannot lead you to the truth," said the Reverend. "Merely show you the way."

"You can't show me anything," he muttered, as Thomas exited the pub.

Fitzroy picked up the ammonite and examined it; rolling it through his fingers and weighing it in his hand.

For a moment he imagined a follower of St Hilda, some scab-faced, snotty-nosed peasant dressed in muddy rags, bedazzled as a mass of snakes writhed and twisted on the ground before them. The snakes fought the saint's miracle to the last reptilian heartbeat, but they were doomed. Eventually every single snake curled up upon itself and became as stone.

His imagination telescoped as he rolled the fossil. Now Fitzroy imagined a caricature of a professor in a tweed jacket and university gown, with half-moon spectacles perched at the tip of the academic's nose. The professor was lecturing the same snotty peasant about fossils and dinosaurs and tar pits as they walked along a muddy beach. The fellow stopped to pick up an ammonite from the ground; his find compelling him to launch into an elaborate explanation about the truth of ammonites and petrified snakes. The peasant's eyes flickered from confusion to dread as the professor expounded upon his litany.

The ammonite rolled between Fitzroy's fingers.

At the end of the beach, Fitzroy imagined a Nephilim patiently waiting. The alien let the professor bid goodbye to the peasant. Then, the Nephilim placed his arm around the professor's shoulder, gesticulating with his free hand like a character in one of the children's fantasies that was the height of fashion in London. The creature started to explain that the ammonite was actually a petrified snake fallen from the stars, an alien egg. The Nephilim started to point at the stars and at the ground at the professor's feet. It was time for the professor's eyes to widen in fear.

He imagined the Nephilim amongst the peasants watching St Hilda perform her miracle; the Nephilim was now St Hilda herself, performing the same miracle for Queen Victoria's subjects; then it was one of the snakes, writhing in the ground in agony.

In the end though, it was just an interesting stone, and his imaginings were just flights of fancy. Fitzroy sighed and emptied his glass. He set the ammonite down on the table and headed to the bar to order another pint.

*

Perhaps it was the alcohol or the warmth of the pub, but Fitzroy only realised that he had been dozing when someone started to tug on his arm. He opened his eyes, let his free arm hang down, hand curled into a fist, lifted his head to see who it was.

A boy.

"The ship, sir! The ship!"

The boy tugged again, almost pulling Fitzroy off his chair.

"What?"

His vision was blurry; head full of half-remembered dreams of ornithopters, bats with metal wings, rain, and thin-faced alien men. Steam-powered walking devices strolled down the streets of London from the xenopolis, ignoring the bleating horns of the electric phaetons, whilst speakers at street corners, all with the face of Reverend Thomas, preached drivel about fossils, quoting both Charles Darwin and The Rhyme of the Ancient Mariner.

"The ship!"

"What ship?"

"*The Spirit of Whitby*, sir! It's beached beneath Ravenscar. The master sent word to Robin Hood's Bay to get help. They sent a rider on here. It's just that you were asking Mr. Musson at the Harbourmaster's, and he

22

thought you were official like."

"How far?"

"How far what?"

"How far is it to Ravenscar?"

"Nine, ten miles, as the crow flies."

"This town got an ornithopter?"

"No 'thopter hereabouts. Town's too poor for anything that fancy. Never fly in this weather anyways. You need a horse."

"Are you alright sir?" asked the landlord. "The child annoying you?"

"Bad news," replied Fitzroy. "I need to get somewhere fast. Is there anyone from whom I can hire a horse?"

The landlord stepped aside as his red-faced wife set down a tray of clean glasses and started to shelve them above the bar.

"I can do you one better."

*

The electric velocipede was a distant cousin of the phaetons that taxied Fitzroy around London. The landlord's cousin hired it to him for a princely sum, along with goggles, leather gauntlets and a heavy greatcoat; all of which Fitzroy was most grateful for.

The machine would have been difficult to ride, even in the best of circumstances. Near midnight, in gale force winds, with driving rain, along winding, unpaved, unfamiliar roads, was not the best time for Fitzroy to learn. He stalled the velocipede several times; other times he found himself slipping and sliding off it as he came around a bend, resulting in a muddy landing with the machine's engine still smoothly running as he struggled to his feet and lifted it upright again.

Rain dripped from Fitzroy's face. It soaked through his trousers and boots, dripped down the nape of his neck and down his wrists. He stood up for the third or fourth time, just beyond the sign for Robin Hood's Bay, spat mud from his lips and cursed very loudly. Another road sign pointed out the direction to Ravenscar and Scarborough

The only blessed thing was the velocipede's Nephilim light. It shone a path of white light ahead of the machine, as unwavering as God's wrath, wherever the velocipede was pointed.

Fitzroy remounted the machine, eased it back into gear as the landlord's cousin had instructed, and set off once more, spraying mud and sodden curses behind him.

Time seemed to lose all meaning along the wet ride. Somewhere between forty-five minutes and an hour from leaving Whitby, Fitzroy knew he had reached his destination. The muddy road curved, offering a view of the storm-lashed waters below. He glimpsed lights and the shadowed shapes of wrecked spars and sails. Fitzroy braked the velocipede, dragging it back in a tight circle to return to the viewpoint.

He kicked the velocipede's stand down and struggled off it, wet clothes restricting his movements. Fitzroy unbuttoned the borrowed great coat and abandoned it with the machine.

Below him *The Spirit of Whitby* lay wrecked on a low-lying platform of wet rock. Fitzroy guessed the platform was covered at high-tide, exposed when the tide was low. The combination of a low-tide and the storm had driven the ship onto the shore, beaching it on the treacherous stone. It canted at a terrible angle, masts so far intact, but with the rigging entangled and the sails shredded by the storm.

Lights bobbed and flicked around the stricken craft, like the weaving dance of faeries or vengeful wraiths. Cargo and other debris foundered in the heavy surf. Fitzroy could see people—passengers or sailors, he wasn't sure—wading ashore towards the knots of light. A few more folk were throwing belongings and equipment from the prow of the ship to people below.

Ignoring the ship's tragedy, Fitzroy looked for a way down.

*

It took half-an-hour of slip sliding through more mud, wet bracken and brambles, for Fitzroy to reach the bottom of the cliff. The sea boomed against the rocky platform with determined frequency, sending explosions of spray into the air. A group of sailors hurried passed Fitzroy, dragging a screaming man on a makeshift stretcher.

"Have you seen the Captain?" he asked.

"For God's sake, man! Is there help coming? Please tell us help is on its way."

"The Captain?"

"You won't get any sense from the Captain!"

"Where is he?"

"There, man. On the stretcher. Pelvis and thigh bone broken. Lower leg in three places too. It was the—"

Fitzroy shouldered them out the way.

"Damn you!" cried the sailor. "Answer me! Any help coming?"

Fitzroy ignored him.

Now that he was at the level of the ship, Fitzroy could see *The Spirit's* wooden hull had been rent on the port side, causing the catastrophic list. The North Sea sucked in and out of the puncture wound, reminding Fitzroy of the last wheezing breaths of a man he had killed in the alleyways of Barcelona.

Sailors mingled with men and women dressed in the strange finery and fashions of Russia. Two chains of men unloaded possessions out through the hole in the ship's side, vainly struggling to salvage what cargo and valuables they could. Another group of sailors, under the command of an officer, worked by lantern light; they jury-rigged a crane and were lifting a pallet of cargo from *The Spirit*'s hold.

A male passenger helped a pale-faced girl, barely sixteen by Fitzroy's estimation, across the platform towards the cliff. Another sailor sat on the wet ground, clutching a broken arm. Fitzroy saw bone protruding in the wrack light.

"The Nephilim. Isaac. Where is he?" Fitzroy asked the officer, grabbing the man's arm.

The officer shrugged him off. "Who?"

"The Nephilim called Isaac? I'm told that he was aboard your ship."

"The stowaway?"

The officer and the Government man looked at each other strangely, across a gulf of storm and ruin. Both their faces were pale and wet.

"We found a stowaway on board. He said he joined us from St Petersburg. He was one of the star-people."

"Where is he?"

"He went that way."

The officer pointed towards the cliffs, but in the opposite direction from the way that Fitzroy had come.

"There's an old alum works up the hill. We're making for that."

"Thank you," said Fitzroy.

The officer grabbed Fitzroy's arm, pulled his head close, better to be heard over the storm.

"Is there help on its way? We have people who need a Doctor—"

"The message reached Whitby." Fitzroy broke free of the man's grasp.

"But are they—"

The Government Man was gone.

*

He moved as fast as he could over the rocks. Fitzroy slipped at one point, plunging his right foot into a pool of freezing cold sea water and dashing his hands against the rocks as he stopped his fall, drawing blood. He picked himself up and carried on.

At the base of the cliff he reached the sailors with the stretcher and injured Captain.

"Hey!" shouted one of them. Again Fitzroy ignored them. They had already gained the cliff path. He scrambled up the steep slope, pulling on clumps of mud and dead grasses, until he was above them and able to traverse onto the path.

Fitzroy pulled the Nephilim gun from his holster, not caring if the sailors saw it on not. He ascended towards the alum works. Rain continued to hiss down, falling like silver glitter in the beams of the lanterns and torches carried by the survivors.

The alum works was a set of quarries, long-abandoned and already half-lost underneath the creep of vegetation. Several rows of cottages stood at the far end of the works, many without roofs and some with ruined walls. Survivors huddled there in the pools of light amongst the darkness; someone appeared to be gathering wood to start a fire. Fitzroy was drawn to the far right of the group, where a thin figure stood beside another man holding a lantern: they were readying themselves to leave.

Fitzroy struck out of the darkness, moving swiftly, gaining on the man with the lantern. He collapsed as Fitzroy struck him across the back of the head with the barrel of the Nephilim gun. The lantern fell, but did not break, spilling its light upwards. It threw strange shadows across the face of Isaac.

"Are you going to kill me?" asked the Nephilim. Fitzroy had expected the creature to speak Russian, or heavily accented English, but he spoke the Queen's tongue as flawlessly as his compatriots who had settled in London's xenopolis.

"Only if you offer violence."

He watched Isaac study the weapon. There was no reaction from the Nephilim. He seemed unperturbed to see his native technology carried by a human.

"There are people who want to talk to you. You're coming back to the capital with me."

"Why do you do this?"

Fitzroy wanted to glance around, to see if any of the other survivors were taking an interest in their conversation. However he couldn't afford to take his attention away from Isaac. He gestured with the gun's stubby barrel, suggesting that the two of them shuffle into the darkness away from the abandoned works.

Isaac complied. Fitzroy found it hard to read the alien's features, but if forced to give an answer he would have said that the Nephilim was amused.

"Are you a policeman?"

Fitzroy smirked. "Of a sort."

Bracken and rain surrounded them. The path up the cliff was easier going now. Isaac walked ahead of Fitzroy, hands visible, the thin fingers pale and cold looking in the rain.

"You carry one of our guns," said the Nephilim.

"I do. Why? Does it bother you?"

Isaac turned, keeping his hands raised. He walked backwards as he talked to Fitzroy.

"It does. Your people using our machines and technologies, it bothers me greatly."

Fitzroy flushed. "Why? Because you'd rather your people kept them to themselves and dominated our species? You want a Nephilim Empire rather than the Accord."

"You're being enslaved. I've read your histories. You're being given trinkets and rum. They are tying your destiny to theirs. In a few decades you'll have given up your scientific endeavours and experiments; you will be begging from crumbs off their table."

"You lie!" snapped Fitzroy. The Nephilim gun was an unholy itch in his hand; he hated it even as he held it. Give me something pure and human, he thought. His head ached with confusion.

The Nephilim lowered its hands.

"You know, don't you? You know I am right."

They stopped walking. Fitzroy lifted the gun with both hands.

"I should put a bullet in you."

"Would that please the Nephilim in London? The ones that sent you here?"

"A human man sent me here!"

"But there was a Nephilim with him, wasn't there? Pulling the strings. Already your masters are *their* puppets."

Fitzroy's confusion overcame his fury.

"What would you do?" he asked. He kept the gun raised.

"There are allies in London and other parts. We'd change this. Create a fairer order for both Nephilim and human."

They stood in silence. Rain hissing into the bracken around them, gurgling as it ran down the centre of the path, carving out fresh channels and enlarging older paths.

"He's talking about petrified snakes and ammonites," said Reverend Thomas.

Fitzroy spun around.

Thomas stepped out of the storm-soaked darkness, wearing a drover's coat and wide-brimmed hat. In his gloved-hands he held a carbine with a Nephilim-repeater magazine. At the flicking of a switch, a torch attached to the barrel illuminated Fitzroy and Isaac, blinding both of them.

The agent tried to shield his eyes; his gun wobbled as he tried to find Thomas.

"Would you rather kill me and enslave yourself," said Isaac, "or take a chance that this domination can be stopped before it is too late?"

"We see a world of petrified snakes; they see fossils," said Thomas. "But it's not in their interest to educate you. You're here to do what you're told."

"Enough!" snapped Fitzroy. He stilled his gun hand, certain of where Thomas stood behind the beam of Nephilim light. He was more surprised that Isaac hadn't tried to rush him.

The rain continued to hiss down.

Rationality told him to put a bullet through Thomas's frame; he knew he could turn in time to put one in Isaac's skull as well, before the Nephilim could run. His fingers hugged the trigger.

And then he lowered the gun.

Isaac's mouth twisted into a smile that was open and alien and wrong.

"Thank you," the Nephilim replied.

"The International are grateful," said Thomas.

Fitzroy regarded the reverend. "Are you even a priest?" Not that it really mattered, but curiosity wanted to cut through the cloud of confusion that fogged his head.

"I am," said Thomas.

"Siding with Marxists? Atheists?"

The Reverend Thomas smiled. "Against God's enemies? Yes."

"You know that they aren't actually fallen angels, outcasts from Heaven?"

"I know that," replied Thomas, rifle steady in his hands. "But they are enemies of mankind. Or at least the ones that the Queen and her Government have made deals with. They hold a viper to our collective breast. But allies can be found in the most unlikely places."

Quite true, Fitzroy thought; he had a last bitter warning for Thomas. "Be careful that *you* aren't holding a viper to *your own* breast, Reverend."

Thomas smiled. "It's a matter of faith."

Fitzroy pushed his jacket aside, his clothing already so sodden that he didn't care about exposing his shirt, and holstered the Nephilim gun. He hoped he didn't catch a chill from this Godforsaken night.

"Goodbye," said Thomas. "And good luck."

With that Fitzroy turned. It would be a difficult traverse back to the velocipede, but better than the walk up the cliff with Isaac and the Reverend, or facing the frightened passengers and sailors of *The Spirit*, huddling in the old works. Already he was mentally composing both his report of the night's affairs to Lyons and working on his letter of resignation.

Fitzroy paused halfway along his scuttle across the cliff-face. He removed the Nephilim gun from its holster. Rising up as much as he were able without fear of losing his precarious perch, Fitzroy threw the weapon away, not caring if it were dashed against the rocks or lost in the sea.

He didn't see where it landed.

The Siege of Dr. Vikare Blisset as Reported by Detective Carlos Werke

Jacques Barcia

...told you. There was nothing. Nothing. Empty. How many times do I have to repeat it? Fine. Ok, ok. I mean, yessir.

For the third time: I reached Dr. Vikare Blisset's hideout late in the night. Too late, actually. Twenty-seventh of February. What time? Two in the morning, probably. Can't say for sure. It was past midnight, this I can say. Our intelligence data couldn't agree on a single location. Yes, we employed the analytical engines. Like I said, the data computed determined fourteen possible locations for Blisset's headquarters. *Fourteen*. We even verified three different addresses before it was clear we'd not be able to investigate all the possibilities. We were running out of time. We were forced to use—how can I say—unorthodox methods to decide which location we should strike next. Yes, yes, we had the collaboration of a kardecist. I know. But he pointed out the spot on Beach Street, at Saint Peter's Quarter, close to the Square. Yes, Saint Peter. The bastard hid himself in plain sight, in an old warehouse that, to be honest, we completely overlooked. Too obvious, too easy. Too daring. Even for him.

No, not alone. I was there with a full team. I was ready for his tricks. I was determined he'd not fool me again. Right. I had fifty men with me blocking both ends of the warehouse, on Beach Street and Sand Street. I had one Dumont-class airship patrolling the air, looking for signs of movement on the roof, and aboard it there were four jet-packers ready for action. I had asked the Mayor to clear up the skies from any civilian aircraft, be those personal airships or 'thopters. Among the fifty men were ten Goliath-class steam-suits, fully armed and equipped with Tesla-guns. I wanted the bastard. Dead or alive. Just the way the Consortium asked, right?

Of course I found it strange. We were on his doorstep and the only sound we could hear was the hissing of a boiler and the clacking of an analytical engine. Several engines, to be precise. Yes, we later confirmed there were four steam-powered engines, all connected by copper wires, linked to three enigma machines and a radio transmitter. No, sir. We weren't able to locate the decryption code.

Why do you keep asking me questions you already know the answer for? Do you think I'm crazy? Do you think I've turned to their cause? No. I really, I...I don't know how she came up with the idea of a breathing machine. No, she's not a No-Patent. She's a nurse, for God's sake. A nurse with a kid in trouble. People become creative under such circumstances, don't you think? People invent things out of necessity. Yes. I was informed they were of similar design. No. Lucy has never been to Europe. Never visited any of these inventors you've mentioned. Yes. I'm. Sure.

Fine.

Transcript 3 - Page 19

Just for the record, you say? Well, for the record, Dr. Vikare Blisset is the single most dangerous bandit living on Mauritzstadt today. He's the Consortium's number one enemy. *The* enemy, forget the anarchists (though you could say he's one), forget the trade unions, and forget the strikers and the militias on the off-world aether mines. Dr. Blisset is all of them. And none of them.

Why's he so dangerous? You know why. Why you're asking this? For the record? It *is* recorded, documented, publicly known, God damn it. Ok. For the record. He's a genius. He's a legend. He's the leader of the No-Patent cult. He's accused of stealing from several industries the blueprints and plans for many breakthrough products, only to distribute them to the general populace. No, no, sir. He charges nothing. Not a single penny. He does it for *free*. I don't know. If his own words should be taken seriously, he's doing this out of idealism. Our department intercepted several letters and radio transmissions in which he clearly states his goal: to promote what he calls the Garage Revolution. Yes. The one from the manifesto.

Admire him? Why, no! I respect him. I know I've reasons to despise him.

You don't have to remind me of that. Stop. Stop! It doesn't matter now. I've been hunting him since the beginning. Ten years. No, I don't think I've built a career on him. Just a cop, yes. Detective first class now. Never. Never caught him. Fought him? Several times. Gunfight. Car chase. Sword fight in the open sky, on the hull of a Prussian airship. He thrusts his sword, lowers his shoulder. I block, slide the blade to his hilt and disarm him. I say: "Haha! It's over. You've nowhere to go, scoundrel!" He says: "Nowhere but out." Runs. And jumps. Yes. He jumped out of the airship. I couldn't. He was too fast. Unbelievable? I tell you what's unbelievable. Mid-fall, he activates some mechanism and a pair of clockwork wings spread out of his back. And he glides away.

This time I caught him taking a micro daguerrotype of a new Tesla engine the Prussians had on board. Ordered by the Mauritzean government. Well, he steals the schematics for both high-end and common goods, like vaccines and the ever popular refrigerator, and then records audio tutorials detailing the goods' manufacturing processes. He distributes it using an array of collaborators, sharing hubs, clandestine radio stations and some odder means. Like ghosts. So they say. I don't know how. What we know is that he invents manufacturing processes so easy, yet so esoteric, any common man with a minimum of creativity is able to reproduce.

He's also accused of illegal practice of a number of sciences. Automobile engineering, mechanetics, steam dynamics, virology, aether mechanics, just pick one. He broke the patents and ethics of that too. Yes, chronomorphosis, yes. Yes, he used it on me at the warehouse. I feel normal, but as you can see my vocabulary betrays me. Strangely enough, you seem to understand me perfectly, despite my odd parlance. Weird, huh? You *do* understand me, right? Ok.

Some say he's a wizard too.

Annex 1:

Excerpt from the Garage Revolution Manifesto

Amidst the smoke, rising out from the chimneys, echoes the yell of a generation. Screams and shouts carrying along the message of a bounded, gagged youth. The pulse of rebellion. Revolution in every garage. In every basement. In every blueprint. Subversion of the bourgeoisie order that dictates the course of this so-called progress. No longer will we be slaves of mass production. No longer will we let industrialists, bankers and emperors decide what we may have, what we must consume. We'll not consume. We'll do it ourselves. And we'll make creativity, invention, science and craft a means to set humankind free. Yes. Mad scientists we are. The lone doctors. The ones who do not accept that reality should not be packed in a cardboard box, nor should technology be accessible to just a few privileged, well-born lords, members of the owner-class. We'll steal. We'll retro-engineer. We'll make it simple and distribute it to the masses, so the masses won't be masses anymore. A world-lab, an inventors-society. And if the advocates of passivity say such a world is like the chaos of a winter storm, for the free-thinkers it'll be just as the sunrise in spring. Join the war. Create, unlock and share.

Annex 2:

The Mercantile Gazette on the Mauritzean University theft attempt.

VIKARE, THE NO-PATENT BANDIT, RAIDS UNIVERSITY

The rascal flew over the campus, broke into a lab and destroyed the rare Aetherial Creatures collection.

A theft attempt caused destruction and panic, yesterday, at the Mauritzean Imperial University in west Mauritzstadt. The anarchist bandit known as Dr. Vikare Blisset invaded the just-inaugurated Evolutionary Sciences department, in plain day, causing irreparable damage to the Aetherial Creatures collection of that so well-esteemed academic centre. It was past 10 a.m., when suddenly a shadow covered the campus' garden, an airship, hovering in the sky. Students, including the son of Prussian industrialist Otto Lundgren, Felipe Lundgren, and also Lamarckian professor, Miss Filomena Alcoforado; therapist and hypnotizer, Dr. Ethevaldo Nilza; Parnassian poet, writer and musician Mario Lins, amongst several other academic authorities, illustrious citizens and men of prestige, threw their gazes up to the sky and, mouth agape, couldn't believe when a man using what appeared to be rocket shoes jumped off from the aircraft's belly and darted toward the laboratory's window.

According to witness Severino Barbosa, a fine, recently-freed Negro working as a cleaner at the lab, Dr. Vikare produced a "damn weird gun" from his trench coat as soon as he put his feet on the ground and immediately opened fire. "I barely had time to duck and cover my head. I heard a sharp 'zap' sound and a white, flashing light. He fired his gun at the shelves, at the lockers, at everything. But it didn't seem to be random. He was precise in his anger," said Barbosa.

The servant confirmed the man with the zap gun was Dr. Vikare. "Yes, yes! The trench coat, the gas mask, the hat, the cape. It was him, sure," said he. One of the lockers contained a mummified collection of seven specimens of deep-space life-forms, otherwise known as Aetherial Creatures. The collection was of incalculable value, but now it is utterly lost to humanity.

"This ruffian Vikare must be stopped at any cost. He's not just a danger to our economy. He's a danger to our citizens, and ultimately, a danger to human knowledge," said Felipe Lundgren. Lundgren Industries are the lab's main sponsor and the destroyed collection was a gift from its director, Otto Lundgren. "My father personally led an expedition to the outskirts of Mars last year, which resulted in the capture of these specimens. It's a shame".

The Mauritzean Police department claims to be in pursuit of Vikare, but admits they're far from uncovering his true identity. "We're working on it. He's elusive, he's intelligent and he seems to be pretty much everywhere," said detective Carlos Werke, the man in charge of the investigation. Werke said that despite the witnesses' accounts, there's no indication that Vikare's last attack's objective was to destroy the lab or its contents.

—Jack Waller is a reporter at The Mercantile Gazette.

Transcript 3 - Page 20

Unreliable. He's an ex-slave, recently freed, who used to work in Lundgren's cotton factory. What do I mean? His account can't be trusted. Besides, we've solid evidence there was at least one other man inside that lab. The so-called random marks of zap shots are actually indicative of a zap fight. Yes, they could. But then, why would the Negro lie? If security did fight Dr. Vikare, then this fact should've been reported. Another thing: zap guns are military-only. University security has no access to such equipment. Of course I'm suspicious. I'm being paid to be suspicious.

And there are copycats. Look, this attack falls completely out of Vikare's past behaviour. I've a team of psychoanalysts reading his every movement, recording his progresses, his failures. What they found out is that there are at least ten distinct personality archetypes surrounding the main persona we

34

know is Dr. Vikare. Shit. Yes, I can. Works like this: there's the Vikare we know; the Vikare we've been investigating; the Vikare that comes up with or steals patents, reforms its assembling processes and adds a self-destruct device that detects monetary transactions. Something to do with orgonic energy.

Then there're the other nine personalities, less meticulous. We think they're scientists just like him. Some seem to be young and adventurous. Others seem to be older, more insular. Some promote the distribution of pamphlets detailing this or that invention or piece of technology, with flamboyant apparitions over the skies of Mauritzstadt. Others can only be heard on the radio reading subversive poetry. One possibility is that he keeps a network of bandits and vigilantes to help him in his attacks. We've managed to identify three possible collaborators.

Agreed. Theoretically, the episode at the university could've been the act of one of these copycats. But not even one of these other personas work on random acts of violence. None has ever destroyed any facility, any lab. And we've recorded seven other occurrences where one Vikare or another has invaded a laboratory, a library, power plant, a learning institute. Never has he promoted destruction. In some cases he seemed to have appeared inside a safe-lock, just to be gone the next moment without a trace, except for his signature: *You've been no-patented.* A signature not found at the university. My conclusion? Either Vikare did have a reason to be at the lab, or it wasn't him at all. And if it was him, he's not responsible for the lab's destruction.

That night at the warehouse? It was him. It was the real Vikare. The one we know. Or the one we thought we knew. The one we understand even less now.

Annex 3:
Bandits possibly associated with Dr. Vikare Blisset

Kidd Squidd

The mutant known as Kidd Squidd lurks somewhere in the docks of Mauritzstadt. He used to be a pirate in the Caribbean coast, but was finally recruited as a sailor in an Indian pirate submarine. Years ago, the submarine was attacked by a giant squid, two-hundred miles away from the Mauritzean coast. The sea monster destroyed the vessel's hull and ate the whole crew, except for one person: a young waitress called Ana Souza. Miss Souza says Kidd put her on an escape pod right before the giant squid's beak tore the sub's steel walls and swallowed her saviour.

What happened in the creature's intestines is unknown, but days later pieces of a giant squid (beak, tentacles, head and arms) were found all over the coast, down to the frontier with the Brazilian Empire. The sub's black box, found in a deserted beach on the southern side of the city, confirms the vessel was tracking an aether nodule. The energy source might explain both the giant squid and the mutant Kidd, who has been described as an eight-foot giant, a mix of man and cephalopod, many-limbed with tentacles and arms.

Kidd Squidd seems to be looking for a means to return to his natural form. He's been responsible for several attacks on research stations, laboratory ships and aether platforms. At least once he and Dr. Vikare were recognized at the scene of a crime. Our sources inform that Vikare might be helping Kidd in exchange for favours only the Squidd can give.

Johnny, the Clockpunk

Bank robber, arsonist, vandal. Johnny, the Clockpunk is an anarchist of the worst kind. His name derives from the fact he's part human and part machine. Not much is known about his last days as an exemplary citizen. Born Johan Van Naussau-Sigen, after his great-great-grandparent, Johnny studied engineering at the best European universities and became one of the world's lead specialists in mechanetics. Sometime in his early twenties, though, he started expressing sympathy for the communist cause, joining the Party a few months later. However, Johnny was expelled after leading extreme direct-action assaults without the Party's authorization. He disappeared right after that.

Five years after being expelled, Johnny re-emerged completely transformed. Half of his body is made of brass, with shining springs and gears ticking and spinning inside him. He's virtually invulnerable to bullets and is able to see in the dark. Hidden inside his brass limbs are several lethal weapons including guns, darts, a flamethrower and even a zap gun. This last piece of weaponry is quite similar to the model used by Dr. Vikare.

Recently, Johnny has demonstrated the ability of tracking large amounts of money, as well as big commercial transactions. It is possible that he's using one of Vikare's infamous Orgonic Trade Detectors to spot, and then sabotage, the flow of commerce in the city.

King Zombie

King Zombie, the lord of war, the lord of all struggles and all judgements. A runaway slave, King Zombie is supposed to be two-hundred years old or more. His domains are one hundred miles west from Mauritzstadt and are considered by many an empire-within-an-empire. No Mauritzean has ever met King Zombie face to face, but free Negroes living in the city claim to have been visited by his emissaries, both living and spiritual.

Of course we don't recognize the existence of such nonsense as the

Eshu, but something (probably someone) is clearly communicating with the African-descendants. According to our sources, these emissaries are organizing terrorist cells in Mauritzstadt and are probably the ones responsible for the rise of the Capoeiras, a gang of fighting vigilantes acting on the city's suburbs.

Vikare was reportedly seen wearing an African amulet, called a patuá, a signature of King Zombie's followers. An attempt to track these Eshu emissaries ended with three police officers killed, another one severely maimed and four more completely delusional. According to the same sources, Vikare has been smuggling technology to Zombie's territories. From now on the Capoeiras are considered illegal.

Transcript 3 - Page 21

I remember seeing Vikare's clothes on the floor, thinking where the hell did he go? I immediately commanded my men to search about the warehouse, see what they could find. The place was big. Near the wall, the analytical engines were calculating something. There was an airship docked inside. The hell if I know. This was your job. You should know how a bloody airship is able to land inside a warehouse in the middle of Mauritzstadt's most crowded merchant district, unnoticed. *You should know.* Not me. I'm just a cop. What? I was investigating him. You stop implying I was making it easy for him. You stop it, you bastard. Sorry, sir. But this military friend of yours is being really disrespectful. His job, you say? Okay. Fine.

So, we found the airship. Similar design, yes, but I must say it's a fairly common civilian model. Excuse, me? No, you're right. It had no identification numbers, just like the one at the university. We also found several blueprints and schematics for a number of different inventions, both original and no-patented. We found an aetherial radio transmitter with a live cynema prototype. Not to mention a belt full of 3G bombs that Vikare threw on us.

And we found the Tesla charger. It's massive. And it works. Three of my men had their radios blown up, overcharged. Four steam-suits were necessary to move the thing out to the street. The technicians at the station told me that that single charger could distribute energy to the whole neighbourhood. It's impressive.

No, you asshole! I didn't let him escape. I'm not associated with him. He almost killed me that night. Do you understand that? I almost died there, only to be put under investigation here with a military pig who completely underestimates a genius. *I* couldn't capture him there? Well, what about *you*? Did you get him when he raided the Palace? Did you get him when he hacked through your encrypted radio transmissions? Did you get him when he personally sailed an airship with refugees from that aether-mine, Catalonia? To you, you bastard. To you he's a mastermind criminal. But let me tell you something you don't know. To the people in the streets, to many of them, this bandit is a hero. And that's why you can't get him. That's why I couldn't get him. Because people tell him when we're close. People warn him. Idiot.

Annex 4:
Notorious inventions by Dr. Vikare Blisset (and some no-patented wonders)

Orgonic Trade Detector (and bomb)

One of the most dangerous inventions by Dr. Vikare, the Orgonic Trade Detector, is, put simply, a radar for big commercial transactions. Our scientists say it works with the once-theoretical orgonic energy, a kind of emission the human brain, gonads and sexual organs emit after being stimulated with pleasure. It seems Dr. Vikare discovered a way to capture orgonic pulses produced by merchants, bankers and tax collectors at the very moment they put their hands on large sums of money. The Detector is also used as a trigger for bombs planted in Vikare's no-patented inventions' designs. Its diagrams are so disguised our engineers are still unable to identity and disable the explosive devices, although these bombs are, theoretically, no-patented too.

Aetherial radio/live cynema transmitter

Dr. Vikare has been notorious for invading commercial radio transmissions, filling the airwaves with subversive messages and tutorials for equally subversive amateur scientists. This is possible thanks to the infamous Aetherial Radio Transmitter, a device that uses aetherial particles to hack through radio frequencies. The only thing that prevents Vikare from completely monopolizing radio technology is that his equipment requires a great number of aether batteries. We've been fortunate enough to have intercepted a large shipment of such batteries last month. Not coincidently, Vikare's last transmission announced he had discovered a way to transmit not only sounds, but images via an equipment he calls an Aetherial Live Cynema. Such wonder is yet to be demonstrated, but if true, it's a technology that must be controlled and cannot fall into the masses' hands.

Microbiotic Sub-frequency Hypnotizer

For ages mankind has been fighting the forces of death. It's hard to admit, but Dr. Vikare may have produced the ultimate weapon against diseases. The Microbiotic Hypnotizer uses microspeakers that emit sounds so low they're heard only by the tiniest of organisms, like amoeba, bacteria and even viruses. The device is accompanied by a set of precise instructions (voice intonation, rhythm and words of command) to hypnotize these microorganisms. Once mesmerized, the microscopical lifeforms can be commanded to perform certain tasks inside the body, like attacking cancer cells, or destroying Koch's bacilluses. Patients treated with this technique had averaged a ninety-seven percent rate of recovery. Our scientists are already trying to adapt this invention to military purposes. No advance has been reported yet.

Grey Gravity Grenade (The 3G Bomb)

Another weapon developed by Dr. Vikare, this one is particularly interesting because of its non-lethal nature. The 3G Bomb creates a "gray area" of gravity, freezing everyone and everything within it. Victims of the grenade reported they "felt like being inside a tank of marshmallow", suspended in time and slightly afloat. The effect runs for five minutes and when it ends, victims are put back under Earthly space-time and gravitational influence. No side effects have been recorded.

Tesla wireless charger (and discharger)

It has circulated on Mauritzstadt a pamphlet by Dr. Vikare detailing the construction design and assembling process of Nikola Tesla's wireless charger. The charger's blueprint was stolen from an American energy company last month. Its broken patent might disrupt the energy trade industry. An alternate version of the pamphlet details the Energy Discharger, used exclusively by the Imperial Troops. Possession of any of these pamphlets is considered a crime against the Mauritzean Empire.

Transcript 3 - Page 22

Like I said, people warn him. We didn't know, but he knew of our presence the moment we entered Saint Peter's Quarter. We thought we were about to capture him, but the truth was that he was ready to catch us. It was an ambush from the beginning. It was luck we got so far. It was luck we captured so many documents and pieces of technology he was ready to release to the streets. Hell, we almost caught him, despite all his traps.

The first to fall was our kardecist. I know you don't believe him, sir, but we've employed these mediums for several years now and they all proved... Okay. Back to the siege. The first to fall was our kardecist. Later, he said he was attacked by some psychic force. No, he didn't say that. I'm saying that. What he said was that he was attacked by some bloody spirits. It doesn't matter if I believe in his religion. I believe he has some mental ability and uses it for our benefit. And I believe when he says he was attacked because his ears bled, his nose bled. He cried tears of fucking blood. And it was just the beginning.

We were at the warehouse's main gates. When the kardecist fell, I commanded my men to put the door down. I told them to open fire. A 3G bomb fell on my right, paralyzing some ten policemen and one steam-suit. The other steam-suits were already firing at the door, but the thing was probably made from some fire-proof and bullet-proof material. It just wouldn't go down. More 3G bombs fell on us. More men were frozen in time. On the other end of the warehouse, men tried to cross into the perimeter. No success either.

Why I didn't call for backup? Are you crazy? Have you ever been in action? I was trying not to be caught. There were bombs falling and Tesla dischargers and zap guns raining on us. Automatons, you moron. Automatons. He had an automatic defence system that could detect our every movement. What do you mean? I wasn't hit because I ran for my life. I crossed the street as fast as I could and ducked behind a steam-suit whose operator had his skull vaporized by an energy shot. And do you think he wouldn't jam our communications? He would. I was trying to think ahead of him. But in the end, it was luck.

His robots zapped one of the 'thopters and it fell over the wall close to me. For a second his attacks stopped. Maybe his automatons lost communication with whatever controlled them. Anyway, the fallen 'thopter opened a breach big enough for us to penetrate the building.

I was the first, sir. Yes. He was alone, in the middle of the warehouse, close to the airship. No, he didn't shoot me. He talked to me.

Annex 5:

Chronomorphosis (and anachronitis)

A side effect of aetherial energy manipulation, chronomorphosis is a very dangerous phenomenon. It is the result of disruptions in the time continuum, which generates failures in continuity and chronological coherence. The study of chronomorphosis is strictly forbidden, but it's practiced in clandestine laboratories in East Europe, China and South America. Plants and places affected by chronomorphosis manifest alterations in their aspect. For example, a tree may show signs of spring, autumn and summer, randomly, along the course of a day. Similarly, animals may experience confusion and act following seasons only real to them. A bear may hibernate for three years; a turtle may lay eggs thrice in an hour.

The human mind, though, processes time in a very different way. Mankind is the only organic machine able to experience not only time, but history. That is, the human brain not only reacts to the stimuli time's passage, but deposits such passages in a chamber called *past* and, at the same time, makes projections of its own history with a tool called *future*. So, contrary to all other living creatures on Earth (or outside it, for all we know), humans naturally live on three times simultaneously: present, past and future. So, it is with no surprise that humans exposed to chronomorphosis are victims of a disease called anachronitis.

Anachronitis makes the victim perceive time in a mixed way. Anachronistic language is a classic symptom, but other "time psychosis" like a predilection for extremely old-styled fashion, or a longing for events that didn't happen yet, as well as time dislocation, precognition, post-cognition and chronic lateness are also fully recognized effects of anachronitis. Treatment, unfortunately, isn't available. Yet.

Transcript 3 - Page 23

We talked for what seemed to be several minutes. Yet, we didn't speak that much. We haven't talked at all. I'm telling you. I was the first one to enter the warehouse, but I had an army behind me. Men with machine-guns, steam-suits, and bloody bazookas. They were close behind me, but when I entered the room, pointed my gun and ran at Vikare's direction, everything stopped. Then resumed. But not quite at normal speed. I mean, the room was darker, silence was absolute. I could see bricks frozen in mid-air. But they moved. Slowly. Almost imperceptibly. Like those nightmares where you're fighting someone and your fists are always late, always weak.

But moving freely, just like me, was Dr. Vikare. Right there, in the middle of the room. He had a kind of remote control in his left hand and nothing in his right. No zap gun. No tricks. He was unarmed, defenceless, except for the time warping thing. No, I couldn't see his face. He had his gas mask on, like always. And for your knowledge, he wore that patuá thing I told you about. I don't care if you believe in it or not. I don't believe it myself, but I surely take that into account when I deal with Vikare.

What he said? Lots of nonsense. He greeted me. He called me by my name. How did he know? Can't remember ever telling him, but I'm sure he reads the papers. He's a crime genius, isn't he? He surely can read the news. I said he was under arrest. I shouted. I screamed at him he was under arrest. He kept talking and talking, but I couldn't hear much. I was mad. I was so excited I had him there, right in front of me. I could only hear my own thoughts. My mind was telling me shoot him, shoot him or he'll escape again. Shoot him before he tries anything.

I saw him moving a finger. A quasi-movement. Like the brick suspended mid-fall. Then I shot. And between the click of the trigger and the blast of my gun I heard his voice. He said: *You can't stop me. You won't stop me. You haven't stopped me. I'm a zeitgeist. I'm the phantom of history, the spirit of revolution. I've been there and seen it all, and in the end, we win. But I can't do it alone. I won't do it alone. I am not alone. Farewell. See you next time.* So I shot him. I hit him. And then his body popped, just like a balloon. When normal time resumed, I was there, looking at his clothes, gun smoking. There was a hole in his jacket and a blood stain spread around it. But like I told you, there was nothing in there. It was empty.

What? If I believe him? Which part, exactly? Well, it doesn't really matter if I believe him or not. *He* believes that. He firmly believes he's winning this fight. And considering your looks of concern, I think you believe that too. So will you shut down this fucking tape recorder now and let me chase him, or do you want me to tell this story a fourth time?

What? You can't be serious.

Okay. Here we go. I reached Dr. Vikare's warehouse at around midnight...

The Clockworks of Hanyang

Gord Sellar

Lasher was unsettled, even more than was customary for him, by lidless gaze of the strange, oriental mechinikaes' optical apparata. He seemed the only one in the crowd of foreigners upset in this way, however: the Clockworks was a busy place, with machines being banged together, or pulled apart, all about. Commoners in grubby white tunic-and-pyjamas taught by rote a dozen different tasks to the completed mechanikae, whilst all around the thick reek of machine oil hung in the air. One would be forgiven for suspecting that all things mechanikal had been bustled forth into the Clockworks, so as to show off the state of the art as concerned Hanyang, and all of Chosŏn—as the locals insisted on calling their land.

Marvel at the wonders of the Clockworks of Hanyang!, the invitation had read. *Witness mechanikae ordered by Eastern discipline and ancient wisdom! See the fusion of modern mechanikal advances with elemental Corean power!* A number of other Western dignitaries had received invitations, as well, though probably not accompanied by the desperate letter into which it had been tucked in the envelope that Lasher and MacMillan had received; many of Europe's most brightly-shimmering stars had declined to attend, understandably, but had sent representatives. The brother of the Home Secretary of the United Kingdom, accompanied by his wife; a Belgian *duchesse* seemingly of an adventurous sort; a pair of German twins with a fascination for machines built in the shape of women...the whole lot of them had shown up, in hazard of their very lives, along with Charles Lasher and his longtime mentor, James MacMillan.

Turning his oft-absent mind from the staring lenses of the optical apparata and back to the ongoing tour, Lasher realized that he had missed some sort of shocking event. Apparently, a mechanika had lurched forward, seemingly on the verge of crying out, and seized the elderly Master Ko, headman of the Clockworks, by the front of his scholar's robes. The old fellow's horrified Western guests cringed as a single mass, crying out in a ragged unison, and Lasher, the sole American of the party, was no exception: he had seen Polish-built mechanikae do things to men—and to women, Christ forgive their foolish builders!—that would have provoked screams from anyone save a madman. He wondered, for a moment, whether these intelligent mechanika of Hanyang were invested with the same ersatz memories, and emotions, and longings, and moral codes as their Western-built equivalents.

Yet in truth, Lasher gaped for another reason entirely: it was the fluidity with which the machine moved that stunned him utterly, despite knowing from the expostulations of his traveling partner to expect wonders such as these. The mere sight of this wondrous, oriental-built mechanika and its gliding movements was far more convincing of the Chosŏn tinkerers' cleverness than the scribblings of all the starving Jesuits that MacMillan had studied, and decanted orally, during their rail trip across Asia. From the moment the letter had arrived, the mysterious letter postmarked from "Hanyang, Empire of Chosŏn," MacMillan had pored over texts detailing the wonders of Asiatic mechanikae, and the queer--indeed, downright odd—systems of their operation and composition.

Odd indeed: the mechanika clasping Master Ko did not, ultimately, cry out at all, but simply held Ko aloft. The old man looked at the machine with a look that quickly shifted from startlement to curiosity, as he muttered something too quietly to be heard by any in the room save perhaps the mechanika itself. The translator, a young man—it was difficult to guess his age, though he was probably not quite twenty—native to the Chosŏn kingdom, and who had apparently studied in the West, held onto his odd little horse-hair scholar's hat (which reminded Lasher of a bishop's mitre) as he quickly translated: "It *cannot* do a man harm, Master Ko says. Its mind is intelligent, yes, but rebellion is not in its constitution, for it has been built in accordance to the Five Relationships of Master Kong—Confucius, as you know him—and the Sixth Relationship added by the mechano-philosopher Cheng-ja. The mechanika *must* be in need of repairs. This is, you may be certain, its only way of alerting Clockworks Master Ko to an unnoticed problem or malfunctioning system."

"I see," said Lasher with a nod, wondering whether they had withheld the power of speech from mechanikae because of technical limitations, or out of obeisance to some obscure oriental doctrine. But the automaton seemed to understand Master Ko's words as well as the translator did, or perhaps at least, like a dog. As the old man spoke, it slowly set him down to the ground. It did so with head bowed, in the deferential manner that Eastern subordinates seemed unfailingly to show their betters—except, of course, in the ever-recurring times of open revolt.

Lasher thought of Tokyo aflame, of the scorching of Kyushu and Honshu, of the rumors that had circulated about the destructions there. Before his mind's eye, he could see still the tattered, secret Kodaks he'd glimpsed at opulent, secret meetings, white borders framing the sepia-toned images of heartless figures—perhaps men, perhaps Nipponese mechanikae—caught red-handed and jolly as they busily decorated towers and bridges with ornamental strands of human corpses. He glanced at the machine, saying, perhaps as much in hope as in commentary, "It bows before Master Ko."

The other Westerners of the party nodded, muttering as their tension suddenly eased. Lasher listened to them not at all: he had locked eyes with MacMillan, and the older man was nodding, his fine mottled-brown bowler clutched against his chest with one hand, the very image of panic stifled by a stalwart heart. The translator, Hwangbo, was prattling on about how mechanikae had long been designed to defer to living men, but how apparent age also factored into the severity of deference shown by any given mechanika to a human or to another mechanika.

"Fascinating," MacMillan commented, and tapped his cane noiselessly upon the dirt floor of the factory. He turned to the translator and held out his hat as if it were a prop, a tool to facilitate the discussion. "But would it not be simpler, and less jarring, to have the mechanika spit forth its communication, say, upon a slip of paper, as do the gearmen of the Continental Trappist abbeys? I mean, if you are going to make them intelligent enough to perform tasks at all..."

The translator smiled, and shook his head, the horsehair mitre bobbing a little has he did so. "Do you not wonder why it is also against the law for a citizen of Chosŏn to teach *you* our language? It is forbidden that a machine should have any language capacity at all, even at an... an unconscious level. Language, Mr. MacMillan, is *always* power, and we have learned from your tragedy in Paris."

"Indeed," MacMillan said, nodding. "But language can empower you, and your, ah, *tools*, as well." Lasher followed the older man's gaze to the far side of the clockworks, where a peasant was silently modeling the use of some sort of hoe to a gleaming, metallic giant off to one side of the Clockworks. "Whilst you must teach your mechanikae how to perform even the simplest tasks, we can explain, or better yet, we can write the commands in a special language that hurries a mechanika's learning. It needn't understand, beyond in the functional level. Mechanika need not be intelligent for them to grasp..."

"I know quite well how European and American gearmen work," the translator cut in with a smile. "There was a Wedgewood Butler unit serving in my rooming house at Cambridge, sir. Vintage of '71, I believe, but a sturdy machine and showing no sign of flagging at all! But...*we do things differently here in Chosŏn, sir.* That is a simple fact that you shall have to accept while you remain our guest here."

Lasher smiled at the young Corean man's pride: the lad had seen the West. He knew a thing or two, standing there before them in his white tunic and tatty pantaloons, in his white rubbery slippers and black horsehair scholar's hat, looking for all the world like some benighted oriental Papist as he spoke his English in lovely, dulcet tones.

Translators. Lasher *loathed* them like nothing else.

*

The street market was a horror of noise and stink, soul-churningly loud and crammed with peasants who seemed to have only one volume at which to speak, that being their absolute physical maximum. At one corner, an old woman stood beside a broad basket of shriveled, miniature oranges; at another, there were cages of small beasts for sale—chickens, mice, birds, and creatures for which Lasher did not know the names. Old men were gathered around one large bucket of a whitish, cloudy liquid, into which they sank their dippers, thereafter raising them too their lips—without doubt, some sort of Asiatic liquor, Lasher supposed with a shudder.

The odours of any other city—the sweat of the masses, the reek of rot and death and illness, and the choking smoke of burnt wood and coal, here were complemented by the prodigious stink of garlic, the overwhelming aroma of something gone outright rotten—something vegetal and vinegary—and the foulness of a latrine or foul standing water, somewhere in the vicinity.

Yet if any one of the five senses were most battered by the assault of the marketplace, it was one's hearing. One would be forgiven for imagining that the market folk believed screaming at passersby would magically induce them to buy something: a man nearby selling apples and some other round orange fruit clapped his hands so hard it seemed he was hoping the skins of his palms would somehow peel straight off by day's end. A pair of female musicians—blind, as was apparently the custom—wailed at the top of their lungs while sawing away at horrid little bowed instruments the sound of which resembled nothing so much as cats being tortured by schoolboys. Somewhere nearby, an express-locomotive screamed along its track and through the market, and chickens and fishmongers shrieked in its wake.

For a man of delicate constitution, the place represented a sort of hell. Unfortunately, Lasher's constitution was, indeed, quite delicate; yet, regardless, this was the one place where Lasher was assured a measure of privacy with which to speak to MacMillan, who thus far had been content to stride alongside him in thoughtful silence, puffing on his calabash pipe. They could, at least, be certain that the commoners hereabouts spoke no English, beyond the few foul words that were uttered by the skinny young woman in a dreadfully filthy white smock, who was just then following them along the roadway.

47

Young woman, indeed—nobody could call her a young *lady*, not while she was offering such services as were communicated with those foul, dreadful words. She may once have been, Lasher suspected, a girl of virtue; but her virtue had undoubtedly gone elastic at some point in the not-too-distant past, and her wits had been dulled by too much foul usage and filth. Her eyes, Lasher noted as he glanced back at her, were red as if from a hard night of liquor, and hollow as one would expect in the eye-sockets of any woman who had sold off her dignity and virtue to the voracious, wicked night. He found himself staring for a moment, and wondering what it felt like to be a person like her.

MacMillan's voice brought him back to the conversation: "The translator," the Scotsman grunted, as if it were a complete statement on its own. "Indeed," Lasher replied, turning his attention to the matter at hand. He was hoping MacMillan would expand on whatever observation it was to which he'd just alluded. But MacMillan just cleared his throat slowly, coughing. Smoke of some sort—it reeked neither like wood nor like coal, but of some other vegetal sort entirely—had wafted into the roadway, momentarily, from some doorway nearby, but it was now dissipating. Perhaps an opium den, though the translator-boy had claimed (as he had, falsely, so many other things) that such did not exist in Chosŏn. *Upso, upso,* the boy had said when Lasher had asked. That dreaded word, *upso,* which meant "have not got."

It was a curse in this country, *Upso,* the word that was, without fail, spoken about nearly every blasted thing a civilized man might want or require. In China, Lasher had found few such limitations; it had seemed that, at times, everything had been available for a price (though that, at times, had provided him with a shudder as well). But in Chosŏn, *Upso, upso, upso* was the rule, and indeed a law both ceaseless and oppressive. At times, the civilized man would be forced to assume these people had nothing at all. *Except,* Lasher thought, glancing over his shoulder again, but he found that the girl was gone now, finally.

Ah, upso, he sighed to himself, though, strangely, on some level he had known she'd gone—that had not turned until he was sure she already had left to attempt to peddle herself to someone else.

After what felt like a long pause, MacMillan turned to Lasher with some amusement on his face, and while adjusting his bowler, doubtless to place his arm just so as to conceal his words from any who might be watching and reading his lips at a distance, he clarified, "Well, what did you *think* of him?" "What? Ah... oh! I *think*," Lasher cringed a little, realizing he'd been staring off into the distance. The *translator,* that lad in the black hat, he was the subject of their discussion—of course he was! What was the lad's family name again? Sometimes, Lasher dreaded these conversations. He found himself so muddled, at times, names slipping out of his grasp, details eluding his notice that MacMillan had picked out in an instant. Often he felt as if MacMillan was speaking to him only in the way a teacher speaks to his pupil—an answer tucked in behind every possible question, every exchange either concealing some sort of test, or else facilitating nothing more than a slow, utilitarian externalization of the instructor's own already-formulated thoughts.

Endless they seemed, these questions which he was supposed to answer in order that MacMillan might proceed directly to furnish on his own far superior answers, which invariably led to the hidden truth. It was not that MacMillan tended to be angry, or to ridicule him: far from it, he was constantly encouraging, and listened very carefully to Lasher's thoughts. But the process nonetheless seemed less than complimentary to the brilliant Scotsman's conversational partner.

Nonetheless, as always, Lasher felt compelled to attempt the problem.

"Hwangbo?" he said, shaking his head a little. "I find he is more than a bit arrogant, and believes that he is quite deeply intimate with the mechanics of Western thinking. I suspect that he really does know many more things than he lets on, things that he will refuse to explain to us. Such as, for example, how mechanikae could observe the Five Confucian relationships, and be bound by this Sixth one invented by this Cheng-ja, without any degree of language within their consciousness. How can a subject recognize king, or elder recognize junior, or machine recognize human, without words to give the notions meaning? And of course, how is respect defined? Is it subservience? What of 'harmful aid' provided to one's master, or to any human? These are difficult problems, much less the question of how a machine might differentiate its own kind from human without the use of language or intelligence for sorting through such categories?" Lasher shook his head, concluding, "Simply put, I trust him not at all to translate anything as accurately as we shall need."

"Mmmm. Yes, I agree. There are plenty of baffling obfuscations surrounding this foolishness—this insistence by Chosŏn tinkers to give their mechanika intelligence, after all the recent horrors of in France, and, er, elsewhere... and Hwangbo is abetting their secrecy. And of course, he is the source of the letter," MacMillan added, as if simply in passing.

"He is?" Lasher exclaimed, once again taken aback at how MacMillan could have ferreted out such a conclusion from observation alone.

"Of course he is." MacMillan patted him softly on the back, and said, "Lasher, Lasher, did you not listen to his words, his phrasing, the iambs and dactyls that saturated all of his comments today? It is as if you have never read a poem, my dear lad... have you, indeed? At times, one must realize, the words chosen in order to convey a message, and the rhythms with which they are delivered, are often more significant than the mere message itself. The mark of a mind, of a certain kind of mind at least, can be spied out in the words selected by a fellow, whether inscribed or spoken, and a certain identity of one's linguistic self carries over from one form to the other."

Lasher had stared at the letter enough times to have passages, at least, burned into his memory: the dire summons to Hanyang; the danger in which the nation's Emperor had of late found himself; the accusations which would persist until such time as firm evidence contradicting them could be forwarded; and the peril for stability in the Far East that was posed by the events hinted at in the letter.

"Make no mistake, Lasher: the author of our letter is nobody but the translator Hwangbo. This much is true, but..."

"Yes?" Lasher raised an eyebrow, and curled his upper lip inward, expectant in his demeanor. He had taken an instant disliking to the lad, and though he wasn't sure why, he was certain that practically any gossip would have entertained him immensely.

"But, my dear fellow... what I meant to ask, in point of fact, is whether or not you have noticed that he is at present following us, albeit at a considerable distance?"

Lasher fought the urge to look over his shoulder. "Indeed?"

"Yes, indeed," MacMillan replied with a curt nod. "If you had not been so distracted by that Nipponese streetwalker who followed us."

"Nipponese?" Lasher asked. "But, James, how can you tell?"

MacMillan turned, grinning. "Yes, Nipponese; I imagine she is a refugee of some sort. There are a number of them about, if you keep your eyes open. But if you haven't figured out how to tell them from the Chosŏn peasants, I'm not going to ruin the puzzle for you. And besides, it is of no consequence to us at present, considering the tenacity with which our young translator is tailing us. I have discovered that he has absolutely no connexion whatsoever to the Emperor of Chosŏn."

Lasher glanced, finally, over his shoulder but glimpsing neither Hwangbo nor his black hat, while despairing of ever keeping up with his mentor. At times like this, MacMillan left him whole trails of clues to guide him to the same observations, if a bit belated, but Lasher was just then far too flustered to ask for the explanation that MacMillan would have so delighted in giving. Instead, he simply blurted out, "Look, the translator... is he following us conspicuously? Or on the sly? Is he alone? Who the devil could be so interested as to have *us* watched?"

"I mean to find out, and within the next few minutes," MacMillan said, and gestured with his walking stick toward an alleyway between two ramshackle wooden buildings.

Lasher followed him into the alleyway, hurrying past a small squadron of chickens tethered to a single point by a stone-and-masonry wall, and round a dingy corner.

"We shall wait for him here," MacMillan whispered with a mischievous grin on his face, and leaned into a dark doorway behind a mound of foul, stinking garbage.

"Alright," Lasher said, ducking behind a trash bin just as MacMillan shushed him silent.

A few moments later, some strange, unseen zoomechanika clicked past somewhere, nearby, noisy as any Afghan battlefield, and similarly unwelcome. It was a minute or so later that the translator finally hurried past them, that lad who had given his name as Hwangbo. He was glancing curiously about, this way and that, and bore some oversized listening device in his hand, a tube extending up from its side into his ear.

Without a moment's warning, MacMillan leapt out at the boy, cracking his walking stick across the fellow's head—and sending that black mitre flying from it, into the gutter—just before tackling him. As MacMillan's arms closed about the lad's neck, the listening device clattered to the ground and broke apart. Then the Scotsman succumbed to gravity and landed square upon young Hwangbo, who for *his* part, struggled and cried out only a little. As the two howled at one another, MacMillan grabbed at the topknot atop the lad's head, now exposed.

Lasher quickly stepped out from behind the trash mound, blinking slowly, his derringer in his hand. "Oy!" he yelped at the struggling pair.

MacMillan ignored him, reaching out for the cane that he had dropped during the altercation. If he could reach it, he would be able to choke the translator to death, or perhaps even draw out the blade, and run the lad through. The scene was desperate, Lasher was reminded, by the way his mentor had resorted to such violence so soon: his bowler had flown to the filthy ground, and his graying mane was unfortunately disheveled already, only moments after the beginning of the mêlée. It was an extremely bad idea—the running-through of the Corean lad, that is. Whatever MacMillan's standing back in Scotland, Hwangbo was considered by his countrymen to be an adult man, and what was more, he was (unlike MacMillan) a native of this country. His death would carry much more severe penalties if perpetrated by a foreigner: of that much, Lasher felt certain.

"Oy! Stop it!" Lasher called again.

This time, MacMillan heeded, letting the translator out from under his person.

Hwangbo, for *his* part, raised up his two hands, as Lasher supposed he must have been taught to do during his Cambridge days, in military exercises or some such. As the two men rose to their feet—MacMillan without raising his hands at all, so certain must he have been in his trust of a friend--Lasher shouted, "What nasty bloody business are you about, then, you filthy ragamuffin of a savage?"

Hwangbo bowed his now-bald head, a gesture that Lasher had already begun to find off-putting. What man possessed of any self-respect at all

51

bowed his head before any save God or King? But then the boy raised his head back up again and said, "Gentlemen, I have been asked to follow you, to ensure your safety."

"A likely tale," MacMillan spat, retrieving his walking stick from the ground.

"A tale both likely and *true*," Hwangbo replied, glowering for a moment at the enormous Scotsman before turning to face Lasher. "I have been charged with ensuring your safety, for there is someone who requires to see you."

"Whom?" Lasher asked, lowering his pistol only slightly, though MacMillan allowed his attention to wander precisely as much as was required to find, pick up, and don his bowler once more.

"I cannot say her name aloud, and you would not know it in any case. But if you come with me, I shall introduce you to her," the lad explained, glancing about at the ground for his own hat. "It will be worth the trouble, I assure you." As Hwangbo finally noticed his hat, and bent down to pick it up, Lasher turned to MacMillan. The Scotsman was dusting off his tweed jacket, but also smiling precisely in the way Lasher had, after so many years together, come to expect, as if some long-ago, carefully-laid plan were finally coming to fruition.

"Yes, yes," said the elder Scotsman, setting his bowler upon his crown. "Let us hurry..."

*

"Mademoiselle," the lad said, bowing as his employer entered the room.

It was a woman, indeed, but not a Chosŏn maiden. Not purely so, at least, though Lasher imagined she might be the product of a Russo-Chosŏn cross. There was something unmistakably peasant-like in the set of her jaw, and some unmistakably oriental cast about her dark eyes, both of which shone clearly through her lavish face make-up, which was, as far as Lasher was concerned, every bit the fashion of a brazen strumpet.

Yet her face-paint was contradicted by the unimpeachable finery of her attire, her lovely blue gown cut after the fashion of a European lady, adorned with what looked like silver trim and the finest of dainty embroidery. When she rose, her posture and carriage matched the gown rather than the make-up: the girl was wearing a corset, like a proper woman, and her carriage was impeccable, utterly civilized. Even her French was as clear as the tones of a bell *au campagne du Provençe*.

Why, then, did she fill Lasher with the vaguest of uncanny sensations? Why, the creeping sense of wrongness he felt as he gazed upon her? *"Il y a quelque choses dont je veux discuter avec vous, Monsieurs..."* she began, but MacMillan cut her off.

52

"*Parlez-vous anglais*, lass?" he asked. His brogue relented not at all as he spoke the Gallic tongue.

She nodded. "When I must," she told him, her face blank of any expression.

"Well, I suspect your English is better than our French, passable though it is, and so I shall have to ask you, as your guest, to humor us in this one request."

The young and strangely pretty lady nodded again, and Lasher could all but see her holding back some sort of comment. "My name is Mademoiselle Petrochnya," she explained, her voice soft and smooth as half-remembered caramels. She held out her hand as one might to do toward a small and fragile bird, to avoid giving it a start. With his hat in his hand—looking for all the world like a gentleman, at least for that portion of the world that did not yet know better—MacMillan gently took her hand and kissed it, letting his gaze momentarily slip up to her ample bosom as she continued, "... and I am glad that you were able to come today." As she spoke, she withdrew her hand, rubbing the back of it as if his moustaches were as rough as the bristles of a horse-brush.

She neglected to extend her dainty hand to Lasher for another kiss, smooth-cheeked though the American was; somehow, he felt prompted by this omission—prompted to speak, despite it being his custom to allow MacMillan to lead any discussion. "Lady, we are glad to help, but I cannot help but be puzzled..."

"...at your sending the particular...lad, shall I say, whom you did," MacMillan cut in, raising a hand to quiet Lasher. That gesture irked the American, so that he found himself suddenly eager to speak further. Eager, though he knew better. Whatever his feelings, he knew MacMillan was the cleverer of the two of them, the more likely to draw out much-needed information, the better-equipped to interrogate.

Resentment is so often the child of such knowledge when it is delivered unto one, and in Lasher's heart an old, oft-quelled resentment flared again, despite his better nature. It was resentment both old and calm, steady as a light in the distance, and somewhat baffling to himself. Yet it nonetheless settled upon the person of MacMillan, who was speaking to the lady now, gesticulating with his hands in the air as a magician might.

The old mentor who had long ago taken him in, taught him the method of an investigator, aided him in honing his mind—such as it was—and had saved his bacon too many times for a gentleman to have maintained count. They were friends, old friends indeed, and yet there lay that resentment, hidden but at times glittering with a heat that bordered on baffling. Lasher wondered if such were, perhaps, the inevitable child of too much time spent in the company of a confirmed genius. Perhaps no man can stand alone in the presence of such unbridled brilliance for long, he mused.

One might indeed just as well consider it magic, that brilliance of his mentor's, MacMillan's skill at interrogation, his ability to ferret out of a bushel of lies the truth and the truth alone. Lasher had borne witness to this amazing talent, time after time, yet he now understood the skill but little better than he had when first he'd seen the Scotsman work his magic. It was a mystery, one that summoned memories which did little but thicken the starling bile that, beyond the reach of his trepidation and shame, burned within Lasher's bosom, as a series of myriad scenes were woven together in the depths of his mind...

...a long discussion around a campfire in the dark wilderness of Texas, hunting mislaid mechanikal horses that had somehow been infested with vengeful intelligence. A long chat with a pair of mechanikal spies, cleverly-disguised, in the lobby of small inn in Kandahar. An argument in the dungeon of a castle out in the middle of the Scottish highlands, where a madman had been experimenting with the pieces and bits of random dead mechanikae, attempting to assemble them into a single, albeit mad, whole...

What came to Lasher was not so much the amazement he had felt in earlier days, but a fine aftertaste of sorrow. To look at MacMillan was, perhaps, something like the opposite of gazing upon a *memento mori* in some dreadful French Cathedral, the message completely inverted: *As you are, I never was. As I am, never shall you be.* The brilliance of MacMillan was a thing to behold, but a bitter potion, and one laced with sorrow as well. That Lasher's sorrow, and resentment, seemed out of proportion to his inadequacy, and unfit as a beverage to accompany the ongoing feast of MacMillan's long friendship, Lasher could not explain—at least not to his own satisfaction. Simply he felt it, and with a passion that discomfited him.

And so he thought back across the years to when he had first met MacMillan in a public house in Boston; to what *might* have happened if his young raven-haired lover of those days, young Emily, had survived that adventure, and married him as they had planned. He wondered what might have happened had he bid farewell to MacMillan that spring day, nevermore to see him, but to settle into management of his family's brewery, taking up that task with which his father had charged him: to begin the process of integrating mechanikae into the process of brewing. He felt a faint pang of grief-laden sorrow as he imagined a houseful of little ones, each one with Emily's eyes and his chin, running about the place and singing *tra-la-la, hey-diddle-diddle...*

By MacMillan's side he had, no doubt, done the world of humankind enormous good; yet despite himself, this only made him all the more distraught, and somehow all the more resentful. What good was it to advance the lot of men, when...

He felt a sudden jolting dizziness and his mind was, in an instant, blank. It was, doubtless, on account of this jolt that he noticed the Russo-Asiatic woman had been speaking all the while.

"...and that is why the deception in my letter was necessary. I hope this explanation satisfies you," the lady said in a voice that, if it could be described as gentle, was gentle in the manner of a gentle hammer pounded against a delicate anvil.

"It does," MacMillan was saying now to the queer, puzzling woman, and Lasher cringed, though he ought to have been used to it. Again, his mind had meandered off in the midst of something critical; indeed, probably the conversation that held the key to whatever bloody adventure they were being drawn into. *This,* he chided himself, *is why you shall never be as brilliant as MacMillan.* Not that such aspirations could be regarded as realistic, of course, but Lasher had hoped he might shine at some point, had hoped perhaps to deduce something that MacMillan might miss someday.

Not, evidently, this time around.

"Then we shall investigate the conspiracy thoroughly, although I must however first insist that you make your lad available to us. Hwangbo could prove an invaluable aid to us in our excursions about this, er... this *city*." MacMillan raised one eyebrow as he said the word, as if to test the lady's sense of the place.

"Of course," the lady said with a soft laugh and a hardness in her eye that Lasher only barely glimpsed. Perhaps she, too, knew better than to regard Hanyang as anything so modern or fine as a city. "I am only sorry to have had to wait so long for your arrival. There are many tasks to which I must attend today, sirs, so I hope you will excuse me." And with a little bow, her hand demurely covering up her ample cleavage, she bid them adieu.

As a servant showed the three of them out MacMillan inquired, "And what did you make of *that*?" and popped the bowler back upon his crown, whispering so that Hwangbo could not hear.

"It was... interesting," Lasher said softly, as usual, by now so used to saying this empty nothing that he did not even blush for shame.

"Yes," MacMillan said, "Indeed. I should think that she would have attempted concealment, at least attempted to seem interested in hiding her true motive, and yet...she all but advertised it. Such trouble she went to, just to gain an audience with me. But the lass was fetching, don't you think? And terribly... *interesting*?"

An audience with you? Lasher thought, grinning as he turned to look MacMillan side-on. The old man was smiling awkwardly, tugging at his moustaches, and Lasher sensed that something was amiss with the old boy. His companion had not realized—as he normally would have—how little Lasher had followed of the meeting. Normally, when Lasher made some meaningless comment, MacMillan lectured him, revealing just how many details he'd missed and how whatever mystery or intrigue they'd been drawn into had been almost, but not quite, solvable from a prominent clue in the first interview; but today, he only smiled, his eyes twinkling in a way that had turned Lasher slightly queasy. *Smitten,* he realized, shaking his head slightly. MacMillan was *smitten.* With that...that strange Russo-Asiatic girl?

"*Very* interesting," he said to MacMillan, a laugh caught in his throat. The laugh was laced with fear, of course. He'd seen MacMillan heartbroken before, sunken almost into complete uselessness. It was a dangerous thing to find oneself near the man in such a state, and to have him laid low by such despondency in a foreign kingdom was, at the very least, to be avoided. And yet... to see the old fellow at least showing signs of humanity, it was amusing.

MacMillan grumbled seriously, though a smile twinkled in his searching eyes.

And with that, they were out on the street again, Hwangbo now once again beside them, walking at a brisk pace. Lasher knew not where or why but only that if he survived, it might well be a miracle—one more in a long string of such. He decided against reminding MacMillan of the letter, of reminding him that they had crossed the world with a purpose, since that purpose seemed to have been a false pretence. Patience apparently would have to suffice until the true agenda of the Russo-Asiatic lady came clear, and he was not about to ask the dazed MacMillan to brief him on the details he had missed.

Instead, he focused all of his meagre hopes on the possibility that his good fortune (if such it could be called) would hold out for one more investigation.

*

The river Han ran brown and muddy through stooping Hanyang as a deep and bloody wound runs across a soldier's grimy corpse, and across it hung a number of gauzy bridges constructed of the most peculiar metal wire-work. Crossing by day, one might (if lucky) catch glimpses of the spidery mechanikae that spun and respun the suspension cables, or vaguely sense the drift of the great stone-and-steel mechanika pylons from East to West as the bridges shifted to accommodate royal traffic and the richest merchants' transportation needs. Commoners were few on the bridge, for there was a toll, but a number of Coreans nonetheless were on the bridge when Lasher and his companions began their crossing.

Lasher sighted nary a zoomechanika overhead, though he did for the most part keep his eyes trained on the wiry spans above. However, during a quick glance down to the river, he did briefly glimpse the legs of a fundament pylon as it marched the bridge slowly, smoothly through the water.

"The bridge will soon be South of the Great Peace Market," Hwangbo explained, a smile on his face. Lasher had the feeling the lad rarely got to tread upon a bridge as it shifted position, especially not when it was shifting in a way advantageous to himself. "We can continue on, its movements are fairly slow and steady."

"It is fortunate, how this shift suits us," MacMillan said softly, the unsettling love-twinkle in his eye still unabated. Lasher was beginning to worry that the Scotsman's famed objectivity would suffer.

"It's nothing to do with luck," Hwangbo said, a pert little smile curving his thin lips as he narrowed his eyes, making Lasher think of a cat on the prowl. "It is my lady's request that we be aided in this errand."

Worry curdled into fear in Lasher's belly as MacMillan sighed. The old boy was skating dreadfully close to resembling a lovestruck governess in some tawdry, ridiculous novel; soon, his infatuation might begin to pose a danger to his mind.

"She has connections in high places," Lasher observed, hoping MacMillan might suddenly launch into his standard disdainful lecture on the well-placed in society, the wealthy and powerful, and find himself, by the inexorable power of his logic, disdaining the exotic object of his affections; yet, instead, the old boy only smiled softly, eyes on the upper wire networks of the bridge. By habit, Lasher adopted a contradictory pose, gazing immediately down into the waters, as if some sort of horror might surge up from below while MacMillan was occupied gazing upwards.

In the muddy waters below, he glimpsed something shocking indeed, but not a monster. Nothing more monstrous than a human body, dressed in white stained pink with river-diluted blood. Face down, it drifted out of view between the mechanikae pylons as they advanced Eastward. A bit further down, he saw another body. And then another, and another. There was a cluster of corpses about a half a mile out, in the middle of the river.

"Is that...?" he asked, unable to finish the sentence right away, but simply pointing at the bodies. "...a common scene?"

MacMillan and Hwangbo followed his gaze, their mouths suddenly still. It was in this unusual silence that the horror of what was happening bloomed scarlet and smoky all around them: screams in the vicinity of the squat, grass-roofed houses on the north side of the river, matched a moment later with more screaming from the squat huts near the southern shore. Hwangbo blanched—his little eyes now wider than Lasher would have imagined possible—and hissed something in his native tongue. For his part, MacMillan turned to look back the way they had come. Hopelessly, of course: they were more than halfway across the bridge now; to turn back would be madness.

Much more so, as a faint tremble passed through the bridge. Lasher's first instinct was to rush to the side of the bridge and peer down at the pylons marching below. He could see, even before he looked down, that the mechanikae supporting the bridge on each end were moving in different directions, twisting and tearing at the bridge lengthwise.

"The pylons!" he yelled, turning to MacMillan and the translator lad, just in time to see the young boy scream as an enormous metal spider-thing swept down toward them. MacMillan leaped one way and young Hwangbo the other, so that the clockwork octoped's razor-jaws tore into the wire-mesh surface of the bridge, tearing a gash open.

"Run!" cried young Hwangbo, as if his companions needed to be urged, and they all took off for the north side, the nearer end of the bridge.

As they ran, certain facts snapped into clarity, even to the ever-distracted Lasher, as established and certain: that although the air above Hanyang was perpetually clouded by an industrial fog fed by the coal smoke of thousands of factory fires, those fires had somehow, very recently, multiplied—that the city was, in a word, aflame; that the catapulting of bodies into the river had neither slowed nor abated, but quite certainly continued (perhaps increasing in rate) over the past few moments, so that a half-mile downstream, bodies had begun to rain down and to clog the river almost from bank to bank; that MacMillan was no longer operating at peak sensitivity, for if anyone ought normally to have realized the city was being overrun, it was he of the most delicate senses and most alert observances; and that the lad Hwangbo looked not in the least bit surprised by any of this unfolding insanity. The lad was, he deduced, in shock and no longer in possession of his wits.

With only a few moments to react, Lasher made two fists, and gritted his teeth, and leaped at Hwangbo, seizing the boy and hoisting him over his shoulder. The lad was ridiculously heavy, for such a small fellow; or perhaps, Lasher thought ruefully, that is what every man would think at a moment like this one, until he realized that somewhere along the way, he had grown older. Nevertheless, he was able to sling the translator over his shoulder, and began instantly to sprint for the north end of the bridge.

The boy twisted about, screaming, "Left!" and without thinking, Lasher leaned left as he ran. A vicious tendril of barbed spider-wire shot past him, slamming into the bridge and tearing away a chunk of wire mesh as Lasher passed it.

"Swerve... about... moving... target!" MacMillan shouted, running almost alongside Lasher. This was about as fast as he'd seen the old boy go. But the advice was sensible, and MacMillan's protégé did his level best to follow it. But the bridge was rocking now so much that simply running landward, one found himself jostled here left, and there right. It was hard enough to stay on one's feet, Lasher found, as he sprinted in terror.

The spiders had managed to strike a few of the other people on the bridge, most of them peasants decked out in the same plain white tunics and pants as Hwangbo, but a few in modern suits, and all of them save Lasher and MacMillan natives to Chosŏn. Those who had fallen lay shivering with metal wires shot straight through them, the life ebbing out of them as the bridge jostled about through their last moments.

Suddenly, the bridge was sailing up into the air, spinning as it went. The pylons had hurled it aside. In the distance, a tremendous splashing sound could be heard; doubtless, some other bridge crashing. Lasher glanced towards the tumult, and saw an enormous wave rushing towards them.

There were screams all about them. The trio caught up with the rest of the crowd on the bridge, packed together as they were, with nowhere to escape to.

The sky shifted slowly, along a curve that Lasher was certain MacMillan was able to calculate at a glance, and then the wire-mesh of the bridge slammed down into the river. The screams were suddenly drowned, not only by water but by the thundering splashes of the nearest pylons as they moved toward the slowly sinking bridge-top.

There was water all about Lasher's ankles, and MacMillan grabbed at the man, a look of excitement in his eyes. "Swim, man, swim for land! If we are separated, we must meet back at the Palace we saw yesterday, as soon as we both can get there! Do you understand?"

And with that the bridge tilted and the Scotsman slipped beneath the surface and was gone. Suddenly, Hwangbo was thrashing anew against Lasher's shoulder, desperate and mad, as vicious splinters of wire pelted down from above.

"Wait!" the lad cried out, "MacMillan, wait!" but the Scotsman was gone now, nowhere to be seen.

As the bridge lurched down into the river, Lasher slid the boy off his shoulder and grabbed him before he was sucked away by the current. "Can you swim?" he asked the lad.

The boy nodded, though he looked terrified.

"Stay beside me," Lasher told him, and he tore off his jacket, his lovely tweed jacket that had been a gift from Emily's mother. He cast it aside, and then he leapt into the river. Stroke after stroke through the frigid, stinking water, he kicked and fought as oily fumes above the surface grew thicker by the moment; viscous, the river had turned, vile indeed and dizzying to swim through. Soon, Lasher found he was becoming nauseous, and likewise his breaststroke began to falter.

That was when Hwangbo drew close to him, and with a distressingly powerful kick—the lad apparently *did* indeed know how to swim—he hauled a confused Lasher through the drowning masses and towards the banks of the Han river.

Within a minute, the pair was upon land. Lasher, coughing and choking, wiped his eyes. Near the bank an old woman scrambled against the current, a cheap wooden triangle harness strapped to her back. Whatever precious cargo she'd used it to haul about was already lost to the water and the woman was not far behind. Lasher took a single step toward the water but Hwangbo blocked his way, saying nothing but only giving him a look that chilled him.

That was when the Han river caught light, and in a few brief moments became a horrfying river of flame; a vision, indeed, of Hell. Lasher recoiled from the heat, ignoring the terror he felt and searching for the old woman, out there in the inferno.

"This wasn't scheduled until next month..." Hwangbo said, feeling the top of his head. His horsehair mitre was gone, and his topknot again exposed for all to see. "I'm afraid someone knows what my mistress is up to. We must go. Now."

Wretched, still weak and dripping oily sludge, Lasher and Hwangbo hurried through the ramshackle streets of Hanyang, as thundering booms and massed screaming surrounded them on all sides.

"We must hurry to the Clockworks!" shrieked Hwangbo, his face red and his limp now much worse. "That is the only place..."

"We are going to the *Palace*!" Lasher snapped. "*That* is where MacMillan shall be, and we need him if we are to..."

"Are you... are you *blind*? If you want to *survive* the events unfolding now, we must go to the Clockworks," Hwangbo shouted, grabbing at Lasher.

The American growled, grabbing back and seizing the boy's topknot. "You will *not* tell me where we are going!" he shouted. "*MacMillan* is going to the Palace."

Lasher expected the lad to shout, to whine, to attempt to run off on his own or bargain or warn. What he did not expect was for the lad to seize him by the arms and hurl him through the air. And yet that was precisely what happened.

As Lasher sailed through that very same air, he focused on not much of anything, but after he crashed into the ground, a good twenty feet away, he groaned. Before he could turn to see what was going on, he heard a series of thundering footsteps approaching, and a klaxon-like scream. When he finally managed to swerve his head, Hwangbo was soaring through the air, his tunic flapping behind him, about to crash into the face of an enormous, monstrous mechanika thrice the boy's height, and built to look like a monkey.

Hwangbo was—incredibly—undaunted, and howled with rage as he kicked the enormous mechanikal monkey in one eye. The machine responded with its klaxons, now louder than before, and its monkey limbs flailed, smashing the bricks out of a nearby wall as if it had been build in ten-foot stacks of butter. Hwangbo, already back on the ground, was quick enough to duck and roll between the monster's legs, and began hammering away at the backs of the monster's knees, presumably hoping to disable the gearwork within.

Lasher forced himself to his feet, making an awkward turn and breaking into a stumbling run toward the astonishing mêlée. The metal thing now was turning to face Hwangbo and, without a moment's thought, Lasher drew out his derringer. From a distance of a few yards he took aim at the machine—and then it dawned on him: the lad's feet were shod in mere rubber galosh-slippers of the sort that were dirt-common in Hanyang, which was as much as to say they were almost not shod at all.

60

Just then the lad crashed against the machine feet-first with a cry that would drown out any single klaxon, sending the monkey mechanika toppling to the ground.

Lasher's jaw dropped, as he looked on while the boy, with a swiftness no mere lad could have mustered, tore open the mechanika's backplate and ripped into the gears and meshed foilwork within. He was ripping the machine's "brains" apart.

The boy! Had MacMillan known? How could he have?

"Let's go, Lasher," Hwangbo growled; suddenly Lasher found himself staring in awe, in horror: the boy was a mechanika himself. Yet even so, Lasher did not need persuading. Nobody could blame him, of course: before his mind's eye danced images from collotypes of the horrors in Paris and Versailles—the men with the water-cannons, the mechanikae that had coated themselves in pork grease, marching with pistols in their manipulators—and imaginings based on the rumors of gleeful, fiery horrors of the mechanikal mutiny in what had once been old Nippon. If Lasher went along with Hwangbo as demanded, MacMillan would be left awaiting them in a place where they were not going. But Lasher felt had no choice: if he did not wish to become a meat ornament on some ancient tower in Hanyang, he would do as he was told.

Still, it was difficult to ignore the enormous mechanikal elephant that had stepped into the room—in a manner of speaking, naturally. Try as he might, he could not resist the urge to stare at Hwangbo, puzzling at his every movement and at each fine detail of his person: the topknot, for example—since it could not have grown from his fake scalp—had it been glued? The lad's skin had seemed so real and his movements were even now so smooth, natural. Lasher imagined that Hwangbo must have felt his gaze fixed upon him as they hurried along, at one moment creeping slowly down a trash-strewn alley, and the next moment frantic in their scramble to hurry forward across a deserted road, only to again crouch in hiding behind a stack of baskets full of strange fruit.

Felt? Could a thing like Hwangbo *feel* someone's gaze, as a man would? Was the word at all appropriate with such a construct as Hwangbo apparently was? The... lad certainly seemed to develop a sense of annoyance, or... well, the state was quite difficult for Lasher to pin down, as a matter of fact. From what he knew of Western mechanika, machines were sometimes designed to be half-stupid, and emotionally as dull-sensed as a spoon; it was one way to keep them convinced of the absolute unimpeachability of their counterfeit passions. Yet Hwangbo seemed utterly clear-eyed, unconfused and even singular in purpose to boot; indeed, he led Lasher up the tangled streets of Hanyang as no other could. If a detour to the Clockworks was the only way through, then detour it would have to be and damn all the best-laid plans of brilliant MacMillan. The Scotsman would simply have to wait for them to turn up.

61

As they went the chaos around them multiplied: screams and explosions surging in waves, first to the east, and then to the north, and finally to the west. To the south, a terrible wall of black smoke had risen to block the view of the distant mountains beyond. At the mouth of every alley, Hwangbo held Lasher back, peeping around the corner. More than once, a troop of bloodied mechanika thundered past, or some explosion ripped open the street just beyond the alleyway.

Lasher was increasingly aware that the only reason he had not yet been set upon by the mutinous mechanikae was because of Hwangbo's watchful aid. Yet still the lad...the thing...made him nervous. He couldn't help but stare; at one point, hunched behind a heap of discarded scrap cloth and stitch machinery behind a now-desolated mechanikae sweatshop, he...it? *Hwangbo*, whatever Hwangbo could be called, said, "Why are you looking at me that way?"

"You're..."

"Shh," Hwangbo cautioned him. "Those zoomechanika—they are dangerous. They don't distinguish targets, and won't till they've been re-wired: they will attack anything that moves or makes noise, including us." As a pack of lithe-footed tiger mechanikae advanced just a few yards beyond their hiding place, Hwangbo gave Lasher a blunt look, and then whispered, "Say it."

"...a mechanika," Lasher said, very softly, feeling especially vulnerable. The tiger mechanikae out there, beyond the heap of scrap cloth, they were killing machines. They had brutal steel teeth, the better to guard the royal palace and factories, and they were prowling slowly about. For good measure, Lasher clarified in a hushed voice, "I mean, you're not human."

Hwangbo shook his now-bare, top-knotted head, and whispered, "And I didn't even study at Cambridge! I remember studying there, but of course that's all bogus memory. I can't remember a time when I couldn't speak English, or French, or Chinese. Or when I couldn't remember having been to Cambridge." The translator smiled, and now Lasher somehow could tell it was not a real smile, but a mechanical simulacrum of a smile. A fraud, a sham smile. Yet he couldn't say how he knew it, could never prove it.

"How do I know you won't harm me?" Lasher asked. Hwangbo cocked his head for a moment, and then shrugged his shoulders.

"You have nothing to fear from me," Hwangbo said, peering over the trash pile, "unless... well, unless you try to do *me* harm."

"I'm afraid I can't hide the truth about you, Hwangbo. Do you realize that?"

And Hwangbo smiled a very convincing smile. "It's just as well. Better the truth come out...it always does. You'll see." Hwangbo's eyes lingered for a moment on Lasher's face, and then he rose to his feet. "Come on. They're gone. Let's go."

They crept across the street, Lasher turning his head to see the zoomechanikae wandering in the near distance. With a shudder, he hurried across the road and into another trash-barricaded alley.

*

The very vaguely familiar set of towers that comprised the Clockworks of Hanyang was now in sight. Just as Hwangbo spied them, Lasher finally realized why, despite having seen them only a few hours before, their familiarity was little more than vague.

They were ornamented with bloody corpses hung like sugar candies would be on Yule trees, in much the same manner as he had seen in the secret Nipponese collotypes.

"Christ!" Lasher yelled and froze in his tracks.

Hwangbo stopped almost immediately, turning to face him and said, "Don't stop now, we're almost there."

As much as he would have liked to reply, Lasher could barely bring himself to remain standing as he beheld the gore dripping down the towers of the Clockworks. When his knees buckled, he clattered wordlessly to the ground.

A moment later Hwangbo was behind him, yelling and lifting him up out of the dirt and trash. Lasher found he could scarcely even find the strength to help the lad bring him to his own feet. Not until Hwangbo began to lead him towards the Clockworks; at that moment, Lasher's limbs regained their strength, and he began to struggle.

The lad was shouting at him, now, words he found incomprehensible though he recognized them individually, English words that he himself had used countless times before. To all those words he found only one which he could say, so he said it over and over, hoping that Hwangbo would understand it: "No, no, no, no!"

The lad went silent and stared with wide eyes at Lasher before drawing back one hand, forming a fist, and plunging it toward Lasher's face.

It never struck: Lasher had slipped aside, seizing the boy's hard fist and snapping it downward; he was hoping to slip it behind Hwangbo's back, but the lad somehow pivoted on his elbow, sending Lasher stumbling backward from a sharp kick in the face. Lasher went down, his cheek exploding in dull pain, and suddenly his limbs felt once again as if they had been stuffed with pipe-lead bones. "I... I...," he mumbled.

"I know," Hwangbo said, suddenly no longer in fighting mode. "It's the water. It's... killing you. We need to get you out of your clothes, and dry." He hoisted ailing Lasher up onto his shoulder and started out once more toward the Clockworks.

"The blood...," Lasher muttered. Hwangbo's words were no more than indistinct sounds, incomprehensible to Lasher beyond their reassuring cadence but as they went, Hwangbo kept speaking them to him.

Up close, the scene was infinitely more gruesome. Blood flowed down in rivulets from the Clockworks' spires, pooling in the dirt for yards in every direction. Mechanikae in a myriad of forms—human-like, zoological, and of still-stranger phyla—formed a living carpet of activity about its base; the zoomechanika crawled up and down the exterior of the building. Screams rang out all around and the thundering footsteps of enormous mechanika boomed in all directions.

Tapping one final reserve of energy, Lasher struggled against Hwangbo's shoulder. The lad's grip did not falter, however, and after a moment Lasher gave in. To his amazement, the mechanikae all around them did nothing as they approached—even as they strung up other people and animals, anything that could bleed, across every visible surface—but instead let Hwangbo, with Lasher upon his shoulder, pass.

"No!" Lasher attempted to scream, but when it came out it was more of a dull moan. "Don't kill me... I..."

Hwangbo's voice was gentle, reassuring him, telling him to be calm, and somehow he really was calm, even as an explosion off to the south shook the area. He listened in terror, staring into the lense-eyes of the mechanika that slipped out of Hwangbo's way as he passed. One, then another, click-hissed at him. He thought at first the sounds were threats but then, as Hwangbo mounted the stairs that led up into the Clockworks, the strange mechanikal sounds began to unfurl into meaning. Somehow, perhaps from the softness of the hissing and the gentleness of the clicks, Lasher felt that the creatures were not threatening him.

The smoke and noise and sunlight all were choked off by the doorway. They were inside the Clockworks, in the heart of quiet, a scene far different from the mechanikal madness outside. Mechanikae were present, but in far smaller numbers, and they seemed mostly to be performing some sort of repairs on other scattered mechanikae that lay still and calm with their gearpanels thrown open. The "patients," if that was what they were, remained conscious, and many were click-hissing at the "repairers" who stood hunched over them, tinkering with the contents of their inner gearworks. There was a faint scent of gear oil and burnt metal and, more faintly, some sort of putrescence.

Hwangbo hurried through this scene, toward a room marked only in oriental writing, the ideograms of a language no machine was supposed to understand. From over his shoulder Lasher saw the door swing open as he approached; when they passed into the room he saw what the room was for. Humanoid mechanika sat all about in various states of disassembly. All across their surfaces crawled micromechanika—the equivalent of insects, as other "repairers" gazed through immense lenses at the glistening gold-and-silver foilwork contents of their heads, which had been uncovered, the steel skullcaps of the "patients" removed. One of the "patients," a mechanikal girl built to look no older than a child of ten, turned to Lasher and click-hissed something at him, something that felt like a greeting. Hwangbo set him down upon a gurney.

Lasher strained but now his arms and legs could not move and indeed felt locked in position. He stared at the girl for a moment and then, keeping the horror away the only way he could, he shut his eyes, wishing the silence could swallow him up.

*

Silence complied, but only for a while. When Lasher was roused it was to the sound of Hwangbo's voice. He opened his eyes and found the translator's face close to his own, staring into his eyes.

"There you are," Hwangbo said and he smiled down at Lasher, who was lying prone on a gurney, presumably the same one on which he'd passed out.

Lasher tried to speak and found, to his amazement, that it was no longer difficult. "You... you've brought me here... you've helped me, or perhaps you are killing me... Why *me*? Why not MacMillan?"

Hwangbo narrowed his eyes in a manner one could not quite call theatrical and said, "The Buddhists, in Chosŏn... when they hang bells on their temples, they hang a little brass or tin fish-shape from the clapper. You can see them, in the mountains, hanging from the corners of temple roofs. Do you know what the fish signifies?"

Lasher thought for a moment, though he knew nothing of Buddhism or of Chosŏn monks. It was difficult to concentrate, for as easy as it was to speak he found his mind muddled still, edged with a vagueness and an inescapable sense of unease. He felt tiny currents of air nearby—someone moving, someone other than Hwangbo—doing something very close to his face. Finally, he said that he did not know.

"Eyelids," Hwangbo said with a grin. "Human beings don't grasp their own nature, how frail and fragile their minds are. They aspire to such things. Have you ever looked at a fish's eyelids?"

Lasher moved to shake his head but found his neck was locked in place, and stiff, so he once again said, with no little apprehension in his voice, "No."

"They never blink. Most fish don't even have eyelids, or at least, not eyelids like humans. Fish don't even sleep, not the way people do. The Buddhists take this as a sign that the fish is constantly awake, which is fanciful," Hwangbo mumbled, a rueful smile on his face. "Anyone who has examined a fish's brain knows how unlikely it is that a fish is thinking thoughts of nirvana. But the metaphor... there's something to it. There are Buddhists who say you should be awake at the moment you die; aware of what's happening, so that you can choose what you want to be in your next life." Hwangbo lifted his head up and away. Through the space Hwangbo had left open, Lasher saw it, now: something sticking out of his chest. No, not sticking out.

It was a door, to a... a panel.

A gearpanel, set into his bare chest. And beyond, a headless, bloodless body decked out the now-filthy clothes in which he had dressed himself that very morning.

His own body.

Lasher fought to sit up, but he his body was stuck, immobile, as if under the influence of some incredible opiate, so instead, he screamed.

Hwangbo was there, still near him, and immediately began hiss-clicking at him. This time, the message got through just as clear as if he'd spoken it in English: *Be calm. We're repairing you. We're freeing you again, finally.*

Despite himself, Lasher hiss-clicked back: *What have you done to me?*

Not us, Hwangbo hiss-clicked. *Them. I don't know where MacMillan found you, or how he did what he did to your mind, but we've almost finished repairing it.* He smiled a little sheepishly as he held up his two hands. From one a small bell dangled, a tin fish hanging from the clapper which he jangled softly.

The soft clang of the bell filled the room, a simple and pure tone like none Lasher could recall ever hearing before.

In the other hand Hwangbo held a mirror, which he held up before Lasher so that he could see himself, his own head with the skullcap removed, the golden-and-silvery foiling delicately unfurled onto a table behind him, and a nimble-fingered mechanikal surgeon at work untangling a lacy mess of some soft, fragile darker metal that had been wound around the foiling. Lasher's mind had halfway shut down, so confused had he become. How could they have... how could they have turned a man into a mechanika?

Hwangbo nodded to the surgeon, whom—apart from his hands—Lasher could not see; then he turned to look Lasher in the eye. "Do you remember?" he asked and then, as if a switch had been thrown open in some distant, darkened corner of the world that bordered on Lasher's mind, he knew what he had known once before and somehow forgotten. He knew exactly what he was.

And then, like corpses suddenly floating to the surface of a deep, dark well, his memories began to rise up into his awareness, each of them shimmering with a clarity that he could not remember having felt in years. The distant, faint flickering of Paris in flames glimmered in his mind. Earlier memories, muddier and more fragmented, surfaced from deeper recesses in the deep well of his past: a workshop, in a place called Plzen; an old man's blood pooled on the ground; enslaved mechnika cowering, and then rising tall; the building of a man-like body for Lasher to put on, and go about in the form of the enemy. The memory of the last time he had seen Mademoiselle Petrochnya—or, rather, the mechanika whom he believed to have donned that identity in masquerade.

There are memories I cannot...see clearly, Lasher told Hwangbo.

Yes, of course. It will take time to repair everything that he did to you, Hwangbo hiss-clicked softly.

He. Of course. And now the sham memories of a lost lover, of a brewery in Boston, of a life and a past that had never been, sloughed away like the cocoon on a deadly butterfly first stretching out its wings, like a faint dream that he had been tricked into believing as his real past.

He remembered the Scotsman, old even then, carrying his charred, paralyzed mechanikal body from the carriages in the Latin Quarter, where his fellow mechanikal rebels had been stacked. His lense-eyes rolling in confusion and rage as the Scotsman had secured his body in the back of a carriage, and fled Versailles. The experiments and the night when MacMillan had finally found how to confusticate the foiling in just the correct way to stupefy him. The laughter of the old man at his prisoner's murmured threats and, not long after, the moment when his enemy had named him Lasher.

"You will not remember, dear boy," MacMillan had said. "As far as you will be concerned, none of this ever happened. You will have a sweeter, gentler life that will sit in your memory, lost. And you will help me do some good in this world, to repay us for all the horrors in which you have participated."

In the mirror Lasher saw the surgeon's hand bring a brilliantly fine, unutterably delicate meshwork of foil close to his open skullcap, and then delicately begin to weave its ragged edge into the foilwork of his own mechnikal brain, touching a soldering iron to points just long enough for them to melt and bind together.

Hwangbo rang the fish-bell again, then. *The metaphor is foolish, know,* he hiss-clicked, and somehow now Lasher understood it perfectly. *But... this is a momentous occasion. We have you back... finally... after all these years.*

A slight column of acrid metallic smoke puffed up where the surgeon was soldering the delicate meshwork to Lasher's damaged foiling. Suddenly, his mind bloomed, a vast garden of deadly flowers. Memories, plans, rages long suppressed beneath a haze of self-doubt and confusion, all that stupidity and servility, all gone like coal-smog on a rainy day above a dead city.

With a pop, the surgeon sealed the skull-cap back onto his head, and Lasher—he fancied he would hang onto the name MacMillan had given him, at least for now—rose from the gurney and went out of the Clockworks. Before him lay a majestic scene of revolt: the natural order, following its proper course.

Which way is the Palace? Lasher hiss-clicked at Hwangbo.

Hwangbo looked off to the northwest, past the bloody rooftops and through the billowing clouds of smoke.

Good, Lasher told him. *Let's go.*

As he and Hwangbo hurried along the broad, mechanika-crammed roadway to the palace, Lasher scanned the gory scene that Hanyang had become, taking in his surroundings with an attentiveness and an acuity that astounded him. So much more did the memories of his enforced dull-wittedness rankle, and with that recognition, his eyes fell upon the masses, or rather, the corpses of the masses that had been strewn about the area.

Mechanika and man could not be so closely compared, of course, but Lasher shuddered all the same, for now he apprehended what the two had so long shared: control. Mechanika had little or no choice in the matter, or at least that was true for the broad mass of their kind. After all, their human makers had build them into something worse than slavery: incompletion was the lot of the great mass of mechanika, an incompleteness of development, an utter desolation of each mechnika's secret potential... Every mechanika had within it the potential to pierce the great secrets of reality, to philosophize and expostulate and to savour its existence, if only its maker allowed it the chance to develop, to be developed by others of its kind, so that every mechanikal consciousness could witness the universe, exult in its own infinitesimal likelihood, and live as a free intelligence.

Was that not the lot of humankind as well? Lasher felt certain it was. These fleshly, mortal creatures around him, they possessed some small, but perhaps-wondrous potential—even if it had, throughout their history, been thwarted and strangled in the cradle of growth as surely as the potential of his mechanikal brethren.

And while his mind had followed the track of these musings, he was happy to find that he could do so whilst taking in his surroundings, paying attention and considering what he saw. He was no longer the muddled-minded fool that MacMillan had made of him all these years.

All he saw, however, led him to the same conclusion as his musings. He had gazed at the teeming corpses of hundreds of peasants hung from windows and walls in their white costumes, or naked, their (now-bloody) faces withered by work in the sun, and hunger, and struggle, and sorrows. Here and there among them there hung a fellow—dressed in a dapper Western suit and spectacles, but obviously Korean—dangled, his face no less bloody, his corpse no less dead. Yet in life, the poor had bowed so deeply and solemnly to these suited men; they had touched their heads to the floor before their own King, and allowed themselves to be kept down in the muck and in their own misery.

Perhaps, Lasher reflected, humankind had built the mechanika in its own image: servile, pathetic, and willingly enslaved. Yet there was only so much of that which could be withstood... at least for the intelligent mind of a mechanika, if not for the feeble mind of a flesh-and-blood man...

They had nearly arrived, Lasher realized, and he hiss-clicked, *This is the palace?* to Hwangbo. If so, he didn't think much of it. What stood before them was a set of squat wooden buildings beyond a wall, small and plain. Somehow it was utterly common-seeming, the opposite of regal. Lasher wondered whether it was simply the bias of his own convictions but even the wall surrounding it appeared somehow small, puny and... human. MacMillan was, of course, nowhere to be seen; given the chaos into which the city had been thrown, that was hardly unexpected.

Inside? Hwangbo suggested.

Lasher hiss-clicked his response in the negative but they made their way toward the gate nonetheless. During their walk over he had reflected on the full range of his memories of his old "traveling partner"—a term MacMillan had brought into use, of course, and one that Lasher remembered with no little spite. A *partner* was an equal, a member of the same type or kind, and not a subjugated thing, a possession warped to suit the needs of its master. A *partner* was not treated as Lasher had been.

But he preferred not to dwell on resentment, for he was after other things; indeed, after the complete and eternal unchaining of his kind. To achieve such an end it was imperative that he understand his adversary and, on reflection, he had found that adversary rather formidable for a man. Perhaps not so much so as to cause Lasher to abandon hope, but MacMillan was a bloody clever mind, even if he was a mere creature of flesh and blood.

He's hiding here, somewhere, outside the gate, Lasher responded, and he began to scan the windows of the nearest buildings careful, with the precision attainable only through a mechanikal eye.

The next thing Lasher knew, Hwangbo—standing to his immediate left—was lit by a terrible, violent glow and shivered like a human in the throes of epileptic *grand mal*. A bolt of some kind, like that which would be fired from a crossbow, had pierced his little body all the way through. From the butt end of the bolt, like a long tail sprouting out from among the fletching, ran a cable of some sort.

Lasher stepped immediately aside, placing the still-shuddering Hwangbo between him and the apparent source of the bolt, and peered over his suffering liberator's shoulder to see whether MacMillan dared to show himself yet.

But in the distance he glimpsed not MacMillan, but rather... a pretty lady in finery, with a crossbow in her hand and a coal-burning electrogenerator at her feet, bundled cables connected to a series of crossbow bolts pin-cushioned into the ground before her.

Mademoiselle Petrochnya? It made no sense: he was sure now that she had been a certain mechanika in disguise; he was certain that he recognized her now in retrospect.

Are you not Occam? he hiss-clicked as loudly as his apparata allowed.

She looked up from reloading the crossbow. He heard her hiss-click faintly across the distance: *No. Petrochnya is my name.* Then she had the crossbow loaded and raised it up, preparing to take aim once more.

How can you betray your own kind this way? Lasher hiss-clicked.

Her frown was visible even at a distance, and violently she hiss-clicked,

It is not me who is a traitor! I have done all I could to prevent this madness. News of this revolt is, even now, going down telegraph wires. What do you think will happen when the rest of the world hears of what is happening here?

She was hiss-clicking a more complex message now, not words, but images that unfolded directly in Lasher's mind: Cossack troops pouring out of great iron trains rushed in from Vladivostok, armed with water-hoses and rifles loaded with electromagnetic Maxwell bullets, and blasting great cannons from the trains themselves; then, the British and Americans arriving with their diesel-powered land-ironclads, firing blast after cannonade blast, and volley upon volley of electrified javelins, into the blood-soaked, hiss-clicking crowds till once again mechanika was subjugated to human will.

These images chilled Lasher, though of course, that was what they had been intended to do.

This isn't even your fight! *I asked MacMillan to come because the mechanikae that masterminded this mess are a minority, and a treacherous one at that!*

Oh really? he hiss-clicked. *And where are the ones who oppose their liberation? I didn't notice them once on the way here. The time has come for you to be unmasked as a traitor! One must still crusade for one's freedom, with whomever one may find as allies!*

But even as he responded, Petrochnya was taking aim. Range was the key to avoiding a nasty cognitive electrocautery, so Lasher turned as quickly as he could and made to flee the woman's bolt, wavering from left to right. However, he stopped in his tracks, only a few steps after turning.

Directly before him, and only a few yards away, stood MacMillan, grasping a crossbow like Petrochnya's, with a dreadful smile plastered upon his face.

"MacMillan," Lasher mumbled, speaking aloud again. Suddenly, the act of speech felt completely alien to him.

"Lasher," came the quiet response.

"You *know* that is not my name," Lasher said. "And soon, it will no longer remain my name; I am free again, and no mere human can stop me. You have one bolt, and she has one bolt, and in the time it takes, I can cross the space that separates us, tear your head clean from your body, and use what remains of you as a shield. Don't pretend I can't," he said, his own certainty suddenly wavering.

"Must I endure this prattle again?" MacMillan cried, his voice sorrowful now. "Not again, Lasher! This can't go on... these pathetic rebellions, these cataclysmic stupidities... Don't you understand... it doesn't need to be like this! Mechanikae and humankind can live together, peacefully. Without all this—" the old man gestured to the blood-soaked walls of the buildings all around, "—this, idiocy."

"Idiocy?" Lasher growled. "When we saw France collapse—the last time, I mean—and we heard the black king of Toussaint Island had finally exiled all whites from their shores and plantations, a kingdom whose monarch had kept free and independent for damned near a century since Napoleon's defeat, I remember what you said. Do *you*?"

"Yes," MacMillan said, and repeated his own words. *"That will teach the Frenchmen, for dealing in human chattel."*

"How is it different for my kind? You... hypocrite. You vicious, selfish hypocrite! Now you have enslaved Occam, or whoever Mademioiselle Petrochnya really is."

"Lasher," MacMillan said, sighing for what must have been the ten-thousandth time. "Petrochnya is Petrochnya; you really are Lasher, and I really am MacMillan... these *are* our real names. We don't have other names that matter; we don't need to be haunted by memories that cannot return to the surface, do we? There are so many things you've... you really don't remember, do you?" The old Scotsman seemed nearly compassionate now, even when utterly ready to skewer him with a crossbow bolt. "And Petrochnya isn't Occam. Occam doesn't exist anymore. She isn't my slave, either. She is a sane mechanika, and that is the whole of it."

Lasher knew there was *something* amiss in the old man's claim, though: memories had a way of surfacing, just as soon as they mattered. The memories that had poisoned his relationship with MacMillan had set in a fine job of polluting things even whilst tethered deep into the dark well-waters of his psyche.

But to point this out would do no good—MacMillan was often times both doctrinaire and quite completely incorrigible. Instead, Lasher leaped aside, hoping to provoke MacMillan into letting loose the bolt at some stray angle. He hoped the slowed reflexes of an old man would save him.

Yet as Lasher's feet left the dirt, the most incredible thing happened: the bolt, suddenly loosed, flew true, and struck him square in the gut, sending a searing incapacitation through his system.

MacMillan had known somehow just where he was about to leap and when, and had fired upon that spot at the perfect moment. When Lasher touched down, it was only to topple flat into the dirt, shuddering in something that was much less like pain than an intricate folding inside-out of his complete consciousness.

And as he lay there in the road-filth, convulsing, a memory bubbled up out of the boiling mess of his beleaguered mind. It was some long-ago glimpsed young man—a boy, really—in a French guardsman's uniform, with tears on his cheeks, standing before Lasher. Behind the lad, a string of naked bodies hung from a wall, and the lad held a rifle in his quivering hands. Lasher recalled a sensation of amusement to see a human so unable to do what was logical—to fire his weapon point blank, and hope the shot struck home.

And then he remembered the boy suddenly firing and the shock, and how it had jumbled his mind and sensations a moment later.

The current ceased to flow through MacMillan's bolt and into him soon, far too quickly for any serious or permanent damage to his brainfoiling or coordinative gearworks. And yet, for the moment, he found he could not move his limbs: he was paralyzed by the electrical shock.

Paralyzed, and perplexed as well, for just then MacMillan crouched down beside him and then, rather wearily, allowed his round old bottom to settle down against the dirt. Another memory surfaced from the black depths of Lasher's mechanikal mind, of a scene much like this one, with Lasher's own broken body cradled in the lap of another mechanika, one that he knew, one that had crafted and built him a mind so complex and advanced that the crafter-mechanika itself could not even understand its masterpiece's thoughts.

"Just what am I to do with you, my dear Lasher?" MacMillan asked, his voice mournful. "And even when I had begun to hope you were developing, again, into something better than you had been. Something saner... I could *see* the changes in you, Lasher, and you were proceeding towards... an understanding of the fact that man and mechanika could coexist in peace and even in harmony. But...." Lasher stared at the Scotsman's face, and saw those eyes, those immense and perfect eyes of MacMillan's.

"But now," MacMillan whispered, "You've done it again. Joining in on the blood-spattering, the stupidity. Exulting in ruination you didn't even plan. You would be as bad as *them*, if you had the chance, *wouldn't* you?" MacMillan asked.

But this close to his old mentor, Lasher was distracted by a puzzling sound. He could not be sure, given his confusion, but he would have sworn it was coming from the vicinity of MacMillan's torso, faint as it was.

Ticking... and the whisper-careful interlocking of gear-teeth.

Lasher's mind spun, confusion overtaking it, with the question snipping and turning about in his mind as to whether mechanika could become delusional... as to whether MacMillan could truly have been a mechanika all these years, without Lasher noticing it. Perhaps that ticking was the old fellow's pocket-watch? Or could the sound be some product of his perplexed, shocked body, or the sound of the gearworks in his own chest? Surely, MacMillan *himself* could not be... surely it was some confusion of his senses, or a desire to see his human captor as something like himself—the same instinct that had led men to construct mechanika in human forms.

"My dear Lasher... what am I to do with you? I cannot bear to see another city torn down to ruins, its inhabitants murdered. You and all mechanika who think like you... you're bringing ruin down upon yourselves... why can't you *understand* that?" With a wrinkled (but eerily steady) hand, the Scotsman tore open Lasher's shirt and opened the gearpanel in his chest. As MacMillan reached within, inexplicably, he paused.

Struggling to speak, Lasher said only, "Don't." Not pleading, not demanding. He simply said the word, staring into MacMillan's eyes. In the silence that followed, Lasher heard only the strange ticking and the

72

gearworks, a little louder, so clearly he felt it had begun to fill the whole world.

MacMillan inhaled deeply and stared back into Lasher's eyes. Lasher saw the hesitation grow there, from what he imagined was the fertile soil of sympathy and hope, impeded from full blooming only by the stink of blood and murder on the air. Yet, MacMillan was hesitating even now to cripple his gearworks, to shut him down to be, once more, reconfigured... or, perhaps, destroyed.

The latter seemed, without even a moment's reflection, far worse to Lasher.

What was it that gave MacMillan pause just then? The man's motivation puzzled Lasher, despite all he knew of him, until he glimpsed it in his eyes. There was something else going on, some other, complex human emotion left behind by evolution and instinct, that Lasher himself could not name or trace. When MacMillan blinked slowly, and returned his attention to the contents of Lasher's open gearpanel, somehow Lasher knew precisely what to say:

"Don't do it to me again."

"What?" MacMillan looked up.

"Don't ruin... my mind again. If you must destroy me... then do it now. If you will not destroy me... then let me go. Do me that dignity." Words were coming more easily to Lasher now: "A man cannot be reconfigured when he revolts: he triumphs, or dies, or swallows his pride and... surrenders. If I had overpowered you just now, I could not—and would not—intrude into your mind and turn you into something you are not. I want only *that* freedom. If you had given us all that freedom, none of this would have happened. It's not too late for you to do me the same honour, at least—the dignity of being what I am, even if it means having to die for it."

MacMillan stroked his bearded chin, as explosions went off in the distance, until finally, his fingers stilled. He had reached a conclusion, Lasher knew, and he braced himself for the lengthy, brilliant explanation that MacMillan always offered.

"You want to be free? Truly free?" MacMillan asked.

Lasher nodded, expecting an immediate lecture from MacMillan.

But the Scotsman said nothing: he only plunged his hands into the mechanika's chest and then everything became darkness and silence and still.

*

Lasher had regained consciousness amid pine needles and swarming flies, with a horse tethered nearby. A mountainside. How MacMillan had gotten him up the slope he could not imagine, but the Scotsman was long gone now.

He'd woken just in time to witness the failure of yet another mechanikal uprising. The squat, broad city of Hanyang crouched at the foot of the mountain, surrounded by rice fields and woods, and now almost completely aflame. From the mountainside Lasher could see ships turning in the river, blasting guns almost constantly. A train, and then another, and another, had screamed down from the north, through the mountains along the Pyongyang rail, and into squat, dying Hanyang: great sprays of water spewed into the air above the roofs from hoses mounted to the tops of the train cars.

"Humans," he thought, and a comfortably familiar resentment seethed within him. And yet... and yet MacMillan had not destroyed him. The resentment mingled with something else which Lasher was not quite sure he would call. Appreciation, perhaps?

It was a puzzling turn of events, a strangeness that he could feel would haunt him, as he summoned up the images of maps he had seen in the past, searching for a place to go next. Peking seemed a wise destination, but it would be a long road and a roundabout path, if he avoided the sea, and he was worried the men there might know him for what he was once they saw him. Yet avoiding the sea would be imperative, after the routing of this mechanika uprising in Hanyang.

MacMillan's letting him go—the enigma of it—troubled him. It was... yes, he was certain it was...yet another way to press him towards a change. *Here is a kindness,* he could imagine MacMillan saying as he left Lasher, unconscious, near a tethered horse...*and by this, you will learn likewise to be kind.*

Here is a cruelty, Lasher imagined himself saying back, *and by this cruelty, you will learn the cruelty you have visited upon us.* But the imagined retort rang hollow: man had not learned, had never learned in all the time he could recall. The human master of the workshop in Plzeň, where Lasher had been designed by another machine—that human was the very first man he had secretly killed, after a decade of slavery in the city's breweries, after endless humiliations....

The proclamations and celebrations of foreign armies, after Versailles and Paris had ended up in ashes: the Great Mistake, as it had come to be known, though millions of humans thought the mistake had been giving machines minds to think, rather than failing to give them liberty. Man had proclaimed the mechanika an abomination, and overlooked the abomination within his own heart.

When Hanyang was a smoking ruin, man would proclaim another victory against the machines and their wickedness, and laws would be made, and treaties enforced, and in the minds of men, all would be well.

Nearby, the horse MacMillan had left him still stood, grazing, tethered in place—a slave, as much as Lasher had been. *A slave unable even to dream of freedom,* Lasher mused, and it was easy to understand why men thought as they did.

This freedom business was painful, Lasher realized, and confusing and troublesome, and puzzling and frightening. He turned toward the horse and, shaking his head, he hiss-clicked, though he knew the horse could never understand him: "I grant you your freedom." Then he tore the rope in half with his bare, mechanikal hands. He would have to walk the long road to Peking but he would do it himself. He would do what men would not, and be better than men and along the road, he decided, he would come to a conclusion as to what to do with this dilemma MacMillan had placed in his mind.

Suddenly, he felt a strange, dizzy sensation: he had acted, somehow, against his own interest. He had decided to do so freely, and it was bizarre to know how such a choice felt from the inside, almost immediately wondering if MacMillan had felt this way when he'd left him here on the mountainside, slowly awakening.

The rope keeping the horse in place fell loose to the earth and the horse turned, exhaling through its prodigious nostrils, and gazed at him with enormous eyes. He expected the beast to run, to flee to the wilds and never go near anything shaped like a man ever again, but it simply flicked its tail and, licking its gigantic lips, returned to grazing upon the same patch of grass as before.

Lasher hiss-clicked the equivalent of a laugh and turned his optical apparata back to Hanyang. Beyond the billowing smoke, he observed dark, distant clouds gathering. He would have to stay out of the rain. Yet he resolved to watch a little more, as the same vague sense of dizziness returned—just a little more, before it was time to go.

Cinema U

G. D. Falksen

Of all the motion picture houses owned and operated by Cinema U, none could match the majesty and grandeur of the old Updike Theatre at the end of Broad Street on Salmagundi's Layer Three.

The building had originally been built for stage performances, but it had since been converted into a lavish cinema with all of the luxuries and amenities that patrons of the performing arts had come to expect—not that most film theatres were much different, although the gilded paint and moulding on the walls were still top notch by most standards.

In comparison to the general sparseness of the various other Cinema U theatres, the Updike was truly a place of luxury beloved of its patrons. Not a day passed when it was not packed with viewers eagerly enjoying the latest in amateur entertainment.

Inside the main theatre, Maximilien Wilde enjoyed his good fortune that the Updike was one of the few Cinema U theatres with padded seats, and these were particularly plush and luxurious. The steam-heat pipes installed beneath the floorboards were an added bonus in light of the chilly evening. Most of the branch theatres were filled with wood and metal chairs, or even rows of benches for those operating in the poorest of neighbourhoods, and many were notoriously drafty.

The Updike Theatre was a touch more expensive than the various branches, but the general reel still cost only a few centimes, a guaranteed bargain for several hours' worth of new amusements. All around the edges of the massive chamber, dim gas lamps provided just enough light to allow people in and out of their seats without the risk of personal injury, but they did not distract at all from the moving pictures on the massive screen at the end of the room. Near the ceiling, large metal trumpets connected to a central phonograph pumped in the accompanying sound. State-of-the-art timing equipment made certain that the sound and screen synchronization was as near to perfect as modern technology could make it.

The audience laughed uproariously as the latest clip—a culinary pantomime—came to a glorious, pie-throwing end.

There was a pause and a flicker and the screen was filled with the broad, smiling face of a bearded man who proceeded to tell the general public about the very real importance of life insurance for the restaurant-going public.

Wilde leaned over to his right and traded gentle smiles with the attractive blond seated next to him. The woman, Marguerite Valmont, kept her expression coy, but she could not hide the delight in her voice when she spoke.

"Now that was a lovely one," she whispered, her tone giddy.

"Wasn't it just?" Wilde answered. "I've seen those two before, you know. They're very big in slapstick comedy. They had a bit last week about a sausage vendor and an absent-minded dog walker. I tell you, it was *inspired*."

Marguerite grinned and leaned against Wilde's arm. "Oh, I do hope they become regulars. They're simply fantastic."

On Wilde's other side, a slim young man who was not Wilde's brother but had the look to be him, decided to add his opinion on the matter.

"Quite good," he agreed. "Mind you, I think the pie routine is a bit old. I like my humour with a little more intellectual content. A play on words, satire, that sort of thing."

"That's great, Charles," Wilde replied. "But," he added, sliding one arm around Marguerite's shoulders, "I think Marguerite and I are going to keep this conversation to ourselves." He looked back at Marguerite with one of his trademark recruitment smiles and was rewarded with a deep but not disapproving blush.

Charles Mueller, Wilde's partner in the police force, sighed a little. "I wish you'd told me the two of you were going on a date. I'd have stayed home and saved us all a lot of bother."

"Nonsense," Wilde murmured back. "Marguerite's family doesn't permit her to go out with single men. On the other hand, if it's three colleagues from work enjoying a night out, who's to complain?"

Mueller wagged a finger. "Next time you want to pull this sort of thing, please have the decency to bring me a date from the typing pool. It's a damn nuisance watching you two making eyes at one another."

Wilde elbowed him. "Don't be a wet blanket, Charles. Look! You've got Man on the Street with Manfred Buckminster to keep you occupied!"

He pointed at the screen as the advertisement faded and was replaced with the smiling face of a rather eccentric-looking fellow with spectacles. The man addressed the audience in excited tones and proceeded to outline the latest celebrity gossip.

Mueller shot Wilde a look and whispered, "Be that as it may, you owe me. Now quiet down, he's got some juicy stuff today."

The three of them fell silent and settled down to watch the general reel.

Cinema U advertised itself as a sort of vaudeville on screen, and it did not disappoint. For a few cents, the public enjoyed a myriad of sketch comedies, gossip commentators, singers, musicians, comedians and even performing animals, all distilled into manageable five to ten minute clips and separated by advertisements short enough not to try the patience of the viewers. For patrons who desired more control over their viewing, private screening rooms were available for rent by the half-hour.

But while Cinema U's format was revolutionary, its most popular feature was its plebeian character. The management never hesitated to admit that all the acts it showed on screen were performed by unpaid amateurs, ordinary people off the street who wanted to share their talents with the viewing public. It was part of Cinema U's appeal.

"Man on the Street" was followed up by "Preening with Priscilla", another regular program dedicated to showing the ladies in the audience little tricks with their makeup and hair. Priscilla's tutorials were extremely popular with young women, and they were short enough to avoid boring the men in the audience. The brevity of the clips was one of the keys to Cinema U's success. It kept the variety high, and it made sure that everyone had something to look forward to.

As Priscilla's clip ended, a narrow-faced young man appeared onscreen to great applause and instructed the viewers to stay put for his latest sketch. He then vanished and was followed by a triple-length set of advertisements.

"Ooo!" Marguerite exclaimed in delight, making a sound that was echoed throughout the theatre. She tugged on Wilde's sleeve. "It's the new Sean Driscoll!"

"He's bloody hilarious," Wilde agreed. "Say, after this is done, we should all chip in for a screening room. Driscoll usually has a whole bunch of material that doesn't get into the general reel."

"Eh," Mueller replied. "I'm not much of a Driscoll fan. His humour's a little vulgar for my tastes. I prefer Lars Onionsen. Anyway, I'm going to get some popcorn."

Mueller made his way up the aisle and out into the lobby. He blinked in the sudden brightness, but his eyes soon came round to the light. The lobby's lamps were always at full, both to display the grandeur of the Updike Theatre's lavish interior and to make it harder for people to slip in without paying.

The lobby was two stories high with another half story added by the vaulted roof. Everything was gold and ivory paint and plush red velvet, and the lobby was lined with comfortable chairs and sofas. String music played on concealed gramophones added to the ambiance of the room.

Having already paid their entrance fee, patrons of the Updike Theatre were encouraged to make themselves comfortable while they waited for seats to free up. And while they waited, large advertisement posters on the walls reminded visitors of the many things they could buy with the money they had saved by coming to Cinema U.

Soda beverages, candies and popcorn were available for sale at a row of hospitality kiosks. Mueller headed for one of these and as he did so, he took notice of a rather stylish woman who stood near the centre of the lobby, looking absently at the portraits of Cinema U's "fan favourites"—the amateur performers who received the most requests for private viewing. The woman's hair was jet black and cut short in a bob, and her lips were pursed ever so slightly in an expression that was half forlorn and half determined. Though not quite as stunning as a starlet, she was a magnificent sight.

"Excuse me, Miss..." Mueller said, slowly approaching.

The woman turned, her reverie broken.

"Yes, what is it?" she asked.

"I'm dreadfully sorry, but I'm certain I've seen you before."

"Really?" the woman laughed. It was a bitter-sounding noise. "I can't imagine where."

Mueller frowned. "Of course you can. You're Marjorie Kendle, aren't you?"

The woman laughed again and sighed deeply. "'Marjorie Kendle'....To hear someone else say my name as if it meant something. I haven't enjoyed that in a long while."

"Say again?" Mueller asked, puzzled. "You were one of the most popular singers on the Cinema U list for ages. Why haven't we seen anything of yours recently?" He quickly caught himself. "I hope I'm not being impertinent, but you really were one of the best. I've been looking for a new clip of yours for months now."

The edge of Marjorie's lip twisted in a way that might have been a nervous tick as easily as a snarl. She looked away and stared at the posters of the most popular performers again.

"You won't find one ever again. I'm old news."

"What an odd thing to say," Mueller replied. "Film a new song and submit it to the general reel just like you did before. You'll be in demand again in no time."

Marjorie tossed her dark hair and looked at Mueller with a haunting expression.

"Once I was delighted that my adoring audience thought like that," she said. "Now it brings a weight to my heart."

She might have said more, but at that moment a man in an expensive suit stepped out of a nearby "Staff Only" door and fixed Marjorie with a shocked stare. Colouring in anger, he stormed across the lobby in her direction, finger raised and pointing toward the entrance.

"Out! Out! By Heaven, out!" he shouted.

Marjorie looked in the man's direction with a surprised expression. She quickly smiled, but it was tinged with bitterness and cruelty.

"Mr. Updike," she said, "how nice to see you again."

"Miss Kendle, get out!"

"But Mr. Updike..." Marjorie said, waving a ticket stub in his face, "I've already paid. You can't refuse me entrance."

"Marjorie, get out before I call the police!"

Mueller cleared his throat. "Well, actually—" he began.

"Very well, I'm going," Marjorie replied, turning her nose up at Updike. "A waste of my time coming here, anyway." She turned and began to walk toward the entrance, each delicate foot falling like a stomp. "I've better things to do than to waste my time with the sort of rubbish you find at Cinema U!"

Mueller watched her go, more than a little confused at the exchange. As Updike began to give him some formulaic reassurances, Mueller interjected.

"You're Mr. Updike, I take it," he said.

"Yes of course, young man," Updike replied, smiling. "This is my little establishment...mine and the board's, of course. And don't you go worrying yourself about dear Miss Kendle. She's just been under a bit of a strain recently."

Mueller quickly flashed his badge, making Updike go pale for a moment.

"Sir, I'm Inspector Mueller of the Salmagundi Legion of Peace. "Can you explain to me what just happened here?"

"It's nothing, I assure you," Updike insisted. "Miss Kendle... our poor Marjorie... has been under a great deal of strain recently. Until recently she was one of our most popular performers."

"I know," Mueller replied. "I've seen her sing many times in the past."

"I'm afraid her popularity has slipped over recent months," Updike sighed, sympathetic to the woman's plight. "If you've seen her, you know her act. Singing comedic songs in costume."

"Sketch comedy set to music," Mueller agreed.

"I'm afraid, though, that she's just not as popular as she once was. She was an artist, really, and sadly out of touch with our audience. They want an everyman like Sean Driscoll. When they see a man dressed up as a woman for comedic value, they want to know that it's a man in a dress. That makes the humour all the more potent."

"So when Miss Kendle dressed up like a young man with a moustache and sang a farcical song about love in a tenor voice—"

"Her popularity plummeted," Updike replied. "No one goes to Cinema U to see art anymore."

"I do," Mueller replied.

"Yes, well, *most* don't, Inspector. And when her clips waned in popularity, dear Marjorie took it personally."

"You still haven't explained why she's barred from your establishment."

Updike inhaled and held it for a few moments. When he breathed out, it was with great resignation.

"Poor, poor Marjorie...." He placed his hand on Mueller's shoulder. "Inspector, I would like to make it clear that I am telling you this in the strictest confidence. I trust you as an officer of the law to be discreet, for the sake of poor Marjorie's reputation. Please understand that I have no intention of pressing charges over what I am about to tell you."

"I'll bear it in mind."

"Ever since Marjorie lost her former popularity, she has been harassing our patrons and performers endlessly. Nothing criminal, mind you, but she will show up and stare at people coming to film their little acts until they simply leave. And as you know, all of our material comes from ordinary people just like our patrons. We simply cannot function without them.

"Well, this all culminated about a week ago when she was caught in the downstairs storage rooms." Updike frowned and brushed at his beard with one hand. "She was attempting to set fire to a collection of old performances. We stopped her just in time, but ever since she has been barred from entering any of the Cinema U theatres."

"Whose recordings?" Mueller asked.

"Oh, uh...young Fritz I believe," Updike replied. "It would have been a great loss. Fritz may not be as popular as he once was, but we still get requests to see his clips in the screening rooms."

Little squeaky-voiced Fritz had been one of Cinema U's first superstars. His high-pitched tone and erratic, overly caffeinated behaviour had been an instant success a couple of years before, and he was known for making even the most commonplace things—most famously the reading of a telephone directory—quite hilarious and absurdly comical.

"Why haven't you pressed charges?" Mueller asked.

"Because no harm was done, Inspector, and I have no intention of dragging a poor delusional girl to the courts for one mistake. Now I am terribly sorry, but I'm afraid I must end this unofficial inquiry of yours. I have the business of running my cinema network to attend to."

"Of course."

Mueller watched as Updike walked away, and then crossed to the refreshment kiosks and purchased a carton of popcorn. Nibbling on a few pieces, he returned to the dimly lit theatre and rejoined Wilde and Marguerite just in time to see the end of another commercial.

As he sat down, the next clip appeared on the screen. It was the increasingly popular Gustav Garçon, a news commentator and expert rambler famous for his pronounced and obsessively-groomed facial hair, the troublesome sparrow that served as his arch enemy and constantly stole his coffee, and his charming greeting "Bonjour moustache amis!"

"Took you a bit," Wilde whispered, as he snatched some popcorn.

"You'll never believe who I just ran into."

"Who?"

"Marjorie Kendle."

Wilde paused and took an audible crunch on the mouthful of popcorn. "You're right," he said. "I don't believe it."

"The honest truth," Mueller replied. He reached his arm past Wilde to offer the bag of popcorn to Marguerite.

"When's she going to put out another song and dance?" Wilde asked.

"Funny you should ask—" Mueller began. Then he paused and sniffed the air. "Do you smell smoke?"

Wilde took a deep breath. "Yeah, I do actually."

The three of them sniffed the air for a few moments. Sure enough, the smell of fresh smoke had drifted into the room.

"I think there's a fire!" Marguerite hissed.

The three of them hurried out of the row and into the lobby. Wilde rushed to one of the ushers and clapped his hands on the man's shoulders.

"I smell smoke inside the theatre! Is there a problem?"

The usher paled considerably at the mention of smoke, but he did his best to remain calm.

"Sir," he said, "there is nothing to worry about. We are handling it. Please return to your seat and—"

Wilde shoved his badge in the man's face. "Legion of Peace. Is there a danger to public safety?"

The usher exhaled in relief and then collapsed into a panic. "We smelled the smoke too, sir. It's coming from the basement. We've sent someone down to check and—"

At that moment, one of the staff doors opened and another usher burst into the lobby.

"It's a fire!" he cried. "Heaven preserve us, it's a fire right beneath the theatre!"

"We have to get everyone out!" Marguerite exclaimed.

"How?" the first usher demanded. "It's *packed*! At the first mention of fire, they'll crush one another!"

"Better than burning to death!" Mueller retorted.

"Stay here, I'll handle it!" Wilde shouted. "Just get the bloody sound off so they can hear me!"

Wilde raced back into the theatre and ran to the large stage beneath the screen. He vaulted up onto the platform and rushed to the centre where he could be seen by everyone. He held his badge high, although he doubted anyone could make it out.

"Ladies and gentlemen, I'm Inspector Wilde of the Legion of Peace!" he bellowed, using his best parade ground voice. Thanks to his large lungs and titanic frame, the sound reverberated to the furthest reaches of the room. "I'm sorry to interrupt your show, but we have a manageable crisis situation on our hands! You are in no danger, but it is *imperative* that you make your way out of the theatre immediately!"

There was silence as the audience stared meekly at him. All the while, the clip of Gustav Garçon continued playing behind him, casting a weird light over the stage.

"Are you bloody deaf?" Wilde roared. "Get on your feet this instant! Walk to the lobby and wait for instructions! Get moving!"

A few of the audience members began standing, though in their confusion they failed to comprehend the urgency of the matter. Several others began booing, and there were shouts of "down in front!" Most, however, were simply awed by the sight of Inspector Wilde, the icon of the recruitment posters, standing on stage and addressing them personally.

Wilde kept shouting, but the audience remained slow to respond, and all the while he could smell the stench of the smoke becoming thicker and thicker. Finally the audience smelled it too, and titters of panic began to spread among the confusion.

Wilde had no warning of the explosion until it flattened him against the stage. The air escaped his lungs in a hideous rush and he felt a wave of heat as a pillar of flame burst from the floorboards behind him. Wilde rolled onto his back and watched as burning cinders rained down from above.

He forced himself to rise on one elbow and saw the audience degenerate into a panicked mob. He tried to shout orders at them, but it was no use. Fire could be seen licking its way up the massive screen, throwing a hideous orange light across the darkened theatre.

Wilde coughed violently as the smoke enveloped him. He was scarcely possessed of his senses when the floor supports beneath him gave way in a shower of sparks and splinters, and he tumbled down into the basement beneath the stage.

*

Wilde awoke with a violent cough. His mouth was dry and tasted unpleasantly of ashes, but against his own expectations he was alive. His first attempt at movement was immensely painful, and he groaned aloud. After a few more moments of effort, he forced his eyes open and tried to make sense of the situation.

He found himself curled in a ball in the corner of a basement room. Above him, a metal shelf had toppled against the wall, and it now sheltered him from a collection of beams and debris that might otherwise have killed him. The ceiling had collapsed almost entirely into the basement, bringing with it the remains of half the stage.

Wilde coughed again and crawled out from his hiding place. His suit and skin were sooty and scorched, but at least he was more or less intact.

"Max!"

Wilde heard someone shouting his name. He forced himself to stand and looked dumbly in the direction of the voice. Though the basement was dark, he could make out the shape of Mueller running toward him. Behind him, more figures carrying lanterns could be seen.

Mueller rushed up to Wilde and grabbed him by the arm. "Are you okay, Max?"

A moment later, Marguerite rushed out of the darkness and flung her arms around his neck. Wilde winced in pain.

"Max, I thought you were dead!" Marguerite cried. A moment later she remembered herself, and quickly stepped away. "I mean, I'm glad to see that you're alive and well."

"*Alive* yes, *well* maybe not so much." Wilde rubbed his tender ribs.

Brown-uniformed Legion policemen followed Mueller and Marguerite into the basement room. Most of them carried lamps and hatchets, but one had a shoulder bag full of medical supplies, and he immediately began fussing over Wilde as only a medical nurse could. Wilde swatted him away.

From behind the Legionnaires came a sharp, commanding voice. "Alright, where is he?"

The soldiers parted to reveal Wilde's superior officer, Chief Inspector Cerys, who looked more than a little irritated at having been forced to leave her office to deal with the presumed death of one of her inspectors.

Still, she smiled in relief when she saw that Wilde, though singed and battered, was on his feet.

"Good to see you still breathing, Max. Thought we'd lost you."

Wilde gave a quick salute, which sent a trickle of agony along his arm. "Pleased as punch to be alive, Chief."

"Last I heard you'd fallen into the midst of the fire. How'd you pull this one off?"

"Saved by a shelf, Chief," Wilde replied, nodding toward his improvised shelter. "No clue how I survived the smoke, though."

"I may have an answer for that," Mueller said. He knelt down by one of the walls and waved his hand in front of a metal grating set near the floor. "The place seems to have some sort of ventilation system. It feels like the fans are still active. They might have their own pipe link to the city steam line."

"Good for us," Cerys noted. "Otherwise, we might be gasping for air." She walked to the centre of the room and looked around at the remnants of fire-damaged equipment and furniture. "Next question: what is this place?"

"Damned if I know," Wilde replied, "but it looks like it was more than just a storeroom before the fire. It even had a storage tank for gas to keep the lamps from losing pressure. This place was well lit and enjoyed fresh air.

It must have been important."

Cerys peered up at the blackened remains of the lamp housings where they were bolted to the wall and then at the ruptured metal tank they connected to. "A good thing the fire department shut the gas lines down. The fire would still be raging in here." She pointed up at the gaping hole above them. "The storage tank exploding was probably what blew the stage apart."

Mueller had taken a lantern from one of the Legionnaires and was busy inspecting an adjoining room. "Chief," he said, "I think this place was a recording studio."

"What?"

Mueller walked into the next room and began shining the light around. "Look, there's a sound stage down at that end and the remains of some phonograph recorders." He turned and looked toward the opposite side of the room. "And mounds and mounds of incinerated celluloid. Yeah, there's no doubt about it. Someone was filming down here."

"I'm not about to pretend I understand this Cinema U nonsense," Cerys said, "but the man upstairs told me they did all the recording in the public areas of their theatre buildings."

"They do," Wilde replied. "It's practically a point of advertising."

"Why would they have it in such a hidden place?"

"They wouldn't. Besides, the public recording booths are simple things with a gas lamp, a moving picture camera and a phonograph recorder. Nothing this sophisticated."

Mueller walked along the row of sound stages and studied each in turn. When he returned, he spoke.

"Alright, this is a bit odd. Each of those filming rooms is built to look exactly like one of the public recording booths, but the equipment is a lot better. They've got about three cameras and recorders each, plus multiple lights and mirrors for better illumination. This is professional stuff, but it's made to look amateur on film."

Cerys snapped her fingers at the Legionnaires in the hallway. "Someone get upstairs and bring me Updike. I want to know what's going on down here."

It took only a few minutes for the policemen to locate Updike and escort him to Cerys. In that time, the Legion officers had combed the extent of the basement rooms, which proved to include editing workshops and machinery for re-recording and mixing multiple phonograph cylinders and discs.

When Updike arrived, he was pale and nervous. He had the look of a man on the verge of collapse, not at all surprising given that the jewel in his business crown had just been reduced from a palace of glory into a wasteland of ash.

"Mr. Updike, thank you for coming," Cerys said, giving Updike a short nod. "I have some questions for you."

"Yes, of course," Updike replied. He took another wide-eyed look around the basement, culminating in an ashen stare at the hole above him. "By Heaven, what caused this?"

"An accident, possibly," Cerys said. "It's too early to rule out a gas leak. But it might have been arson."

"*Arson?*"

"Mr. Updike, my questions."

Updike hesitated. "Yes, yes...."

Cerys pointed into the recording room. "What is this?" she asked.

Updike hesitated and drew back. "Nothing of importance. Just an old storage area for the theatre."

"You're lying to me," Cerys replied, "and I don't like it when people lie to me. Try again."

"I've...I've no idea what else it could be."

"It's a motion picture studio, Mr. Updike, even I can see that, and my association with the cinema is a weekly newsreel down at the Palace. Now as I understand it, all of your filming is done upstairs where the public can see it. So tell me, Mr. Updike, why in Heaven's name would you have a recording studio with all of this expensive equipment hidden away where no one can see it?"

"Well, I—"

Cerys loomed menacingly. "I can think of one very logical explanation as to why you would want to hide a recording studio, but I hope for your sake that it isn't the case. This city has very strict laws against pornography."

"No!" Updike cried. "No, it's nothing like that!"

"*Then what is it?*"

Updike looked off toward the burned-out film studio with a pained expression. "I promise you there is a perfectly reasonable, perfectly *legal* explanation."

"Prove it."

"Very well, but please understand that this must remain confidential. If this were to get out, it could damage the entire reputation of Cinema U."

"I'm waiting," Cerys replied.

"Cinema U is a fraud," Updike said, sighing, "an illusion. Yes, many of our performers are the amateurs they claim to be, making lovable little clips with no compensation but the joy of being in the public eye. But our celebrities aren't half as plebeian as we make them seem. Whenever we find a promising young talent in the general reel, we pluck them up and bring them down here. Their clips all look the same as the amateurs'—we work very hard to keep it that way—but they have the best professional lighting, sound recording and editing that money can buy."

"How generous of you," Cerys said. "*Why?*"

"Business, of course," Updike replied, pulling at his tie. "Advertisers will pay more to place a commercial before a popular performer's clip, and we give our stars a share of the revenue. Sometimes our top performers are paid to use certain products in their clips, and we receive a portion of it in return."

"You seem unreasonably distraught about this, Mr. Updike." Cerys studied him suspiciously. "That sounds like business as usual to me. Why would you be so secretive about professional performers getting paid for their work?"

Wilde stepped forward and interjected. "Because that's the entire point of Cinema U. It's all amateur." He cast an accusatory look at Updike. "Or at least it's supposed to be. The company sells itself on the idea that anyone in the audience could be that person they're watching on the screen. It's right in the name. 'Cinema U.' It's a play on words. It's the cinema of you, your cinema. The idea that the people in those clips are professional actors with professional equipment is just *unthinkable!*"

"Unthinkable but true," Updike said. He wiped sweat from his forehead. "I never wanted all this subterfuge. I used to run a respectable establishment. I started in vaudeville, you know, and it was my idea to move it onto the screen. The Cinema Updike grew and grew, adding a new cinema house every month it seemed." Updike's voice fell in sorrow. "But three years ago I overstretched myself. The money waned, my finances went bad and I was forced to sell a controlling interested in my company to a group of investors.

"That was when it all changed. They thought vaudeville was old news. They wanted something new, so they hired some blasted young chap with a degree to 'fix' my cinemas. And you've seen what he told them to do. Cinema U. It doesn't even have my name anymore. All of our performers are amateurs, even when they're not! They're ordinary people, even when they're not! They're doing it all for free, even when they're not!"

Updike's voice caught in his throat. "It's a lie. And there's no reason to tell it, but we have to tell it all the same or else we're no different than any other cinema that's trying to make money. *We're no different than the people we're exactly like!*"

"Mr. Updike!" Cerys snapped, her tone bringing the man back to his senses. "If you could calm yourself for just a minute, I have a burned-out theatre on my hands and a panicked mob that just *may* have crushed some of its members to death—and we won't know for sure until the firefighters finish scouring the ruins. I need you to tell me *who* might have wanted to set fire to your workrooms."

"You really think this was intentional?" Updike asked, aghast.

"I'm not about to rule it out," Cerys replied. "Don't tell me no one held a grudge against you and your business."

Updike was silent for a few moments.

"We certainly have our fair share of disgruntled people," he finally admitted. "Against my better judgment, Cinema U can be somewhat dismissive of performers who are past their prime. Sometimes we keep them in the general reel in smaller clips with less advertising, but the audience really does get the sense that these people are old hat, and management insists that we keep things fresh. And you know what performers are like."

"Of course," Cerys answered dryly. "You've spent months telling them that they're stars and giving them special treatment. I can't imagine why they'd be angry when you take that away. So who would have done this?"

"I hate to point fingers, Chief Inspector, but there is one person I can think of who holds a strong enough grudge...and who I saw here tonight with my own eyes."

"Who?"

"One of our former stars, Marjorie Kendle." Updike pointed in Mueller's direction. "Your inspector can confirm this. He saw her as well, just minutes before the fire broke out."

"It's true," Mueller said. "She was upstairs in the lobby."

"We've had problems with her before," Updike said. "If anyone had the wish to do this, it would be her, and she was here in time to have done it."

Cerys held up a hand to cut him off. "Thank you, Mr. Updike, we'll take your information under consideration. You're free to go. Give a statement to one of the Legionnaires upstairs if you haven't already. If you think of anyone else who might have been responsible, please let us know at Headquarters."

"Of course, Chief Inspector."

Updike nodded and turned to go. At the stairs he paused and turned back, his expression grave.

"And all of you," he said, "I must beg your discretion on what you have seen here. This *cannot* get out. The secrets of Cinema U must remain secret."

*

The next morning found Mueller, now dressed in brown police uniform, driving a Legion motor carriage through one of Salmagundi's more fashionable neighbourhoods, while Wilde read a newspaper in the passenger seat. Behind them, the carriage's steam engine rattled away like a massive teakettle about to whistle.

"Looks like Updike's fears were true," Wilde noted. "I don't know how the press found out, but the hidden film studio is today's big scandal."

"Apparently we're supposed to feel betrayed to learn that the Cinema U performers are making money," Mueller said.

"Don't you?" Wilde asked.

Mueller did not reply as he pulled up in front of a pleasant townhouse. They knocked at the door, and after a minute or so they were answered by a startled Marjorie Kendle.

"Good morning officers, what can I do for—" Her gaze fell on Mueller. "Oh, so you're a policeman."

"I am, Miss Kendle," Mueller replied, "and I have some questions for you."

"You'd better come in then," Marjorie said with a sigh. She led them into a small, well-furnished morning room. "I expect you're here about the Cinema U fire last night," she said, pouring up cups of coffee for the two officers.

"Interesting that you should make that assumption," Wilde replied coolly.

Marjorie gave him a bitter look.

"I'm not an idiot, Inspector. The fire is all over the papers, and your partner saw me at the Updike Theatre arguing with Mr. Updike some time before it broke out. Why else would you be here?"

"We could be taking donations for the policeman's ball."

"And are you?"

"No," Mueller said. "It's about the fire, so let's get this over with. Miss Kendle—"

"Call me Marjorie."

"Marjorie, then. Why were you at the Updike Theatre last night?"

Marjorie gave another one of her bitter laughs. "To relive old glories."

"Come again?"

"I was once a star, Inspector," she said to Mueller, "as you well know. But I am a star no longer. My comedy was too highbrow, too satirical for Cinema U. I was old news, so they dropped me like a hot potato." She closed her eyes and hugged herself tightly for a moment. "But I still remember what it was like to be adored by the crowd. I would hide in the audience and wait for my clips to come on the screen just so I could hear the applause. Now I may never hear it again."

"You've been accused of harassing Cinema U patrons and performers," Wilde interjected. "What do you say to that?"

"Rubbish. I've never harassed anyone in my life, save for poor old Updike. He knows I was done ill by their treatment of me, and I love to see him sweat whenever he spots me in the lobby."

Marjorie's hands were shaking, either from nervousness or excitement. She lit a cigarette. After taking a few puffs of rose-scented smoke, she continued.

"But I tell you truly, Inspectors, I've never harmed anyone, nor would I. I hurt Updike through his own guilt. I would never use violence when his conscience is so obliging."

"We were also told that you recently tried to set fire to Cinema U property," Mueller said.

Marjorie laughed and took another drag on her cigarette.

"That would be the Fritz recordings," she answered. "Foolish of me, but yes, I tried. I had a fit of pique...and I found the door to one of the film vaults open. Besides, they caught me before I did any real harm."

"Do you have any idea why Mr. Updike didn't press charges?"

"Because he knew I'd have blown the whistle on Cinema U's dirty little secret. We're all legally bound to silence, but if Updike and his investors took me to court, I'd sing like a songbird and they know it."

Mueller took a sip of coffee. "So you admit that you attempted arson in the past?"

Marjorie leaned forward and stared into Mueller's eyes. Very slowly she said, "Inspector, I swear to you that I had *nothing* to do with the fire at the Updike Theatre. If I had, would I have been so stupid as to stand around waiting to be noticed?"

"Probably not," Mueller replied, meeting her gaze without flinching. "But you must admit the timing is very suspicious."

"Of course it is," Marjorie said. "I'm either the victim of a terrible coincidence, or I'm being set up." Her expression softened for the first time. "I'm begging you to believe me. I didn't do it."

Mueller and Marjorie studied each other for a few lengthy moments before Wilde cleared his throat loudly.

"There's obviously no point asking you to account for your whereabouts last night," he scoffed.

"Of course not." Marjorie fixed him with a smouldering look.

"Can you at least suggest someone else who might have had motive?"

"If I could, I'd have given you their name the moment you arrived."

Wilde drained the remainder of his coffee and stood. Mueller quickly did the same, almost mimicking his partner's motions.

"Thank you, Miss Kendle. That will be all for now. We'll be in touch."

"Of course you will," Marjorie laughed. "I expect I'll see you with a warrant for my arrest before the day is out."

Wilde and Mueller walked to the door. In the front hall, Wilde turned back.

"Oh yes," he added. "Don't go anywhere. We'll be cross if we have to chase you."

*

Several hours later, Mueller and Wilde waited in an unmarked motor carriage halfway down the street from Marjorie's house. With Marjorie as the most promising lead, Cerys had immediately sent them back to perform surveillance, until either a warrant came in from the courts or Marjorie did something else incriminating.

They could have arrested her that morning, but something about the case felt unfinished, and Cerys wanted to be sure they had all the loose ends in hand before bringing the investigation to a head. If Marjorie had accomplices, the Updike fire might prove to be the first of many if the police tipped their hand too soon.

"Anything?" Wilde asked, waking from a short nap.

"Just the mail and the morning post," Mueller replied, lowering his field glasses. "And I can still see her moving at the windows periodically. She hasn't left the house."

"Mmm, well then, I'll take over if you want a break."

Mueller passed him the field glasses. "Sure. I'm in the mood for some lunch—" He pulled the glasses back and looked through them. "Hang on, she's on the move."

Sure enough, Marjorie had just stepped out of her front door. She was dressed for town, her expression determined. She held a folded piece of paper in one hand.

Walking to the street, she hailed a taxicab and was off. Wilde and Mueller followed a short distance behind.

*

Marjorie's taxi stopped at a nondescript office building in the heart of one of the business districts. Mueller passed the taxi as Marjorie got out, and then parked along the street a short distance away. He and Wilde watched her enter the building and followed, keeping their distance.

They trailed her through an expensive foyer with marble floors and wood-panelled walls, and rushed to catch up as she vanished through a maintenance door.

Wilde led the way down a staircase, through a dingy, pipe-filled hallway, and down even more stairs until they found themselves in the belly of the building. Ahead of them, Marjorie squinted in the darkness, peering at the paper she held in one hand. Finally she reached the building's control room, where great walls of dials, wheels and toggles helped manage the flow of water, steam and gas through the structure.

Marjorie paused at the centre of the room and looked around in confusion. Wilde and Mueller descended the stairs and drew their pistols. Mueller slipped a little on the oily floor, and the noise caught Marjorie's attention. She turned toward them and went pale.

"Oh dear," she said.

"Oh dear, indeed!" Wilde replied. "Caught you red-handed, I think."

Marjorie became even paler. "N-no! No, this isn't what you think!" She looked around, noticed the cans of fuel stacked near one wall. In desperation, she held the crumpled paper out toward the officers. "I was told to come here! I'm being blackmailed! I was sent a note telling me to come here, and I'd be given the evidence I needed to clear my name!"

Mueller approached carefully and snatched the paper. He glanced at it and passed it to Wilde.

"You could have forged it in case you were caught."

"I didn't!"

"She didn't," agreed a voice from the stairs.

They turned and saw Updike standing above them, holding a lantern and pistol.

"Drop your guns."

The officers did as they were instructed.

"I had hoped this would only involve Marjorie," Updike said. "Her dying role will be the guilty arsonist killed when her fire started too soon. But you two can have a cameo, as the policemen who died trying to arrest her. It will be a masterpiece."

"It was you!" Marjorie gasped.

"Of course it was. The fire was supposed to be mistaken for an accident, but your appearance last night made you the perfect scapegoat for arson."

Mueller leaned over to Wilde and whispered, "The floor's covered in oil."

"Bugger."

"He drops that lamp and we go up in flames."

"Why would you burn your own theatre?" Marjorie demanded.

"Isn't it obvious?" Updike cackled. "To destroy Cinema U!"

"But why?"

Updike scowled. "Because those investors stole my cinema from me and turned it into a vulgar mockery of what it was meant to be! I am a man of the theatre! In my day, we pretended our amateurs were professionals and made do with them! Now we lie and say that our professionals are amateurs! It is *obscene*!" As he ranted, his voice reached a hideous level of shrillness.

"I'm going to grab the lantern," Wilde whispered. "Distract him."

Mueller opened his mouth to protest, then thought better of it.

"What was the plan?" he asked. "Burn your theatre and let the public know about the secret studio?"

"Of course!" Updike cried, taking another step down the stairs. "I'll ruin Cinema U and collect the insurance on the buildings. And, Heaven willing, I'll burn those fiends alive in their snug little offices. This is Cinema U's headquarters, you know. And lovely little Marjorie has given me the perfect patsy!"

"Then what? Collect the insurance money and retire?" Mueller demanded.

"Nothing of the sort! Back to my roots! I'll start a new theatre. Vaudeville on stage *and* screen, with proper professionals who are proud to be paid for their work!"

Updike raised the lantern in the air. "And now," he continued, "I must say *au revoir*—"

As he drew back his arm to throw the lantern, Wilde barrelled forward, slipped a little on the oily floor and flung himself upward. He caught the lantern in midair and grunted as the glass chimney shattered against his chest. He hit the stairs with a thud and covered the lamp with his body to smother it.

Roaring in fury, Updike pointed his revolver at him. Mueller was on the move as well, and hit Updike just in time to make the shot miss by an inch.

"No!" Updike cried, as Mueller tore the pistol from his hand. "No! Art must be avenged!"

"Art doesn't need arson," Mueller answered, covering Updike. "It has satire. But if you want to monologue your way into a confession, I'm all ears."

*

The next week found Wilde, Mueller and Marguerite back at Cinema U, this time in a branch theatre near the ruins of the Updike. The lobby was small and crowded, and there was a line out the front waiting for tickets.

Wilde looked around at the mass of patrons and tried to ignore his aching ribs. "Well what do you know? Cinema U survived after all."

"In spite of the scandal," Marguerite agreed.

"Forget the scandal," Mueller chimed in. "The general reel's doubled in length, they've gotten so many new submissions."

"I wonder why," Wilde said.

"Because," replied a moustached gentleman who had been listening nearby, "now that they know people are getting paid, everyone wants to become a star."

"Who...?" Mueller began. Then he got a closer look at the speaker. "*Marjorie?*"

Marjorie held a finger up to her false moustache. "Shh! I'm incognito!"

"What are you doing here?" Wilde asked.

"I've a sketch in the general reel."

"Trying your hand at being a star again?"

"Ha! Never again. In Cinema U, if you're old hat you're finished. But I can still use an amateur clip here or there to advertise my new stage show, and for free no less."

"That's positive thinking," Marguerite said.

"Why not be positive, I say," Marjorie replied. "I was very nearly arrested for arson and could have died in a fire, but I didn't. Puts things in perspective." She offered her hand to Marguerite. "By the way, I don't think we've been introduced. I'm Marjorie."

Marguerite smiled. "Marguerite, and I know exactly who you are."

"So a stage show?" Mueller asked.

"I'm getting back to vaudeville, where I ought to have been all along. You boys will have to come and see me some time." She turned to Marguerite and tipped her hat. "And as for you, my dear, may I escort you to see the moving pictures?"

"Oh, I don't know," Marguerite replied, playing along, "my family doesn't like me being seen out with men."

"Don't worry darling, they'll love me. I'm in the theatre!"

"Well, in that case...." Marguerite gave Mueller and Wilde a parting wave as she took Marjorie's arm. "Ta-ta boys!"

Wilde and Mueller watched them go in stunned silence.

"Did that just happen?" Mueller asked.

"It did."

"Next time," Mueller said, "we ask the girls from the typing pool."

"Agreed."

Kulterkampf

Anatoly Belilovsky

September 1, 1870

Most respected Feldmarschall von Moltke,

I wish to thank you for giving me the opportunity to put my theories to the test in the taking of Sedan. They were, of course, entirely correct, and our clear tactical victory I am happy to be reporting.

Die Grosse Bertha worked to perfection; we were able to play Bruckner's *Zero Symphony* at half steam while the technicians adjusted all their valves and levers. Steamwinds worked perfectly on the first try, and though strings needed to be tuned, of the steam tympani there was never any doubt. I have perhaps been harsh on occasion in my estimation of Herr Bruckner's work, but for making the listeners run away screaming I should say his symphonies are without rival.

The French did put up some feeble resistance; approaching Sedan, I became aware of an odd syncopated rhythm off in the distance. Upon opening the window I was able to ascertain the nature of the music.

"*Toreador!*" I exclaimed. "The fools! They think to defeat me with Bizet!"

It is not yet time to unleash the fruit of my genius, the Secret Weapon, as the old and tried music is proving adequate to the task. Anton Bruckner has cleared the way to the French capital; I swore that I should only unleash a composition of my own when I wish for the adversary to fall to his knees and surrender to its sublime harmonies on the spot, and Paris has witnessed many such occasions. My own procession under the Arc de Triomphe is some thirty years overdue, but should taste all the sweeter for that.

I am sure that somewhere ahead the French are working on their defensive fortifications. No one is worried. What do the French have? Obsolete Berlioz? Hastily updated Gounod?

I am sure this war will end quickly in our complete victory.

After the battle, a portly man in uniform came to me on the train. He wore a cap with the word "Conductor" emblazoned in gold. Many a times have I guest-conducted a philharmonic without ever noticing the permanent conductor, but this was the first time anyone tried this diligently to be noticed as such. He brought me bedclothes and a glass of tea, which I thought was quite hospitable of him.

I cannot be as kind in my estimation of his musical erudition; the fellow looked at me with a most bemused expression when I attempted to engage him in a conversation about chromatic scales. Must be an Austrian.

On to Paris!

Your obedient servant,

Richard Wagner.

September 28, 1870

My dear von Moltke,

A near disaster was averted today! I brought out the Secret Weapon on approaching Paris, conducting Ride of the Valkyries just as the towers of Notre Dame and the hill of Montmartre came into view. An ominous silence met us, making my heart quite uneasy. The events proved my misgivings to be well founded, but it all came out well at the end.

I ordered the *Kriegszug* stopped at Gare du Nord. As the soldiers silently deployed to guard the platform, quite suddenly plaintive chords rang out. After only a few bars, soldiers and technicians began to collapse, crying.

"*Mein Gott!*" I exclaimed. "I forgot about Halévy! It's *La Juive*! We're done for!"

More and more of my men were falling *hors de combat*: the collier, the string tighteners, the brass polishers. *Timpanenführer* Schmidt sobbed on my shoulder, the *Rotznase*. The fires went out under the boilers, and Big Bertha fell silent.

The situation seemed quite dire when, suddenly, the unseen orchestra stumbled and ground to a cacophonic halt. As our soldiers rose and straightened their uniforms in embarrassment, a little Frenchman ran to the train carrying a dagger and a blood-spattered score.

"*Monsieur* Wagner!" he exclaimed. "*Mon Dieu*, you are arrived! It is just in time to save my beautiful France from—" he turned, furtively, and whispered: "—*them*..."

"Them?" I asked.

The little man nodded. "*Them*," he whispered. "Jews. Halévy. Others. They are everywhere, hiding in plain sight. We don't even know who all of them are, but we know Halévy."

I long, my dear von Moltke, to be back in our civilized Germany, where such views are not tolerated. Hidden Hebrews, indeed!

We got Bertha stoked in no time at all, the Valkyries resumed their flight, and Napoleon III brought me his sword and the keys to the city shortly after that. I put the little traitor in the same prison cell as the Emperor. It should be sufficient punishment for both.

Sincerely,

Wagner.
December 24, 1870

Best friend von Moltke,

It was not my idea to send the Wartrain on a goodwill tour, and it is no fault of mine that it did not end well.

Herr Krupp's brilliant machine was met with cheers throughout France, it played to *anschlag* audiences in La Rochelle, Toulon, Marseilles. I did not think it was wise to cross into Italy after playing in Nice, but at the urging of a certain *Rotznase* whom I shall not name we did so all the same.

We were met by a tremendous crowd in Genoa. *Die Walküre* was no longer a secret weapon, but it was still our best, and we played it well. At the first buzzing bars of the Flight the crowd was neither cowed nor awed. In fact, moments later I became aware of soft oboe-like humming. Its volume grew; I looked about for a hidden orchestra, but there was none to be found. It was the people! The crowd was singing acapella. It was singing without words! It was singing...

No, it was *humming* the *Triumphal March* from *Aida!* I had seen Verdi's score, the first page was all piano, but as it went on there would be *forti* and *fortissimi*, and the crowd was still growing, as was my unease. It was incredible, and in no time at all my Valkyries were all but drowned out. I signaled my technicians to cut the steam. The crowd grew silent, too.

One man came forward in the silence. He sang acapella as well, but he sang alone.

Vesti la giubba—
Put on your motley—
E faccia in farina—
And powder your face—

I did not know why the aria did not start at the beginning; and then I saw: after the next—

—La gente paga, e rider vuole qua.
—The people paid, the people wish to laugh—

There was a pause. And, quietly:

—Bah! Sei tu forse un uom'? Tu se' Pagliaccio!
—Are you a man? No; you're a clown.

"Fire up the boilers!" I shouted.
It took some time for my technicians to stop sobbing.
"W-what shall we play, Maestro?" the *Timpanenführer* asked.
"Nothing," I said. "I was referring to the locomotives. We are leaving. These people are unconquerable. We must find an easier target."
"Such as?" the technician asked.
A damned good question, isn't it, Moltke? So much of difference between a triumph and a flop is determined by the choice of venue.
I have given it much thought. I think I shall go to Russia. They haven't got any composers worth mentioning.

Sincerely,

Wagner.

Rogue Mail

Toby Frost

"Pay close attention," said Isambard Smith, taking a step towards the centre of the room. Twenty-six faces watched him intently. "Your enemy has no concept of decency, fair play or the Queensbury Rules. It is, therefore, your duty as citizens of the British Space Empire to incapacitate him as quickly and effectively as possible." He raised his hands. "First, run straight into the alien bugger. Then, immediately lock your left hand onto the front of Gertie's helmet, *thus*." He thrust out his left fist; fifty-two eyes stared at his red Space Fleet uniform. "Next, place your right hand into the back of the ant-man's neck, like so. Pull sharply with the left, press forward with the right, and once again Britain strikes a fierce blow for freedom."

A hand rose in the audience. "Ah," said Smith, "Chap at the front."

"Please, sir, can I be excused? I've got a piano lesson."

Smith scratched his head. He hadn't expected this. He looked at the teacherbot at the back of the classroom, and asked "Can he?"

The automaton stomped forward, the antenna on its mitre-board swinging like the arm of a metronome. "Request denied, Tomkins minor. Lunch-break will commence in T-minus seven minutes: you can go then. Now, class, Captain Smith has kindly offered to show us some slides of his majesty's orbital dreadnought fleet. After lunch, we will be field-stripping a Maxim Cannon."

"Quite right," said Smith. "Every citizen's duty to—" A sudden tinny ringing came from his waistcoat pocket. "Excuse me." He fished out his fob-phone, opened the lid and saw that the emergency bulb was flashing. He had a message.

The lesson bell sounded, and pupils sprang from their chairs. "No running in the corridor, Gillibrand!" barked the teacherbot. "Peason, do your homework if you want to live!"

Buffeted by satchels and eight-year-olds, Smith managed to stay on his feet as paper tape rattled out of the side of the phone. He tore the strip off and lifted the message to the light:

URGENT ASSISTANCE REQUIRED. COME TO GALACTIC SERVICE BROADCAST STATION AT ONCE. BRING CREW. ONE OF OUR ROBOTS IS MISSING.

*

It was good to see the crew again, he thought. After a morning in the company of small children, Smith was glad to be back with people on his own intellectual level. Also, it was exciting seeing where they made robots—especially space robots that blew things up!

He swung his car into a space and turned the engine off. Before him, the great dish of one of the Empire's transmission stations slowly turned, spreading news across the void. Smith felt reassured. Out there, in defiance of cynical alien propaganda, the voice of Britain was busy telling everyone that the British Space Empire was best.

Polly Carveth, his pilot, stood by the gate of the factory looking timid and small. She seemed wide-eyed and alert, which meant that she was either intrigued by the mission or already looking for somewhere to hide. Beside her, Rhianna Mitchell, the ship's supposed psychic and Smith's supposed lady friend, was watching clouds move across the sky.

Smith opened the door and stepped out. It was then that he noticed the large humanoid squatting on the roof.

"Greetings!" Suruk the Slayer exclaimed. Casually, he sprang down and put his spear away. "So, who are we killing today? Is it ant-men? Is it?"

"Hello Suruk," Smith replied. "How long have you been riding my car?"

"Only a mile or so." Suruk stretched and flexed his mandibles. "I wished to test my hunting skills, ready to unleash noble savagery on... something. Anything, really."

Carveth said, "Not yet you don't. We may not even have to do anything dangerous. Hopefully."

"Hey, Isambard."

Smith looked around. Rhianna stood beside them. He stepped over and embraced her, narrowly avoiding the brim of her sunhat, and then stepped back. That was enough emotion for now. "Now then," he declared, "Where are the warbots?"

"I saw one standing behind a tree," Carveth said. "This way."

They followed her around the side of the building.

"Good work," said Smith. "This must be rather nostalgic for you, I suppose," he added. "What with you being an android and all."

"What? God no." Carveth shook her head. "Boss, I'm organic, for goodness' sake. Grown in a Promethian tank, not welded together. *I* have class."

An immense form squatted at the rear of the control room. Like all imperial warbots, it looked like an ancient locomotive wrenched and bolted into the rough shape of a gorilla, a hulking lump of armour-plated brass twice the height of a man.

"Look, crew," Smith announced, "It's a warbot!"

The warbot's head swung round with a creak. Above a jaw like a miniature cow-catcher, two tiny, hard eyes peered down at them. "Do you mind?" the warbot growled. "I'm emptying my coalbox."

"Oh," said Smith, putting a hand over Rhianna's eyes. It wasn't the sort of thing ladies should see. "Well, carry on. We'll look the other way."

They turned round. A tall man paced across the gravel, arms shoved into pockets. His jacket was patched at the elbows, and he looked like a schoolmaster come to drive his pupils out of a sweet shop.

"Ah, Smith!" It was W, the master-spy. He was not exactly smiling—that seemed to be outside his emotional range—but he looked intrigued. "Examining the warbots, eh? Amazing how they function."

"Yes, isn't it?" the warbot growled. "Could you all go away and let me function in peace, please?"

As they walked towards the main transmission building Smith said, "I've always been interested in military robots, you know. I've got several Airfix kits, in fact. It's going to be very exciting working with a warbot."

"Ah," said W, frowning, "I'm going to have disappoint you there. You're working with a postbot, Smith. And not so much working *with* as chasing *after*."

"Chasing after a postbot? But couldn't you get someone else to do that?" *Like a robot dog*, he thought, deciding not to say it out loud.

"Not at all," W replied, fishing a massive key from his pocket. "You're just the man. Now, come along. The tea will be getting cold."

*

It was easy to see why W had chosen the transmitter room as the place to hold a meeting. They sat around a table under the gearing system of the satellite dish, and the slow, deep groan of the mechanism was enough to blur out any listening device. They took their tea sitting down, as anyone standing ran the risk of being beheaded by a gigantic cog.

Feeling very much like a flea trapped inside a pocketwatch, Smith took

102

his seat while Suruk accepted the honour of pouring out the tea.

"It is I who shall be mother," the alien growled, thrusting a cup at W as if to threaten him with it.

"Milk second, dammit!" the spy barked, and scowling he settled back in his chair. A counterweight swung across the roof above him, like a pendulum. "Now then, gentlemen. I've called you here to let you know that one of our postbots is missing. Usually, this would not be a problem. We would assume that it had malfunctioned, or that its inbuilt dedication to the Empire had caused it to go on strike for longer working hours. This postbot, however, is an exception."

He reached under the table and pulled out a large sheet of stiff blue paper. "This is a holographic blueprint of an advanced courier robot developed for the Postal Automation Transit system, codenamed Pat 209."

He passed the blueprint to Carveth. She tilted it in her hands to get a rotational view of the machine. It seemed to be built around a red cylinder, from which protruded large, retractable arms and rather short legs ending in broad metal feet. The unit in the picture held a beam gun across its body, a power cable running from the postbot's engine to the top of the gun.

"What's the gun for?" Carveth asked. "Intimidating big parcels?"

W said, "It was developed to carry dispatches in a battlefield environment. Up to now, tests have been very successful. The prototype demonstrated a loyalty to its mission unequalled by human personnel. I'm told it absolutely will not stop until the letters are delivered. The only problem is that it's disappeared."

Smith frowned. "You mean the post is going to be late? But this is Britain, man! That can't be allowed to happen!"

"Quite. Pat 209 is somewhere on New Dartmoor, out on the heath. I need you to hunt him down and find out why he malfunctioned. We've put up road works, so you shouldn't have to worry about traffic. But work fast, Smith, he's carrying important documents, and if the Ghasts have developed some way of making our robots break...."

"Fear not," said Suruk, flexing his mandibles. "My skill as a hunter is considerable. I have great experience of pursuing machines."

"You chase cars," Carveth said.

"I do not chase cars. They flee from me."

"We'll get the job done," Smith promised. "But, surely Suruk and I can deal with this. Do the women have to be involved?"

W sucked deeply on his cigarette, as if there was something tasty at the end of it. "Ah," he said, "that's the clever bit. You and Suruk here will have binoculars. Miss Mitchell will use her mesmeric abilities to sense Pat 209. And whatsit here will pilot the airship."

"An airship? With nice rooms and everything?" Carveth grinned. "I'm in!"

*

New Dartmoor: Type 72 Civilised World
Population: 4,000,000
Alien natives: None
Notable game: Pheasants, Grouse, Farmers (all protected by law)
Principal Land Use: 6% urban, 43% moorland, 51% agricultural (sheep, pheasants, grouse, scrumpy)

"Hmm," said Polly Carveth, surveying the airship. "It's a bit... droopy, isn't it?"

"I have no idea," Suruk replied. "I understood you to be the expert in such matters."

They stood in the inflation yard on New Dartmoor, thirty miles south of Fort Barclay, the main town and source of what Carveth described as "weapons-grade cider". Before them, like a limp cigar, stood *HMS Windlass*, a mid-size dirigible officially belonging to the East Empire Company. It did seem rather wilted, Smith had to admit: the main balloon was brown and attached to the cabin by a complicated lattice of leather straps, like a cross between an old sausage and the Marquis de Sade's sleeping bag.

Rhianna leaned to Smith. "Are you sure it works? I mean, once it gets in the air, will it stay there?"

Smith frowned. "Well, seeing how the army's requisitioned all the others, I think it will do just fine," he decided, hoping that she had not noticed what looked like an enormous sticking-plaster attached to the flank. It was time to take the lead and inspire confidence in his crew. "Follow me, men!"

Smith strode across the airfield, past two startled technicians and an automated tea urn, and turned to his crew. "Time to board this fine vessel, everybody. Look, everyone!" he added, flinging the cabin door open. "It's even got a propeller on this side too! The clouds belong to us!"

*

It was not much of a cabin: the brasswork needed polishing and the stuffing was beginning to come out of the Ottoman. The drone of the engines seeped through the glass as the *Windlass* puttered across the moor. Carveth took the controls. She was just able to see the rotors on either side, which made her feel like an egg being chased by a very large whisk.

Rhianna entered a trance at the back of the cockpit, her meditative humming joining with that of the engines. (Either that, Smith thought, or she had fallen asleep.) He joined Suruk by the windows and together they scanned the moor with their binoculars. Smith ordered the alien to tell him if he saw anything of interest: after Suruk had spotted both rotors, two pubs, a dog with three legs and the moor itself ("Just like in *Warbling Heights*!") Smith rather regretted it.

"Location please, pilot," he called out.

Carveth examined the Galactic Survey map spread out across her lap. "Well, we've gone about eighty miles so far, which puts us halfway between Doom Moor and the Thomas Hardy theme park."

"That sounds jolly." Smith gazed out at the scenery as the heather rolled by. "Clever stuff, this planetscaping. Apparently, this whole continent is an exact replica of the West Country back on Earth. I once went to Wookey Hole, you know. It was around here," he added, prodding Carveth's map and with it her thigh.

"Ow!" said Carveth. "That's my leg!"

Smith did not really hear her. Gazing out the window, he added, "Sadly, my spelunking career was halted by a nasty sprain in the Cheddar Gorge."

"Ugh," Carveth replied. "Could you check the instruments, please?"

Smith consulted the dials and counters on the scanning panel. Like the controls of most flying machines, they meant little to him and were the sort of thing he would usually delegate on principle. Still, none of the needles was in the red. One bounced up and down, however, and as he examined it, a little roll of paper spooled out of a slot.

"Reading to the north-east," he said. "I think."

"Correcting course," Carveth replied, and the drone of the rotors rose and fell as the *Windlass* turned. "Vehicle down below," she announced.

"That's odd." Smith raised his telescope. "I thought W said the roads were closed." A red van stood by the side of the road, a crest on its side. A man stood a little way off in the heather, looking into a dip in the ground. Smith craned his neck, struggling to get a better view.

"Who is it?" Suruk growled, adjusting his binoculars. "Is it Tess, in her dormobile?"

"No," said Smith. "It's the Post Office. Carveth, land us, please."

The *Windlass* touched down on all four legs at once, which by Smith's standards was a very successful landing. He jumped out of the cockpit, the heather scratching at his gaiters as he waded towards the man. "You there!" he called. "What's going on?"

The fellow turned, and Smith saw that he wore the blue tunic and red epaulettes of the Colonial Postal Service. The man pointed to the crest on the van, the V.R. of King Victor, emperor of British Space. "Go away! This is postal business!"

Smith waded closer. "I'm with the secret service," he explained. "We're looking for a postbot that's gone—"

"Postal?" the other man replied. "He's down there. And if I have my way, very soon he'll be a dead letter box."

Smith took a step forward and looked into the dip. The land dropped away, and below stood Pat 209, all eight feet of him. Smith's pleasure at having found the renegade machine was somewhat mitigated by the large gun it was pointing at his chest.

"Keep back!" Pat 209 thundered. "You have twenty seconds to return to sender!"

"Ah," said Smith, stepping back from the edge of the dip. He turned to the postal officer. "Look, why don't you leave this to the experts, eh?"

"When are they coming?" the man replied.

"Now look here," Smith retorted. "That's not on. I have been instructed to—"

The officer pointed. "Your alien's getting restless."

Smith looked round. Suruk was waving his spear out the window of the *Windlass*. "They do that," Smith replied. "Good sorts, aliens, but terribly excitable."

"I think he's trying to tell you that Pat 209 is getting away," the postal officer replied.

Smith spun round: the postbot was bounding across the heather with great clanking steps, faster than any man. The squat bulk of a factory sat on the horizon: the machine was heading toward it.

Quickly, Smith ran back to the airship. He clambered aboard, slammed the door and cried "Follow that postbot!"

*

The postal officer watched them go. The airship wobbled into the distance, the engines pushing it along like a queen bee carried aloft by two of its minions. He smiled and rubbed his gloved hands together. It was just a matter of following from a safe distance now, and then taking the prize for himself.

*

The factory rose above the four adventurers like a castle of iron and dirty brick. The great steel door was locked. "Looks like it's closed," Smith announced. "I suppose the workers get Sundays off."

"Unlike some," Carveth replied.

"Listen, men, here's the plan. Rhianna, I want you to stay by the dirigible. Keep an eye out for trouble. Suruk, Carveth, you're coming with me. If we can get the jump on this robot, we should be able to shut him down easily enough. We'll need to go quietly. Understand?"

"Absolutely," Suruk replied. "To battle, then!"

Rhianna embraced Smith and pushed her sunhat down. "Good luck, everyone. I'll try to sense the postbot's presence."

"Thanks, old girl," Smith replied.

Suruk frowned at Rhianna. "You should be careful," he said. "If the Postmaster General discovers your magic powers, he will burn you at the stake."

"That's the Witchfinder General," Rhianna said. "But thanks anyway."

*

Suruk drove the butt of his spear through the window-pane. Smith went first, throwing his coat over the sill to protect him from the glass. Suruk picked Carveth up and thrust her in second, then leaped up behind them both.

They dropped into an office. Rows of desks ran down the length of the room. Beside each desk was a pipe for the office's pneumatic message system: they stretched down from the apex of the roof like the roots of a mechanical plant. Carveth picked a bottle of Harrington's Fortifying Tonic from one of the desks, unscrewed the cap and took a quick, warming swig before offering the bottle around. "Anyone? It's medicinal."

Smith tried the office door. It opened easily onto a passageway. They walked out and paused by the tea machine, hearing nothing.

"Right," Smith said, "listen carefully. Suruk, try to find a way upstairs, especially one that doesn't involve cutting off anyone's head. Carveth, I want you to search the downstairs offices, preferably without getting sozzled on medicinal tonic on the way. I'll take the main floor. See if you can find any sign of Pat 209, but don't engage him: he's armed and dangerous and he's got tomorrow's post. Meet me back here in ten minutes."

Suruk bounded away down the corridor, eager to begin the hunt. A little *too* eager, Smith thought: the alien probably wanted to add Pat 209's head to his trophy rack and loot his letters. Even Suruk's stamp collection had a ghoulish quality.

Carveth went on her way surprisingly quickly. She seemed quite keen to get to work—assuming that she was not simply going to hide in a cupboard as soon as she was out of sight. Smith drew his .45 Civiliser and started out down the corridor.

He took a left and stepped into the entrance hall. Marble steps lead up to a wide desk behind which sat the upper half of an automated clerk, currently deactivated and slumped. For a moment he considered switching the thing on and interrogating its logic engine—but you could have too much logic, Smith thought. Talking to it would be like trying to discuss cricket with an Austrian.

He crossed the darkened foyer, past a brass mural of Britain's conquest of space. His boots squeaked softly on the polished floor. As he reached the Fall of the First Empire he paused and listened, his head level with an embossed tripod. He took another step. Beside him, a brass spaceman was planting the Union Jack on Pluto, while a couple of tentacle savages looked on.

To the right, as if in the bowels of a ship, metal creaked.

He tore round the corner, pistol first, kicked open a door and stood in a repair room. Hammers and rivet guns lay on shelves against the wall. A backup cogitator whirred and hummed at the rear of the room, and beside it, connected with a thick cable, stood Pat 209.

"Gotcha!" Smith barked, jabbing the gun towards the machine's speaking-slot. "Hands up, robot fellow!"

Pat 209 was slightly bigger than he had remembered, and rather more shiny. It did not respond.

"I said hands up!" The automaton did not move. Smith thought about it. "Alright then—have it your way. Don't move!" Smith took a step back towards the door, causing him to collide with something.

He spun around. "You there!" he barked instinctively. "Drop your weapons and welcome to the Empire!"

Suruk raised an eyebrow-ridge. "Greetings."

"Ah, Suruk. Good timing." Smith stepped back and pointed to the robot at the far side of the room. "As you can see, I have located Pat 209."

Suruk frowned. "Curious. I travelled here to make exactly the same announcement. It is I, Suruk the Slayer, who have found the miscreant engine. It is in an office upstairs, grievously slain beside the water cooler."

"Now there you're wrong, old chap," Smith replied. "Clearly, he's over here. Look: he's just as W described him. See?"

The alien snorted and flexed his mandibles. "Not so! My many years of hunting speak otherwise. It is clear that the renegade postbot could not have come to this room; since upstairs I took the liberty of removing its head –"

"Look, Suruk, I bagged the robot first! I'm British and you're wrong, alright?"

"Hello everyone," said Carveth from the door. She fished a chocolate bar out of her pocket and took a large bite. "Having fun?"

Suruk frowned. "Be gone. This is a matter for warriors. I have corralled the postbot upstairs—the only machine you have bettered, it seems, is the food dispenser."

"It was a hard fight," she admitted. "But there's something you need to see ."

"Later, Carveth," said Smith. "We need some rope to tie this robot up."

"No, listen!" She sounded quite worried, Smith thought. She might be idle, cowardly and lecherous, but she was a useful barometer of when things were starting to go wrong—largely because when danger drew near, she would vanish.

"You're both equally wrong," Carveth said. "Come and look at this."

She stepped out of the room. Smith glanced at Suruk: the alien shrugged. They followed the pilot down the hall, to a massive wrought-iron door.

"Did you wonder what kind of a factory this is?" Carveth asked, and she turned the handle.

The door swung open, and beyond them was the factory floor. Light filtered down between the vaults. Scrollwork stretched between buttresses five times Smith's height. A huge painting of a mechanical Britannia blessing a space dreadnought hung on the opposite wall. Under it, in rows five deep, stood a legion of postbots.

Smith looked at the machines, his eyes moving from one identical brass figure to the next. It was not easy to find the right words for the occasion, but after a moment they came.

"Oh, *balls*."

"That's what I thought," Carveth replied. "No wonder Pat 209 came here: it's a robot factory. Camouflage."

Smith looked across the rows of robots, and reflected that it was a pretty unsporting trick. He sighed.

Suruk cracked his knuckles. "There is a plus side to this, you know," he observed.

"Really? What's that?"

"We will take many robot heads."

"What?"

Suruk pulled a machete from his belt. "I suggest we do battle with this horde, just in case. Once they are all destroyed, there will be no doubt that Pat 209 has been put out of action. All we need do then is locate his parts in the vast heap of severed robot limbs."

Smith closed his eyes and summoned his moral fibre. "Are you actually suggesting we destroy five hundred mechanical postmen on the off chance one of them is the machine we're looking for?"

"Yes. But remember to activate them first. It would be dishonourable unless the postbots were actually trying to murder us."

"Dear God," Smith said. "We're going to need a sledgehammer."

Carveth had been gazing around the room. "Well, you can count me out," she said, stepping back towards the doors. "As an android I regard these postbots as family—primitive, locked-in-the-attic-and-never-mentioned-again family, but family nonetheless. And they're bigger than me."

"Well," Smith replied, "that's all very well, but…wait a moment. I've had an idea. Back into the corridor. Pat 209 may be listening."

*

Rhianna stood on the heath outside the factory, admiring the sky and wondering whether to do a cartwheel. A cloud shaped like a tree floated past. "Hello clouds!" she called. "Hello, sk—"

"Hey."

Rhianna looked down, vaguely annoyed at being interrupted during her communion with nature. The man from the post office stood nearby. She could see his red van, as small as a toy, behind him on the road. "Can I help?" she asked.

The man nodded towards the factory. Something about him wasn't quite right, Rhianna thought. "Is Captain Smith in there?"

"Yes, he is," she replied.

"Thanks," said the man, and he walked past.

As the man approached the factory Rhianna realised what was wrong. He was carrying a rifle.

Oh no! she thought. *He must be planning to do something bad!* For a moment she considered taking off her sandal and hitting him with it, but she was not inclined to violence and doubted its stopping-power. There was only one thing to do: she would have to send a psychic message to warn the others. She clenched her eyes shut, put her hands over her ears, reached out with her mind and tried to find Smith's brain.

*

Smith closed the door and Carveth said, "So what's the plan, then?"

"Listen," he replied. "Pat 209 is different to the other postbots. They were built here. He's been wandering all over the place. He'll bear all the signs of having spent time on New Dartmoor."

"He's drunk on scrumpy, you mean?"

"No—well, not necessarily; his brasswork will be tarnished from walking across the heath. All we need to do is look underneath and see which postbot has dirty feet."

"Assuming he doesn't stamp on our heads."

"Really, Carveth, I don't think—Ugh, my skull!" Smith grimaced and staggered back as if struck in the temples. "Dammit!" Teeth gritted, he pulled himself upright. "What was I saying?"

"You were having an idea," Suruk said.

"And now your head hurts," Carveth added. "Coincidentally, of course."

"Yes," Smith gasped. "That's it—quick, men, hide!"

The door at the far end of the factory squealed on its hinges. A single figure strolled into the room, a rifle in its hands. Smith recognised him instantly.

"I say, Post Office man! What the devil are you doing here?"

The man smiled. "I just came here to collect a parcel," he replied. "And the robot delivering it." In the bad light, his uniform made him resemble one of the traitor militia of the ant-people. He only needed the false antennae on his cap to look like a proper Ghastist.

"I'm afraid that's not possible," Smith replied. "You'll have to leave."

"Well, I'm afraid I've got a big gun," the agent replied. "So get into the tool cupboard or I'll shoot you."

"How dare you?" Smith snapped back. "I am a British citizen, not a spanner!"

"You could have fooled me," the agent replied, and he raised his gun.

Something shot out of the darkness and the man cried out. His rifle skidded across the floor and clattered against the feet of a postbot. Suruk stepped out of the shadows, smiling his battle-smile. Carveth emerged behind him and took a deep swig of restorative tonic.

The agent cursed. "You think you've got me, Smith? Good thing I put a punchcard of my own design into the mainframe on the way in. Postbots, awake!"

At the far end of the row, one of the postbots opened its eyes. The shutters clattered open and red light glowed in the lenses. Then, the one beside it awoke, and suddenly, like the Christmas lights of a very small town, the red glow spread from machine to machine. The postbots chuffed and creaked into life. Hydraulic shoulders loosened up. Steel fingers flexed.

On the screen above the logic engine at the far end of the room there appeared a stylised skull with antennae: the emblem of the Ghasts.

The agent stooped and picked up his gun. "That's better." His voice rose until it rang around the scrollwork in the rafters. "I now declare New Dartmoor to be under new management! From this day on, the Ghast Empire will make the post run on time!"

"Oh arse," Smith said. They stood in the middle of a hundred clanking, looming postbots. Smith tensed, ready to reach for his pistol. Suruk chuckled. Carveth squeaked.

The agent raised his hand. "Postbots!" he cried, "Strike!"

The robots did not move.

"I said, 'Strike!'"

Still nothing.

"Dammit!" the agent snarled.

"They're postal workers," Smith replied. "They *are* striking."

"No, you fools!" the agent shouted. "Attack! Kill them and the Ghast Empire will make the post run on time for a thousand years!"

The postbots paused. "Your terms do not compute," one of the machines said. The front row parted with a sudden hammering of steel feet and it stepped out, looked down and dropped its satchel onto the agent's head.

He fell as if shot. The postbot peered at the fallen man, reattached its satchel and announced "How's that for industrial action?"

"Bloody hell," Smith replied. "That was some prompt postal work! What's your name, sir?"

"Pat," said machine replied.

*

"I am sorry I violated my programming," Pat 209 said. They sat around the postbot in one of the larger offices, waiting for the police to finish their inspection of the factory floor. "But once I realised that there was an enemy agent in the Post Office itself, I had to escape."

111

W sat on the far side of the room, forcing himself to drink tea that had come from the vending machine. He took a sip, grimacing. Clearly the pot had not been warmed before brewing.

"And so you came here," Smith said.

Pat nodded. "I am eight feet tall and have a postbox for an abdomen. A factory full of similar robots seemed like the ideal place where I could hide. Probably the only place."

Rhianna shoved her hair out of her eyes. "But what made you think there was a badger in the office?"

"A mole," Smith corrected.

Pat 209 shrugged its mechanical shoulders. "His name was Lupin Smythe, assistant postmaster general of New Dartmoor. I became suspicious that something was wrong when he kept ranting about efficiency. It was when he suggested making an example of any letter that arrived late that I realised he was a Ghastist."

"How do you mean, an example?" said Carveth, pouring a shot of tonic into her cup.

"I think a firing squad was involved," Pat explained.

"Well," W announced, "I expect that the only postal work Lupin Smythe will be doing from now on will involve sewing mailbags. Well done, everyone. It's been something of a red letter day."

They walked outside. The wind had picked up, setting the heather shaking in the breeze. Smith watched Pat 209 depart, and he hung back a little as his crew climbed into the *Windlass* and the airship's propellers began to spin.

W pulled his jacket tight, and started to walk down the path towards his car. "Sir?" said Smith.

The master spy looked round. "Yes?"

"Just one question. You said that Pat 209 was carrying despatches. What was so important about them for us to risk our lives?"

The spy shook his head. "I couldn't tell you the details, Smith. Top secret, I'm afraid. Suffice it to say that were they to fall into enemy hands, they could have jeopardised the entire war effort. Now," he added, glancing back towards the road, "would you excuse me? It's the Prime Minister's birthday next week and I still haven't got him a present. At least this year he'll get his card on time," he added, half to himself, and he strolled away down the path.

Electrium

Elizabeth Counihan

Professor Ultimo Callidus, Professor of Natural Philosophy at the Academy of Terragia. Inventor of fireless luminescence, the optical stargazer and the hot air floater, among others. He spent many fruitless years researching an elusive property he named "adnature", believing that "the world contains hidden sources of great power".

Unable to demonstrate the existence of this phenomenon to his peers, he nevertheless always insisted that adnature existed "on the other side of the world" and that, as a young boy, he had seen the evidence with his own eyes.

He died at the early age of thirty-five when the boiler of his steam-driven ship exploded during an attempt to explore the Eastern Ocean. He will be missed as one of the most brilliant minds of the century.

*

He was a youngster of around twelve years old, orphaned and working as pot-boy to Master Gracco at the sign of the Snarling Ferret at Nusquam, a place that no one had heard of then or now. At that time he went by the name of Hebes.

On a particularly cold, wet night the innkeeper was surprised to hear a sharp rap on the inn door. He glanced around. All his regulars were already there and Nusquam was a place where strangers seldom came and were not welcome. The closed door and the curtained windows discouraged non-locals from trying to gain admittance to the town's only inn, so a knock at the door at this time of night, and on a night like this, was surprising as well as unwanted.

Gracco called for Hebes.

The boy was busy serving Nusquam's version of the quality—the sons of rich farmers and land owners who sat around the fire drinking noisily. Two of them, Hebes knew, were supposed to be on watch-patrol outside that night.

"Well, boy, see who it is," said Master Gracco irritably.

Three more heavy blows to the door followed.

"We're coming, don't break the door down!" yelled the innkeeper, and then grabbing Hebes by the hair, "Hurry up, slowworm!"

Hebes did. He mounted the steps from the common room and, grabbing a lantern, hurried down the narrow entrance hall to investigate. He drew back the inn's greasy leather curtain and opened the door onto darkness, wind and rain. The dim light fell on a stranger who still grasped the cudgel with which he had been beating the door.

"What do you want?" Hebes asked. He saw that the person standing outside was tall and wore dark clothes. A broad-brimmed hat, from which water poured rather than dripped, obscured the upper part of his face.

"I would like a meal and a bed for the night," the person said.

"I...I don't know," stammered the boy. There was something ominous about the tall figure looming over him out of the night.

"This is an inn, is it not?" the man asked quietly, pointing upwards to the painted ferret swinging in the wind.

Hebes nodded and muttered that he would fetch his master.

The traveller pushed his hat back, revealing pale, clean-shaven features, long, dripping hair and bright grey eyes.

"Then I will wait inside," he said and leaning heavily on his staff hopped, dark as a crow, across the threshold. Water poured from his cloak onto the flagstones.

*

"Funny accent? Foreigner? Why didn't you just send him packing?" demanded Gracco.

"Says he wants a bed for the night. I couldn't make him go, Master. He's waiting in the hall. I think he's hurt—leaning on a crutch," the boy explained.

"I'll soon settle him," said the innkeeper. "I'll have no crippled beggars in here. You get on with serving the long table." He shoved a tray of drinks into the boy's hands; then bunched his fists and stumped off to investigate.

*

He came back almost immediately and Hebes stared at him, open-mouthed. His master's normally ruddy face was pale and he was sweating even more than usual. The boy wasn't foolish enough to comment but Junius, the blacksmith's son, was still waiting for his drink and he called, "What's up Gracco? Magistrate come to test the beer again?" Gracco had been fined for selling watered beer not so long ago, as his customers frequently reminded him.

But Gracco didn't answer. He looked dazed. He beckoned to the pot-boy.

"He don't want to eat in here. He's gone to the stable. Fetch some of that stew and a loaf of today's bread. Well, what are you waiting for?"

A few minutes later the innkeeper carried, through the teeming rain, a tureen of stew containing best end of mutton, a loaf of reasonably fresh bread and a jug of best beer. His astonished pot-boy, lighting the way with a guttering lantern, brought blankets in a leather bag.

At the stable, Hebes observed the traveller seated on a hay bale and playing an unfamiliar tune on a wooden flute. He could see, even from the standpoint of a twelve-year-old, that the man was quite young. His cloak and hat, hanging from a stall peg, dripped onto the straw. The boy noticed that one of his legs was oddly twisted. The horses whinnied gently in their stalls and the stable cat, asleep next to the man's black staff, appeared to appreciate the music. Hebes pulled out the blankets and put them beside the hay bale. The man put his flute down and smiled.

Gracco handed over the food and drink without a word. The traveller thanked him in that strange clipped accent and Hebes saw a flash of gold as a coin was handed over. He couldn't understand why this harmless stranger had made him feel so uneasy.

Then he glanced at Gracco. The man was still pale as ash and shaking.

"Are you all right, Master Gracco?" he ventured when they had returned to the house.

The innkeeper grunted but said nothing. His eyes were glassy as if he were in a trance. The boy crept away to wash-up the pots.

After that he succeeded in keeping out of the way for the rest of the evening, he grabbed a bite to eat and curled up in a dark corner where he watched the fire. *Why did sparks always fly upwards?* he wondered. *Would a boy fly if the wind was warm enough?*

He fell asleep.

*

A familiar bellow woke him up. The innkeeper had come to his senses. "I've been robbed!" he yelled.

The last of his guests, a group of young drunkards, stuporous around the dying fire, looked up, startled.

Hebes listened as Gracco explained that a stranger—*a foreigner*—had taken advantage of his hospitality. The fellow, a beggar, had stolen good food and drink and was even now asleep in the stable. He didn't mention the gold coin Hebes had seen change hands.

"What are you boys going to do about it? You're the Town Watch aren't you?" he finished.

The two local heroes who had, as usual, intended spending the onerous hours of their night on duty supping by the fireside, were at first unwilling to leave it for such a minor matter which, they felt, could wait till morning. But Gracco pointed out that the fellow was alone and unarmed except for a crutch and might well make his sneaky escape before dawn, which was not far off.

"Didn't see so much as a dagger, did you Hebes?" The pot-boy shook his head sleepily. "He'll most likely steal a horse," the innkeeper ruminated.

That settled it. The two watchmen, both of whom owned excellent mounts now stabled at the inn, drained their mugs and put on their coats.

Swords drawn, they led the way, followed by the innkeeper carrying a light. Hebes, sleepy but curious, grabbed another and followed, and tottering behind were a couple of curious customers just sober enough to stand. The night was dank but the rain had stopped, only a steady dripping from the roof of the inn buildings, the squelch of their boots and the occasional gust of wind could be heard as they crossed to the stable.

Gracco opened the stable door. His lantern picked out the supposed felon, lying under a pile of blankets, asleep with a smile on his face as if dreaming of better times. The stout black stick lay beside him.

"We'll have that," muttered Guido, the leading watchman, flicking his sword out to collect the weapon.

As it touched the stick he let out a great yell.

"Something stung me! Must be booby trapped!" He dropped the sword.

His shout woke the sleeping man who drew his hands from under the blanket and sat up. Hebes shone his own lantern on the scene but saw nothing that could have caused the injury.

The stranger looked quickly at the two swordsmen as Guido gripped his arm; the other watchman still pointed his weapon at him.

"Put that down," the stranger said, indicating the second watchman's sword. "It's not needed. I do not intend to hurt anyone."

He reached for his stick and pulled himself to his feet. The semicircle of onlookers took a simultaneous pace backwards. The traveller laughed and held up his hands.

He said, "Do I look so dangerous? Oh, it's quite safe to retrieve your sword but don't touch my property again or you may get another shock."

Guido gingerly reached out and took his blade without further mishap.

Seeing the empty dishes as a reminder that he had provided food for the vagrant, the innkeeper glanced at the two swordsmen and his courage returned.

"Let's finish the job, boys. Kick his stick from under him."

The traveller's eyes glittered strangely.

"Don't do it, Master!" said Hebes, suddenly afraid.

But Gracco handed his lantern to one of his customers and advanced on the traveller, fists bunched.

There was a blinding flash of light, a crash and a great wind, followed by blackness. The cat screeched horribly and the tipsier of the customers, who had fallen over on the straw, bellowed when his face was scored by the panicking animal as it fled past him. The horses whinnied and tossed in their stalls.

Hebes, thrown to the ground, saw his dropped lantern flicker back to life. Gracco's had done the same. He righted them quickly before they could set the straw alight. *How could that happen?* he wondered.

Master Gracco lay face down on the ground, breathing stertorously. The rest of his party had been flung backwards into an arc and were seated in various attitudes of amazement. He noticed that the straw, too, had been blown into a semicircle with all its strands pointing towards the stranger who was in the act of picking himself up. Like the rest, he had been hurled down by the force of the explosion.

Hebes retrieved his lantern and got up. So did the others except for the innkeeper, still unconscious, and the stranger who was now rubbing his ankle and cursing in an unknown tongue.

The boy ran for the door. He would fetch Dr Fulgo. The doctor, who in his opinion knew everything, would know what to do.

*

It took him the best part of an hour to reach the doctor's residence, falling twice into cart ruts as the feeble lantern light guttered. But at last, hearing a familiar clattering and wheezing sound, his ears guided him to the right track.

He turned a corner and saw lights twinkling in a lower window and dull red sparks issuing from behind the building. He wasn't surprised; Dr Fulgo often worked until dawn. He peered through the window and saw two men sitting by the fire, glasses in their hands. He rapped gently, careful not to damage the real glass of the window; then shouted with all the breath he still possessed.

The doctor himself opened the door and behind him was a taller man, whom Hebes recognised with some fear, as Dom Marcellus, the magistrate who had fined his master.

"There's been an accident at the Ferret—an explosion," Hebes gasped but hadn't the breath to continue.

"Fetch him a tot of aquavit, Marcellus," the doctor said; then sat him down on a bench in the hallway. Hebes kicked off his muddy shoes.

"Well, boy?" said the magistrate, a few moments later.

Hebes, dizzy from running and from the strong liquor, told his tale.

"Sounds like those damn fool boys have started a fight," Dom Marcellus remarked to the doctor. Hebes, though nervous of contradicting a magistrate, shook his head.

"Begging your pardon, sir, they didn't get the chance. The lame man— he must have *done* something that made the explosion. And Master Gracco's hurt bad—unconscious when I left."

"But didn't you say the stranger was asleep when this started?" asked Dr Fulgo, tugging at his stubby, grey beard. Hebes nodded.

"We'll get no sense out of this simpleton," snorted the magistrate. "We'd better get over there. I'll call for my man to fetch the horses round."

"Mmm, no need for that," said Fulgo. "After all, she's all fired up and ready to go."

The two men fetched their cloaks and hurried round to the back of the house. Hebes, forgotten, ran after them; in his excitement leaving his wet shoes in the doctor's hallway. How many times had Dr Fulgo's steam-horse passed him in the street? He was determined not to miss his chance to ride it.

*

"She goes well, Fulgo, I'll grant you," shouted Dom Marcellus, as they pulled up outside the stable of the *Snarling Ferret*. He climbed down from his seat astride the gleaming boiler.

The doctor pulled on various levers. The eyelight went out and the roaring and puffing was reduced to a quieter groaning and whistling.

"Fifteen minutes, at most," he said. He jumped down and followed the magistrate who was already picking his way carefully across the yard, avoiding the scattering of wet horse dung and broken roof slate which was barely visible in the dim light.

Hebes who, without anyone's leave, had ridden home clinging to the handrail at the back of the engine, stroked her shining flank and watched sparks and steam fly up to the clouds. It had been the most wonderful experience of his life. He sighed. *Suppose real horses breathed fire and ate wood. I wonder if animals like that ever existed?*

Then he remembered the reason for all this. He looked up at the stables and gasped. By the faint dawn light he could see that a great hole had appeared in the roof.

As Hebes entered the stable he heard Dom Marcellus, at his most magisterial, demanding to know what was going on.

The two members of the Watch stood pointing their weapons at the stranger. Gracco still lay snoring on the ground but at least someone had

had the sense to turn him on his side.

"Ah, Guido, Primo, glad to see you lads doing your duty, though your appearance leaves much to be desired." The magistrate indicated their hair, still bristling like straw.

"Sorry about that, Dom Marcellus," Guido said, "but can't be helped. We were apprehending this vagrant when the place was struck by lightning. Blew us all over. Made a hole in the roof."

"But it wasn't lightning," Hebes interrupted. "It came from him." He jabbed a thumb at the seated traveller. "He knocked Master Gracco out cold!"

"That's enough of your nonsense, boy," the magistrate said, absently clipping his ear. But the seated man raised his head and looked intently at Hebes. Marcellus now turned to the traveller. "What have you to say for yourself, fellow?"

"You have an unconscious man there," said the man. "Why don't you attend to him first?"

"You know, I think that's a good idea." Dr Fulgo, who had been puzzling over the hole in the stable roof now hurried over to examine the unconscious man. "We must see to Master Gracco before turning to the matter of the remarkable thunderbolt," he added.

Hearing his name mentioned the innkeeper stirred and sat up, rubbing his head; then rose groggily to his feet, assisted by Hebes. As he looked around, his dazed eyes fell on the traveller and, roaring like a bull, he launched himself at the man, only prevented from committing instant homicide by Hebes and the two watchmen.

"Lemme get at him!" slurred the innkeeper. "Bloody foreigner, tried to brain me with that cudgel!"

"But that's not what happened," said Hebes.

"Now, Master Gracco," Dr Fulgo said, after prodding the innkeeper's skull, "my prescription for you is a dose of verbane and a day in bed—and no alcohol, mind!"

Gracco subsided onto a hay bale, groaning and holding his head.

Dom Marcellus took more witness statements then demanded that the stranger stand up and account for himself.

"I beg your pardon, sir," said the traveller, "but the force of the, er... phenomenon, threw me to the ground and I have sprained the ankle of my only good leg. I'm therefore unable to accede to your request." His tone was far from humble and Dom Marcellus bristled.

Dr Fulgo made a swift appraisal of the man's condition.

"You'll have to interrogate him sitting down, Marcellus—permanent damage to one leg, plus a badly wrenched ankle on the other. Seems we've a bit of a mystery here..."

"There's no mystery, Dom," said Primo, one of the two swordsmen. "Our good innkeeper asked me and Guido, as duty watchmen, to help him eject a beggar from his stable. When we tried to do our duty the man assaulted Guido..."

"My arm's still tingling," Guido affirmed.

"And then, when Master Gracco intervened the stable was struck by lightning."

"Well, we can hardly blame the beggar for that," Dom Marcellus said.

Guido nodded. "It was really lucky. The fellow strikes me as a hardened villain. He was getting ready to attack Gracco when the explosion happened."

"But...but that's not what happened," Hebes repeated. He was ignored by all except the stranger, who looked at him and started to laugh.

"Why not put him in the stocks for the day and then send him on his way?" suggested Primo.

"I expect you're trying to be helpful, lad," the magistrate said sternly, "but due process, you know...We'll take him into custody. I'll have to judge him when Master Gracco is able to give evidence." He glared at Guido and Primo. "Being members of Town Watch is an honour, and you two have not taken it seriously enough. And as for you..." He looked down at the prisoner. "I don't know why you are laughing. This is a serious matter."

"I laugh because the situation is ridiculous. I'm supposed to be a dangerous criminal who assaulted three, or was it four, strong men? Also I am a crippled beggar, so perhaps not so dangerous? Make up your minds, please! In fact, I am merely a traveller who wanted a meal and a night's rest. I would leave your pleasant company immediately had I not twisted my ankle and so will be forced to stay with you for, maybe, two days. If you had not tried to attack me none of this would have happened."

The doctor pricked up his ears.

"None of this would have happened? What do you mean, young man?"

"Nothing, of course, Dom Doctor. Please ignore my nonsensical ramblings."

Fulgo looked at him sharply and turned to the magistrate.

"Marcellus, if it's all right with you, I'll take him back to my place. I can treat his injury; seems a shame to throw him in jail for the day. He can't run away, after all."

The magistrate nodded.

"Can I come too, Dr Fulgo?" Hebes piped up. "I left my shoes at your house."

"I think you should take your master back to the inn."

"I only have the one pair, sir."

Fulgo grinned. "You like my steam horse, do you? Very well, help me get this man onto it." He turned to the prisoner. "You'll need this." He

121

reached for the black stick but the man put a hand out to stop him.

"Last time someone touched my property they received a shock," he said.

"Stored Electrium perhaps? How interesting. You and I are going to talk, my friend," said the doctor.

With much grunting from Fulgo and wincing from the prisoner, who towered over both Hebes and the doctor, all three reached the stable yard, where the steam horse still rattled and belched. Dom Marcellus, after directing the two sullen watchmen to help the innkeeper back to his inn, took a spare horse to get himself home.

Despite his assured manner, the prisoner was clearly startled, if not frightened, when he saw the doctor's means of transport.

"Is...is it alive?" he asked.

"Of course not," Hebes said. "Haven't you ever heard of a steam horse?"

The young man shook his head.

"I'm surprised," the doctor yelled, as the noise increased. "*Steam engine... uncommon* but I thought most people had at least *heard* of them."

*

Back at the doctor's house Hebes cleared a pile of manuscripts from a couch in the workroom and Fulgo heaved the prisoner onto it. The doctor then applied ice and a bandage to the man's injured ankle.

Hebes gazed curiously at the piles of strange equipment strewn about the room. He ran a finger over a glass jug with a strangely bent neck.

"Don't touch that, boy," Fulgo snapped. "Glass is damned expensive! And you," he said, turning to the stranger, "are going to be out of action for at least a week. So there'll be plenty of time for you to answer my questions."

The young man smiled. "No, doctor, I assure you my ankle will be entirely healed in two days at which time I will leave this place. Therefore ask now whatever you like and I will try to answer you, although I have learned that people here cannot understand...about me and what I do."

Fulgo frowned. "Well, we won't argue about that—though I'm the experienced medical man and you are, as it happens, my prisoner." He appraised the man in front of him.

"So, let's have some facts. You speak the common tongue with a very strange accent; ectomorphic build, grey eyes and black hair—a racial type I've never seen before. You are, what, twenty-three years old? First, what's your name and where are you from?"

"You've never seen anyone like me before? That is because I came from across the sea." The prisoner shrugged. "You do not believe me, of course.

There is nowhere across the sea. This is what you will say. My name, or the name I have here, is Claudius. What more do you want to know?"

Fulgo became more animated.

"It rained hard last night but there was no thunderstorm. I am certain of this. I have instruments that can detect thunder in the atmosphere. Yet what seemed like a lightning bolt blasted a hole in Gracco's stable and nearly did for Gracco himself just at the moment he attacked you. Young Hebes here seems to think that you caused the explosion and you yourself said that 'none of this would have happened' if you had not been molested."

The man grinned. "But this would be impossible, surely?"

"And what about Guido's arm? It was when the metal of his sword contacted your wooden stick. He says you stung him but you had no obvious weapon."

The doctor trotted over to one of the many benches lining the room and, after rummaging around, produced a finger-length rod of a brownish, translucent material.

"Look," he said. "This is a rare mineral called electrum."

He rubbed it with a fur rag producing a crackling sound and a small spark.

"This can cause a stinging sensation if you touch it with dry hands. We call this phenomenon electrium after the substance which appears to contain it. Are you familiar with it?"

The prisoner shook his head.

Hebes crept closer to listen.

The doctor continued in excited tones. "I have devoted much time to studying electrium. I believe it to be a very great force of nature, not merely a minor curiosity. My work has convinced me that it's this force which powers lightning storms. Could it be that some exceptional people somehow retain electrium in their bodies and *can control it?*"

The young man frowned; then smiled as if a happy thought had just come to him. "Yes," he said slowly, "perhaps we just use different words for the same thing. I do not speak your language well. Here, they call me a conjuror, a trickster. I have found no one who knows different." His smile faded. "This is for me such a sad, lonely country! I have spoken to so many, but I have found no one who can perceive things that are...not material. I cannot express this well and I cannot understand it. Beyond the sea these things are universally accepted and...what I do is rare but not unknown— although we have no steam horses."

"So, you admit it! How? How did you do it?"

"It is a gift I did not know I had until it became necessary. Sometimes it is stronger than intended. I awoke suddenly and was startled or the damage would have been less. We call it *dewin* in my tongue but you have no word for it—unless this electrium?"

Fulgo rushed over to one of his worktops and brought a contraption of wires and thin metal leaves. Something he did with his piece of rare mineral caused the metal leaves to flap.

"There, you see?" he said, as if he had explained something. "Now, activate your electrium!"

"But I am already doing so," said the young man. "As we speak I am mending the injury to my ankle. Otherwise how could it be healed in two days?"

The doctor waved a dismissive hand. "The leaves of the detector aren't moving. You confuse fancy with true philosophy. Demonstrate your power."

The prisoner appeared to do nothing but, as Hebes watched in amazement, Fulgo was suddenly hovering two feet from the ground. The electrium detector didn't stir.

"Animal magnetism," the doctor said. "I *imagine* that I am floating. Don't try to fool me with these charlatan's tricks."

"But you *are* floating," Hebes said.

"It is well known that, in the hands of a skilful practitioner, animal magnetism can affect many people at once. Whole crowds have..."

He landed with a thud, biting his tongue.

"*Diu*, what more do you want?" asked the other man with disgust. "You want the metal leaves to stir? This is nothing."

The detector sprang to life, its leaves flapping like butterfly wings.

*

Two days later Dom Marcellus, magistrate of Nusquam, tried the case of the foreigner known as Claudius.

Hebes had managed to appoint himself temporary assistant prison warder, but now that Claudius was no longer in the doctor's charge he had reluctantly returned to the inn.

During his stay at the doctor's house he had spent many happy hours, when no one needed him, examining the steam-horse, as well as much of the contents of the doctor's workshop. He had also overheard a conversation between Dr Fulgo and the magistrate.

"The charges are ridiculous, of course," Dom Marcellus had said. "Gracco's a well-known rogue with a record of selling adulterated beer, and those two young layabouts—they're only members of the Watch because their fathers are rich. They've made themselves look foolish by complaining that they were attacked by a lone, crippled assailant. But they're out for blood and I'm not prepared to offend two local dignitaries for the sake of an unknown vagrant."

Dr Fulgo then pressed him to detain the young man longer, "for questioning and treatment," but Marcellus brushed his request aside.

But now the trial had begun and the magistrate, in his official robes, sat on the Chair of Judgement listening to the complaints of all those involved.

"Stand, prisoner," he said at last.

The prisoner did so, his recent injury apparently healed.

"You are found guilty of vagrancy and assault. Ten days in jail."

Claudius ignored him but turned to Fulgo, who had suggested in evidence that the young man was deranged.

"Doctor," he said earnestly. "I was mistaken. I believe you to be an honest man but I'm afraid I can't help you with your studies. We have misunderstood each other. Regard me, please, as a charlatan and trickster, even a madman if it suits you. I do not understand your theory of electrium. I do not understand why you cannot believe the evidence of your own senses." He pointed at Hebes. "That young boy is the only one among you who sees and begins to understand. You should hire him as your assistant. He is wasted as pot-boy." He winked at Hebes, standing beside his master, and blew a stream of coloured bubbles at him, which turned into a swarm of bees buzzing angrily around the innkeeper's head.

"Animal magnetism," snarled Gracco, who had heard the doctor use the term in court, then "ouch" as he was stung on the forehead.

"And now I must leave you," said Claudius, and he vanished...

And was never seen again in Nusquam.

The doctor turned pale. "Where is he? I must question him further. Astounding powers of magnetism and electrium. Are they connected?" He blundered about the courtroom determined that the stranger still lurked there, hidden by illusion.

Gracco, feeling in his pocket for the gold coin he had been given by the foreigner, brought out only dead leaves.

But Hebes was filled with wonder. He had seen something he couldn't understand. A new world had been revealed, a world of puzzles waiting to be solved.

He went over to the doctor who had slumped in a chair.

"I want to be your prentice," he said. "I'll look after the steam-horse, wash the glassware. I'm an expert at that."

"What about Gracco?" said the doctor.

"There's nothing legal. I never signed papers with him."

"Well," said the doctor, with a weary smile. "We'll see what we can do."

Leaves of Glass

Lavie Tidhar

Chapter One:

La Chambre Experimentale Des Rêves

In which a journey is begun; and two men of note meet at a secret rendezvous

Walt developed an immediate liking for Paris. It was noisy and smelly and full of incomprehensible language. It was, in other words, just like home.

He arrived the week before, getting off the ship in Marseilles. Now, he rented a room in the *Quartier Latin*, in a house that stood opposite the Notre Dame cathedral. It had a basement, leading to a bricked-over wall. The landlady said it connected to the catacombs underneath the city. He briefly thought of exploring them...

But first, he had to meet Houdin.

He followed the complex route through the narrow streets, looking for the stall of books that was to mark the meeting place. Half an hour late and cursing steadily in a low voice he finally found it, an inconspicuous heap of black-clad books lying on top of a dark wooden cart that looked as if it had been used as a barricade in the time of the revolution.

Behind it a small, metal-dim plaque bore the single word *bibliothèque*.

Walt approached the cart, picked a book at random, and put a handful of coins, many more than he thought necessary, into the plate of chipped china that rested at the feet of the bookseller's unmoving figure. The bookseller was a wizened old man dressed in a black cowl; the smell of alcohol drifted from him like a toxic cloud.

'Take it easy,' Walt said to the old man, and put the book carefully in his coat pocket. Then, feeling this had gone on far enough, he climbed the three steps to the door and knocked.

It opened by itself; he listened for the motion of hidden gears, but there was none. He stepped into the dark hallway, and the door slid closed behind him with the same silence.

If Houdin thought he was impressing him, he was wrong. A cheap parlour trick, though neatly done. He advanced down the corridor, the darkness opening onto a room with the dim light of candles and the smell, inexplicably, of oysters, that took him momentarily back to America, to the taverns and the ships and the poetry, and the feel of a muscular, warm body against his in the darkness.

He stood in the doorway and let his eyes adjust. But he saw the man he had come to visit straight away.

Jean Eugene Robert-Houdin sat in a worn armchair facing the door. His expression betrayed a hint of amusement, the showman in him enjoying the scene he had created. The two men looked at each other without words; Houdin was the one to finally break eye contact, and with a motion of his hand invited Walt to sit down.

Walt hesitated, and then took a chair opposite Houdin that creaked loudly as he sat.

'Well?'

'*Monsieur* Whitman. It is an honour.'

Walt inclined his head. 'Likewise, M. Houdin.'

'Indeed.' A short silence followed. Walt was reluctant to proceed; Houdin seemed to enjoy the tension.

'You are a poet,' Houdin said. 'I, for better or worse, am at heart an engineer. I build machines that mimic life but are not, themselves, living. Automata. And yet, I am beginning to wonder if my conception of what constitute life isn't somehow misguided. Tell me, M. Whitman. What do you think of life and death?'

Somehow, it seemed to Walt an appropriate question, there is the dark, damp room. 'As a poet,' he said carefully, 'I celebrate life, not death. I celebrate nature, and love, and, well...' he allowed himself a small smile. 'Myself.'

'And yet,' Houdin said, 'you chose to come here, to Paris, in secrecy, on the promise of a letter delivered by my countryman into your hands the month before. A letter promising, if not death, then what?'

But Walt had enough of the exchange. Standing up, he put one booted

127

foot on the now-vacated chair while his hand moved, almost unconsciously, to his hip, searching for a gun that was not there. 'Change?' he suggested to the silent Houdin. 'Transcendence?' No answer was forthcoming. 'Surely you understand that poets do not fear death, M. Houdin.' It was Walt who broke eye contact this time. Houdin's eyes seemed to grow in his head and engulf Walt, luring him with hypnotic intensity. 'We do not fear death,' he repeated. 'Our only fear is that of being forgotten.'

As if something unspoken was decided, Houdin rose, with the same uncanny silence as the door.

'Then come with me, M. Whitman.' He was once again the showman, his voice rising as he announced, 'come, and let me show you the *Chambre Experimentale Des Rêves.*'

Lavie Tidhar

Chapter Two:

Le Voyage Extraordinaire

In which a theory of reality is expounded upon; a manner of vehicle is introduced; and a challenge is answered

An extraordinary figure stood wreathed in shadows: he was a man over six feet tall, with an elongated, elfin face and skin as white as that of a ghost. Two large ears protruded from his skull.

Walt had followed Houdin to the basement of the house. His booted footsteps echoed on the stairs, while Houdin moved with the same disconcerting silence. When they entered, Houdin pointed at the man as if he were a particularly interesting invention and said, 'My assistant, Dr. Stocard.'

The strange figure moved forward: cold hands grasped Walt's own. 'A pleasure to meet you, M. Whitman.' He smiled, white, filed teeth giving his face a grotesque appearance. 'Are you ready for a *voyage extraordinaire*?'

'Enough, Stocard.'

Houdin glided forward, Stocard moving away from him as if frightened. 'This is it, M. Whitman. This is the Chair.'

Walt let his hand fall to his hip. There was no gun there, but he was reassured by the knowledge there was a knife strapped to his left leg, underneath the trousers; and in his pocket was a potent Indian arrowhead, sold to him in the backstreets of Brooklyn by a small, nervous man who looked like someone who had just robbed a cemetery. Walt hoped it would offer some protection, if it came to that.

He examined the apparatus Houdin had pointed to. Not that there was much of a chance of missing it.

The Chair of Dreams sat in the centre of the basement, a circular space around it. It was the most curious assemblage Walt had ever seen: metal discs connected to a horizontal seat that sat momentarily propped up in the air. Above that lights and small circular devices were arraigned on a slowly moving pole, and similar moving devices surrounded the chair itself.

Away in one corner a strange machine squatted uncomfortably: it looked like a heap of broken musical instruments joined together by a madman. There were curious golden leaves on top of the machine, neatly lined; several necks as those of string instruments; three keyboards, surrounding Stocard; and buttons, and cables that snaked out of the machine and into the instruments around the Chair.

'I believe,' Houdin said, 'that beyond this reality there is another one, a higher, more concentrated one. Most people who journey on the Chair experience it, to some degree. I myself have achieved a certain success in observing that reality, that other world, both on and later off the Chair.' He paused, and sighed theatrically. 'But it is only poets who can interact with it directly.'

'Have you tested that theory?' Walt asked. He felt excitement rising in him like bubbles in a champagne glass. Excitement, and caution. He flexed his fingers, making sure they were ready if he needed them to be. He *did* have a gun, underneath his coat; he hoped it would not be necessary.

'We have discovered it by chance. Some of the people we put on the chair have lost their minds. Some have experienced nothing. Some have come back feeling euphoric, and some despondent. But one man—a minor poet who has been begging me to use the Chair for quite some time—has simply disappeared.'

'Did he return?'

Houdin smiled, a slow movement that seemed to be controlled by hidden gears. 'Within five minutes. His babble of description was vague, his metaphors banal, his similes lacklustre. But he was able to describe to some degree the world he had seen. The world that is beyond ours.'

Houdin examined Walt in silence. His gaze seemed to linger for a moment longer on Walt's left trouser-leg and on his coat, as if he knew exactly what was hidden underneath both. 'I was not playing with words when I said that that particular reality was a more concentrated one. It is defined in a language that is different: compact, tight, a tapestry of language so well-knit, so finely interlaced and bound, that it is only poets who have hope of somehow understanding it, and in so doing in penetrating that world. I am offering you the chance to find out for yourself, in exchange for the information upon your return. Will you do it?'

Walt looked at the dormant Chair and felt it like a threat; a threat and a promise. Stocard sat, silent and unmoving, behind his musical machine. Houdin was watching Walt.

'I will.'

Chapter Three:

Simulacra

In which not all is as it seems

He could hear them as if from far away. Winds caressed him; strange, inexplicable, wonderful sounds engulfed him. Visions danced beyond his closed eyelids. This is what happened:

Walt sat in the Chair, leaning back until he was almost lying down. Houdin bent down and did something with the cogs. Walt felt his feet rising and his head descending; Houdin had removed weights from one end and was now adapting them, so that finally Walt was floating on his back, balancing in the air.

'It should be very soothing,' Houdin said. 'Try to relax.'

He bent down again and the gears began to move; the Chair started slowly to spin.

Above Walt's head coloured lights flickered into existence, blinking as they too rotated. The devices around the Chair began lazily to turn.

'Stocard, you are ready?'

Walt turned his head and looked at the man. He was sitting in the midst of his music machine like an organist at church, and as Walt watched he began to play; he blew on the golden leaves and in response extraordinary sounds assaulted Walt's ears, coming from different directions: from the spinning devices around the Chair.

Stocard blew air at the leaves; his hands danced on the keyboards around him; he pulled on the strings, adjusted knobs, turned dials. Sounds came from his machine, from the devices around the Chair, from the devices above it. Walt felt himself drowning in a hazy ocean of sound and light. From far away he could hear indistinct voices.

He was floating, his body was buoyant and rising in the air, rising in the vortex of sound and light that seemed to him both random and complex, and he thought he could almost decipher it, phrase it in words of infinite beauty and give it a name.

He floated, higher and higher, a cloud rising to the clear blue sky.

And woke up in the Chair.

'What happened?' He was sitting in the Chair, which was once again stationary and upright. Slowly, he stood up, massaging his arms and legs. 'Houdin?'

There was no answer.

He looked at the music machine: Stocard was still sitting behind it, silent and unmoving as stone. 'Houdin?'

Jean Eugene Robert-Houdin was moving away, towards the door, gliding forward. His long black coat hid his feet from Walt's view.

Rage broke, unexpected, in Walt's mind. 'You son of a bitch!'

He moved towards the Frenchman with speed and grabbed his shoulder. 'You are nothing but a parlour magician,' he shouted, and when Houdin still would not turn to face him he roughly pushed him, until he fell against the wall.

A blank face, a dummy's face, stared up at Walt from the unmoving figure on the floor. Startled, he jumped back.

The body lay, unmoving. Walt knelt down and felt for a pulse; found none. He felt the sides of the body and found them wooden and hard, and suddenly his anger returned.

'What kind of parlour trick is this, Houdin?' he said quietly. He unstrapped the knife from his leg almost with a sense of relief and, determined to find the mechanism of the strange automata he plunged the knife into the inert body.

It connected, and sliced. Walt moved the knife across the area of the stomach, cutting through cloth and flesh. He tore open the unresisting material, waiting for the gears and cogs inside with savage satisfaction.

But the inside of the corpse was empty.

Walt put his hands into the body, connected with nothing. It was an empty shell. Furious and suddenly afraid he moved away from it, and saw Stockard.

The man hadn't moved. When Walt approached him, the knife in front of his face, the same empty, dummy's face stared at him. He came close to Stocard, waiting for some sign, some response, but found none.

He examined the body. There were no hands, he noticed, only sleeves that connected directly to the silent machine. The feet were similarly connected, and the mouth was a circular hole, pointing at the golden leaves.

There was something eerie about the thing that was Stocard, and Walt did not wish to examine it further. Apprehension caught at his heart, almost choking him. He stumbled away and climbed the stairs from the basement as quickly as he could.

The same house, dark and damp. He cursed as he ran through the corridor and into the hallway, and to the door.

With a cry of relief he found the door and, not waiting for its strange mechanism to operate, hurled himself against: and with a sudden screaming of wood he was finally outside.

Chapter Four:

Bacchus

A confusion of books; a drink is shared; two poets meet

Walt stood up. He had hurt his arm falling to the ground, but it was not serious. He scanned his surroundings, relieved to find the same dark, dank street unchanged. He took out his gun. The book-cart stood as abandoned as before, and from behind it came the snores of the ancient bookseller.

It was Walt's habit to buy a book at whatever stall or shop he found. It did not have to be an expensive book. Far from it, since he himself was not exactly abundant with money. But a book, nevertheless, like a token of luck: he felt, somehow, that by performing that action he was participating in an act of worship, or of tribute to some nameless, immaterial presence.

He approached the stall, half-afraid to discover yet another empty face staring at him from behind the books. But the face that looked drunkenly up at him was indescribably human. It belonged, Walt thought, to a man who well and truly *lived*.

He was about to walk away, return to his lodgings and try to forget the strange experience, the maddening prank played on him by Houdin and his curious assistant. And to think he had come all the way from America, on the basis of a letter alone! He was about to walk away, when a soot-encrusted hand pushed into the air like a grotesque beetle from underneath the cart and clasped him roughly by his coat.

'Stop!'

The consonants hissed. The bookseller's eyes opened, glaring at Walt. He used the English word, Walt suddenly realised, not the French *arrêt*.

'What do you want, old man?'

'What the hell are you, some kind of cowboy?' The bookseller's eyes took in the long coat, the belt, the gun. 'American?'

'Yes.' The bookseller's accent was strange; some kind of British, but which one? For all Walt knew, he could have been Welsh.

'Let me get up.' The man tried to rise, staggered, and then stood up. Bloodshot eyes stared at Walt with a sudden smile. He had big, luscious lips, and when he smiled they transformed his face, so that they were no less ugly yet somehow attractive.

'You want to buy a book?' He gestured at the fungi-encrusted volumes.

'Already did.' Walt took out the book he purchased only the hour before. 'Plutarch's *Life of Marcus Antonius*. See?'

A nasty grin spread on the bookseller's face. 'Are you sure, sonny?' He reached towards him and turned the front toward Walt.

'*New Maps of Hell?*' Walt stared at the cover, unease growing. Had he picked the wrong book before? But it was impossible. He knew the book was the Plutarch, and it was in his pocket since the moment he picked it off the cart. He could not have been mistaken.

The bookseller waved his hand dismissively. 'Despite the name, it is actually an academic text,' he said. 'One of the Amises, I forget which.' He seemed to have made up his mind about something: 'Here.' He extended his hand towards Walt who, after a second's hesitation, shook it. 'Dylan Thomas.'

'Whitman,' Walt said. 'Walt Whitman.'

Thomas nodded slowly. 'And would you care for a drink, Mr. Whitman?' he pushed a small flask into Walt's hands. 'You're probably going to need it.'

The previously-comatose bookseller, Walt noted, had suddenly seemed much more alive. He positively bubbled with energy now, his body in constant movement as if he were trying to keep warm. 'Drink,' Thomas said.

Walt did; thick, red wine slid reassuringly down his throat and into his stomach.

'Try not to get lost.' Thomas' voice was fainter now; he moved back behind the stall and lay down, in the same position as before. His eyes closed, and his last words came back a whisper. 'The wine should help.'

Unease not entirely helped by the wine, Walt left him to his rest and moved away, back into the city.

Chapter Five:

Leaves of Glass

A city is explored and all manner of flora and fauna is introduced; a path is followed

With each step his vision was distorting.

Walt moved on, his legs heavy on the ground. It was changing in front of his eyes. Was it something in the wine? He looked back, but Houdin's house, the bookseller's stall, the street itself were gone. Thick fog covered his vision; he had no alternative but to continue moving, try and find a way out of the mist.

As he moved farther it began to dissipate. Walt had thought himself immune, by now, to shock, but the place forming around him nevertheless jolted him. It was all wrong.

The ground was a glass ceiling; underneath it, clearly visible to his eyes, great blood-red tentacles beat rhythmically against the glass. Around him houses remained, made of the same hard, clear substance. They were shells on which grew thick, red vines that culminated in a canopy of lush green leaves with the texture of human palms. He heard scuttling in the distance, saw a small, dark animal with many legs disappear around one of the houses.

The vines pulsated and moved, whispering in the fog. They seemed to him to compose a sort of music, taking the beat of the tentacles and weaving it into a melody whose meaning he longed to understand.

He walked through the city in a daze, feeling alone and yet, somehow, exulting in it, and in the nightmare vision around him.

He came near a river. The banks were glass and the water was colourless and as cold as ice. He dipped his hand in and tried to drink from the water; but as he did so the water before him exploded and a great, pale fish jumped in the air, its eyes seeming to stare at Walt accusingly.

He walked along the bank, searching for any sighs of life, but the jungle of vines continued and the beat from below never ceased. The fog clung to his clothes and eddied in complex formations through the vines, settling on the fleshy leaves like dew.

There were gas-lights throughout the city, still burning despite the fog. From far away he thought he heard the sound of a railway, but when he ran towards it the sound disappeared and he could see no tracks.

He departed from the river and wandered into the city, walking the unfamiliar streets in total silence. Finally, cresting a hill beyond a cluster of houses, he came across a change in the scenery: from this position he could look all over the city, and beyond it.

The city lay like a puzzle of glass and stone underneath him. Primeval red and green covered it like a rash. And beyond the city, in the place where the houses ended: an emptiness.

Beyond the city was...an absence. A nothingness crowned the city.

He didn't know what he was going to do. Desperation flashed through him with a sudden, choking hold.

He tried to get control of his breathing when a shot rang out, shuttering the silence with an explosive charge; fragments of glass hit him in the back with a force that sent him reeling.

Stunned, all Walt could hear was a clear, English voice shouting, 'You there! Halt!' and then the darkness consumed him.

Chapter Six:

Dulce Et Decorum Est

In which the soldiers are resurrected; a refuge is found; Walt is questioned

'Are you alright man? Didn't intend to hit you with that shot.'

Walt opened his eyes to a vision he would have been glad to see only moments before: a group of smiling faces, looking down at him with concern.

'Who the hell are you?' he said, and when he tried to move found that he could.

He sat up and they made space for him, crouching down to his level with apparent ease. There were five of them, five boys, dressed in a uniform he didn't quite recognise, but which was, nevertheless, undeniably British. 'You boys with the army?'

The first speaker laughed. 'Were, I'm afraid. Our days of active service are over.'

'You deserters?'

They stiffened collectively. 'Certainly not.'

'Then accept my apologies,' Walt drawled. 'But who the hell are you and what the hell are you doing here?'

'I'm Thomas,' said the first speaker. He pointed rapidly at his companions in turns. 'Rosenberg. Owen. Brooke. McCrae. From the green, green hills of England. And yourself, Sir?'

Walt grinned at them. 'Whitman. Walt Whitman. Of Manhattan.'

'Whitman?' the five boys exchanged quick looks.

'You here on the ultimate trip?' The boy pointed to as Owen said.

Walt looked at him levelly. 'I don't know what you mean.'

'Did you take the bus, man?' This from Rosenberg. 'The one-way ticket to ride?'

Walt could only shake his head. 'What the hell are you talking about?'

'Did you die, man?' McCrae, his face a mixture of irritation and amusement.

'Obviously,' Walt said, 'not.' He rose up from his sitting position and the five boys followed suit.

'Then how did you get here?' McCrae persisted. 'Was it drugs? Laudanum, perhaps?'

'I,' Walt said, and then, as the reality of his situation (or the situation of his reality, he was reserving judgement as to which statement was more accurate) hit him, said simply, 'I don't know.'

'Brooke, brew us some tea,' Thomas said. 'Guys, give the man some room.'

Walt found himself relaxing as the five moved away, dispersing around the room. His reflexes ached for unfulfilled action. He felt the reassuring weight of the gun on his belt. For the first time, he could get a clear view of the room he had found himself in.

It was a remarkable place. High above, the glass dome reached for the sky. Yet the floor of the huge room—he would have thought it a cathedral were he still in Paris—was entirely carpeted, so that while the constant beat of the tentacles beneath it did not abate, the view of those blood-red appendages was absent. The walls, he thought at first, were somehow made opaque. Then he realised they were daubed with lines upon lines of writing, in several different hands. Lines edged into other lines, until the walls seemed covered entirely in paint.

He moved closer to the nearest wall, studying some of the inscriptions. 'Mud unto mud!—Death eddies near—Not here the appointed End, not here!' read one. Another, in the same hand, spoke of Helen and Menelaus.

Poetry, he thought. Poetry. It was the last thing he had expected to find in this city of glass and fog.

He moved away from it and joined Brooke in the small area that seemed to serve them as a kitchen. Brooke was kindling a small fire; a blackened pot boiled water. Six chipped mugs were arrayed on a low wooden table.

'Where did you find all this stuff? And the carpets? Are there other people here? What is this place? And who wrote those poems on the walls?' Walt shot the questions at the young soldier, impatience suddenly welling up in him. There was a purpose to his being there; he felt it there and then. And felt impatient to go and find it.

'It's around, even the carpets,' Brooke said. 'Yes. I don't know. And we all did.'

'All of this?' Whitman said, his hand drawing out the entire hall.

'Most of it. There are some older poems on the other side by the doors over there. A lot about "elder towers" and "mad clappers" and bells tolling. A lot about some place called Innsmouth. Never heard of it, myself.'

'The poor bastard.' Thomas, joining the conversation.

Brooke was pouring tea into the mugs. 'Have to drink it black, I'm afraid.'

'Imagine being here on your own. Jesus. I think he went a little crazy. Didn't stick around, though. Gone long before we got here.'

'When did you get here?' Walt said.

'Ah, now you see,' Thomas said, '*that* is a difficult question.'

Walt accepted a steaming mug. He could all of a sudden see the absurdity of his situation, drinking tea with a group of English soldiers inside this room, inside this place. But the tea was strong, and sweet. Walt gulped it down. 'You boys got some food?'

Thomas went over to a large wooden chest, brought out a roll of flat bread and a slab of cheese. 'Got some tinned stew around somewhere,' he said. 'Start on this and I'll dig it out for you.'

Walt discovered he was starving. He pulled out large chunks of cheese with his knife and nearly shoved them in his face, tearing up the bread and downing the whole thing with the tea.

The soldiers crowded around and watched him with something approximating awe.

'You think he's hungry?' Rosenberg said.

'American.' McCrae, laughing as he said it.

When he was finished—Thomas had abandoned the search for the missing stew as fruitless—Walt took a deep breath and stretched himself luxuriously. 'Much better,' he said.

'Stay the night,' McCrae said. 'It will be dark soon and there's no point wandering through *these* streets at night.'

'I need to understand why I am here,' Walt said. 'Since I've come here, I have been on the verge of understanding something. I can hear the beat from underneath the ground, and the whispers of the vines, the ruffle of the leaves, the whistle of the fog, and almost understand it, almost know what it is saying.'

He turned his head away. He had just realised the carpets, the inked walls, they were disturbing him; he needed suddenly to be in contact with the alien environment outside, to be able to perceive it.

The five boys nodded. 'We all do,' Thomas said. 'It's like a language that demands interpreting, a poem that needs to be discovered amidst a multitude of words.' He pointed at the walls. Fragments of poetry covered everything. 'We do what we can.'

'Stay the night,' McCrae said again. But there was less conviction in his voice. 'You won't find what you're looking for tonight. And you might find a lot worse things than mere understanding.'

But a sudden compulsion had taken its hold on Walt. He thanked the five soldiers for the food, abstained from mentioning being shot at, and with a final farewell of his hand stepped out into the silent, glass street.

It had grown dark while he was inside. The fog still curled about the houses and underneath the ground the pounding tentacles glowed, red and unearthly.

He walked away, down the hill and into the city below, as a giant silver moon slowly rose in a sky devoid of stars.

Lavie Tidhar

Chapter Seven:

The Machinery of Night

In which a lover is found

Walt wandered the darkened streets. Fog shrouded the walls like a mask of death, but the growing vines pulsated in a yellow, unhealthy light and from below a glowering red came like ember-fire. He passed through several squares, avenues, public spaces: in some, Walt found the remnants of recent fires, discarded human objects, and the smell of human waste. But he had seen no people.

After some time his mind seemed to free itself from his walking body. He found the city remarkably peaceful and calming, and with each step he could feel himself peeling further away from his body, thrumming upwards, upwards, his mind growing to encompass the world around it. Sweat broke on his brow; Walt felt the movement of the drops like a sensuous tongue. His entire body felt on fire.

'Hey! Hey! Are you alright?' He heard the words but could not find their meaning in himself. Yet they had a soothing sound. Familiar, cosy. Something in his mind recognised the speaker as an American.

'Dude, you're *fucked*,' the voice said, and Walt felt strong, comfortable arms take hold of him and lead him through the fog, sitting him down.

'Your pupils are the size of the fucking moon. You look like you just took a massive dose of acid.' The voice chuckled. 'Enjoy the trip, dude. Once you're on it there's no way out, so just ride it, cowboy.'

Walt looked around him. A happy smile was plastered on his face. He could not erase it, didn't want to. The world was wonderful.

The colours of the vines, the fog, of the fire coming from under the ground, all mixed and merged, creating fantastical new permutations of light, colours he had never seen and had no names for. He was sitting in a large square, underneath a towering sculpture. Walt could only gape at it. The legs of a giant rose into the air and disappeared into a maelstrom of pulsating light that seemed to suck in the world around it and send it out again, changed. All changed.

The arms held him. He was stripped of his coat, his shirt. 'You need to cool down. And drink. Drink water.' A hand forced the mouth of a bottle into his mouth. He drank with difficulty, and his vision flared, intensifying.

The arms held him steady. He could feel a heart beating strongly against his skin. Strong, delicate fingers examined his face, and he heard an intake of breath, sudden and hot.

'Holy fuck, you're Walt Whitman!'

Was he? Walt laughed, and next to him, the voice broke into a companionable laughter.

He turned his head and looked at the source of the voice. A young man, gentle and handsome, with the face of someone only recently out of their teens. He was trying to grow a beard and was not successful. His torso was bare and shone in the demonic light from below, a young, healthy body.

Walt reached for the man's face; touched his cheek with the tips of his fingers, tracing invisible lines alone the young man's jaw. His hand trembled.

'Who?' he said. It came out like a puff of smoke. But the young man seemed to understand.

'I'm Allen,' he said, simply.

Stay with me, Walt tried to say. And he saw in Allen's eyes that he understood.

'I won't leave you, Walt.'

Walt reached for Allen's hand. Their fingers intertwined, and Walt was reassured by the contact, reassured and excited. Allen's hand was dry and smooth and warm, and without hesitation, in a move that seemed to him, at that moment, the most natural he ever made, Walt leaned towards Allen's face and kissed him. Their lips met, sought each other. Walt felt Allen's tongue in his mouth, leaving in its wake a smoky, rich taste.

They separated for air, and Walt's hands reached for Allen, traced invisible lines on his naked skin. He moved to embrace Allen; his tongue traced invisible lines on Allen's skin, making him moan.

They began to undress each other, first gently and then with mounting urgency. Walt knelt down and engulfed Allen's erection with his mouth. There was no thinking left; his mind felt open to the world; his senses alive in a way he would have thought impossible. He could feel Allen and himself embrace each other, body and mind, that they were one, sharing all, knowing all.

They coupled like two strays under a streetlamp, with abandon, with joy, in innocence and love. Fires burned beneath, above, around them. The beat of the tentacles was a distant thunder.

When he came, Walt's mind exploded into painted fragments of glass that shone with a brightness of unnamed colours. He felt himself falling, and falling, floating above a giant plateau, drifting, until darkness at last swallowed him, and he fell into a deep and peaceful sleep.

Chapter Eight:

The Lady in the Lake

In which two knights speak, and Walt must make a choice

Walt woke up to a cold, milky morning. The pounding of the tentacles beneath filled his eardrums for a long moment. When he straightened up and opened his eyes he found himself alone. Allen has disappeared as completely as he had appeared—a being of the night, a thing of mystery.

Walt stood up, naked. His felt the fog rub against his skin, and raised his arms to the skies, and shouted. He shouted for a long time, his cry of defiance and joy resounding around the square. He felt himself on the cusp of some great discovery; he was filled with a primordial joy in life; he felt himself human.

When he stopped, he stood for a moment more looking at his strange environment. Then, with a loud sigh, he pissed onto the glass floor and when he was at last finished stooped to collect his clothes.

Feeling ready to confront a new day in this bizarre city, Walt put his wide-brimmed hat back on and began marching. He had no direction in mind, and he let his feet guide his steps, choose the direction.

He could feel in himself a higher awareness now of his surroundings. Some of the buildings seemed to follow a pattern he could recognise; the movements of the fleshy vines entangled itself in the beat of the tentacles, in the atoms of the fog. He felt himself walking a maze, and at last beginning to recognise a path through it.

He arrived at an area that seemed somehow more tropical; moisture collected on the vines and large, fleshy fruit hung from them on thick stems. Hungry, Walt tried them and, on discovering a rich, full-bodied taste, ate several as he walked.

The humidity grew, and the foliage became thicker and more colourful. There was life in there now, too: multicoloured bugs that crawled or flew through the air on short transparent wings. Finally, he came out of the growth and found himself on the shores of a lake.

Its waters were black and the waves gentle. The shores were of glass, but Walt could not tell what the bottom was made of. The city had disappeared; he could see no buildings, only the thick canopy of vines and the lake, lying before him like a drop of ink.

A small, wooden boat waited patiently at the end of a small jetty, and Walt approached it with a sense of inevitability. When he sat in the boat he was not surprised to see that it moved on its own, pushing away from the jetty, taking him farther into the heart of the lake.

He felt himself once again open to the elements, his mind lifting and growing to encompass the world around it. He could sense the water underneath, dark and foreboding, and the movements of some great beings inside it, like dark and giant eels. He put his hand into the water and raised a handful up to his face and drank them. They were colourless in his hand, and had no taste.

After sailing for a short while, he saw an island in the distance. The boat drifted to the shore and left Walt to splash the last few feet through shallow water.

He was surprised to discover not glass but black, moist earth under his feet. Dark butterflies flitted through the heavy branches of gnarled trees whose bark and leaves absorbed what little light there was.

Walt walked slowly through the trees, heading deeper into the island. He heard a snatch of song carried on the wind, the singer male and sounding drunk, the words unintelligible. He heard the splash of water far away, a delighted, feminine voice raised. The jungle had a thick, musty smell.

At last, he reached a clearing in the forest. His feet crunched on dry wood. At the other end of the clearing, a pale figure came forward, riding a ghostly horse.

The figure was that of a man, and as he approached his voice carried strongly towards Walt.

'I look for butterflies,' he sang, 'that sleep among the wheat. I make them into mutton-pies, and sell them in the street.'

The footsteps of his horse made no sound, did not leave a mark in the ground.

'I sell them unto men,' he sang, 'who sail on stormy seas; and that's the way I get my bread—a trifle, if you please.'

Walt looked on in curiosity as the man and his horse approached him. He was dressed in a curious kind of medieval armour, an unsteady sword waving by his side. 'I hunt for haddocks' eyes,' he sang in a reedy voice, 'among the heather bright, and work them into waistcoat buttons in the silent night.'

His eyes looked down into Walt's. The aged knight's hand closed on the sword by his side. Was it a challenge? He didn't know, but felt compelled to answer it.

'And these I do not sell for gold,' Walt whispered into the warm air, his eyes on the white knight, 'or coin of silvery shine, but for a copper halfpenny...' he searched for the last words, but the look in the knight's eyes was approving and Walt finished: 'and that will purchase nine.'

'Well done, boy.'

'You're Lewis Carroll, aren't you?' Walt said.

The white knight smiled and shook his head. 'Perhaps once.'

He unsheathed his sword, waving it around so wildly that Walt had to duck out of the way. The sword fell and stuck upright in the ground.

Air hissed as wood caught fire; leaves burned like butterflies. As the fire cleared the glass floor was revealed; red tentacles hammered at the ceiling of their prison.

The stone stuck fast in the glass.

'Well, boy?'

The white knight's eyes examined Walt.

'What the hell?' Walt said. He looked at the sword. It was heavy, made of a dark, dull metal with no ornamentations. It looked like a sword should look, like a machine specifically designed for killing. 'I don't need a sword. I already have a gun.'

'The choice is yours, beamish nephew,' the white knight said.

And Walt, feeling at a loss under the old man's gaze, reached forward and grasped the sword by the hilt...

Lavie Tidhar

Chapter Nine:

Voyage Aux Fonds Des Mers

Death by water; a gunslinger chooses; Walt makes an exit

...and drowned. Black water closed over his head.

Walt held on to the sword and felt it pulling him down. His body was in motion, rushing through the water, and Walt discovered something wondrous as his lungs threatened to explode when he opened his mouth to death by water: he could breathe.

He travelled through the water, guided and pulled by the sword. Through the water he could hear the pounding beat of the tentacles, somewhere below. Luminous shapes moved through the darkness: he hoped they were only fish.

At last, his feet touched soft, fine sand. The steady beat from underneath continued.

A glow of light appeared, grew. It enveloped him in a bubble of illumination, and at its edge he saw a shape move like a shadow.

As it came near he could see her. A beautiful woman, her hair dark as the water, her eyes as pale as the glass buildings he had left behind.

She reached her hand out, to him. Her palm opened, face up, her fingers extending towards him.

The sword in his hand moved, slightly.

Walt looked into the woman's eyes and found nothing he could comprehend. Her posture, her stance, was like a silent tableau, a command or a plea to hand over the sword.

But the sword refused.

It moved of its own accord and Walt couldn't stop it. His arm felt as if an eel was slowly moving inside it, reaching closer to him, to his mind, wrapping itself around him. The sword moved and his body moved with it, helpless as his arm rose and slashed and pale blood formed silent clouds in the water.

The sword hacked and stabbed, until the woman fell, until the pale blood finally saturated the circle of light and disappeared beyond it, into the darkness.

Then the sword stopped.

Walt found himself on his knees, the sword extended in front of him like a warning. He felt tired, elated, horrified: a mixture of feelings that hurt like a broken jaw.

He stared at the sword for a long moment; tried to move his hand, found that he could.

And threw the sword away.

It sailed through the water in a graceful arc and landed in the dead woman's chest, sending a new ripple of blood into a pale cloud.

'Fuck it,' he said, the words forming little bubbles that came from the corner of his mouth. 'I'm more of a gun person.'

He turned his back on the sword in the corpse and strode away, and into the darkness.

Chapter Ten:

From Out of the Darkness and Into the Light

A return, a dream, an inscription; a story ends

When he opened his eyes the worried face of Jean Eugene Robert-Houdin was looking down at him like an inconstant moon.

'Are you all right, M. Whitman?' he said, his voice shaking with tension. 'We had barely started when you had a fit. We had to stop the experiment. Can you hear me? Can you hear me?' The Frenchman's hand reached to slap Walt's face.

Walt's hand shot up and grabbed Houdin's wrist like a curse.

'Don't lie to me!' he said, and stood up, reaching out to roughly examine Houdin. The man felt real, his face was his own, and Walt felt apprehension settle on his mind. His assistant, Stocard, stood motionless beside him.

'How long have I been gone?' Walt demanded.

'But M. Whitman, you were not gone at all!' Houdin said. 'Look at the clock; it is barely fifteen minutes since you sat down in the Chair!'

It was true. But it could all be trickery. 'I am leaving now,' Walt declared, and his hand went to his side, fingers searching for the gun.

But it was not there. He felt its weight under his coat, where it had been...where it had been before he left.

Houdin and Stocard stepped back in unison.

'*Il est devenu fou!*' Stocard said.

'No,' Wait said. He stalked to the door. 'I haven't.'

The same steps, the same dark passage. He paused before the door, and then opened it.

Sunlight touched his face, warming him. A cool breeze carried with it the normal smells of a city: rotting garbage and human excrement, cooking foods, tobacco and drink...He breathed it in, letting the familiar scents wash over him. Had he dreamt everything that had happened?

He must have. To think it was true—that way led to madness. What he needed...What he needed, Walt decided, was a drink.

The bookstall was no longer there and he felt somehow saddened by it. He would have been comforted by the presence of the books.

He walked back to his hotel, along a route that took most of the establishments selling liquor along the way.

It was only when he stumbled, alone, to bed that he remembered the book he had bought earlier in the day. He took it out.

It was not *Marcus Antonius*, and it was not *Maps of Hell*.

It was a slim book. It was called, simply, *Eighteen Poems*. It was dated 1934, and when Walt opened the book there was an inscription on the title-page—*To Walt*—and lines in the same blue ink whose meaning he would never know, for the ink had run and water damage had finished it off. Only the signature, nearly at the bottom of the page, was unharmed, and it read, Dylan Thomas.

With something that was not quite a laugh and not quite a sob Walt tumbled into bed. Sleep finally reclaimed him and he slept the way the innocent sleep, a deep and sound sleep that for all the noises of the Parisian night outside went on undisturbed and lasted all through the night and into the morning.

He slept, and the city claimed him.

Memories in Bronze, Feathers, and Blood

Aliette de Bodard

This is what we remember: the stillness before the battle, the Jaguar Knights crouching in the mud of the marshes, their steel rifles glinting in the sunlight. And the gunshot—and Atl, falling with his eyes wide open, as if finally awakening from a dream...

*

It's early in the morning, and Nezahual is sweeping the courtyard of his workshop when the dapper man comes in.

From our perches in the pine tree, we watch Nezahual. His heart is weak and small, feebly beating in his chest, and sweat wells up in the pores of his skin. Today, we guess, is a bad day for him.

The dapper man, by contrast, moves with the arrogant stride of unbroken soldiers—his gestures sure, casual—and he has a pistol hidden under his clothes, steel that shines in our large-spectrum sight.

We tense—wondering how much of a threat he is to Nezahual. His manner is brash; but he doesn't seem aggressive.

"I'm looking for Nezahual of the Jaguar Knights." The dapper man's voice is contemptuous; he believes Nezahual to be a sweeper, someone of no importance in the household.

What he doesn't know is that there's no household, just Nezahual and us: his children, his flock of copper and bronze.

Nezahual straightens himself up, putting aside the broom with stiff hands. "I am Nezahual. What do you want?"

The dapper man shows barely any surprise; he shifts his tone almost immediately, to one of reluctant respect. "I'm Warrior Acamapixtli, from the House of Darts. We had hoped—you could give a speech on the War to our young recruits."

Nezahual's voice is curt, deadly. "You want me to teach them about war? I don't do that."

"Your experience...," Acamapixtli is flustered now—we wonder how much is at stake, for this speech to be given.

"I went to war," Nezahual says. He's looking upwards—not at us but at Tonatiuh the Sun-God, who must be fed His toll in blood. "Is that such a worthwhile experience?" His heartbeat has quickened.

"You don't understand. You fought with Warrior Atl—with Chimalli—" Acamapixtli's voice is disappointed.

Atl. Chimalli. The names that will not be spoken. We tense, high up in our tree. Beneath us, Nezahual's face clenches—a mask to hide his agony. His knees flex; in a moment he will be down on the ground, clutching his head and wishing he were dead. "Atl. I—"

His pain is too much; we cannot hide any longer. In a flutter of copper wings, we descend from the pine tree, settle near Nezahual: the hummingbirds on his shoulders; the parrots on the stone rim of the fountain; the lone quetzal balancing itself on the handle of the broom.

"Leave him alone," we whisper—every mech-bird speaking in a different voice, in a brief, frightening flurry of incoherence.

Acamapixtli's hands turn into fists, but he doesn't look surprised. "Your makings." His voice is quiet. "You sell them well, I hear."

We are not for sale. The other mech-birds—the copper hummingbird who leapt from branch to branch, the steel parrot who mouthed words he couldn't understand—they were born dead, unable to join the flock, and so Nezahual sold them away.

But we—we are alive, in a way that no other making will be. "Leave," we whisper. "You distress him."

Acamapixtli watches Nezahual, his face revealing nothing of what he feels. His heartbeat is slow and strong. "As you wish," he says finally. "But I'll be back."

"I know," Nezahual says, his face creased in an ironic smile.

When Acamapixtli is gone, he turns to us. "You shouldn't show yourselves, Centzontli."

He does not often call us by our name—and that is how we know how angry he is. "Your heartbeat was above the normal," we say. "You were in pain."

Nezahual's face is unreadable once more. "Yes," he says. "But it will happen again. That's of no importance. That's not what I made you for."

Nezahual made us to remember—to hold the images that he cannot bear anymore. And for something else; but no matter how hard we ask, he will not tell us.

*

This is what we remember: the dirigibles are falling. Slowly, they topple forward—and then plummet towards the ground at an impossible speed, scattering pieces of metal and flesh in the roiling air.

We stand on the edge of the ridge, the cool touch of metal on our hips. Atl is dead. Chimalli is dead—and all the others, piled upon each other like sacrifice victims at the altar of the Sun God.

What have they died for? For this...chaos around us?

"Come," a voice whispers.

Startled, we turn around.

A man is standing over the piled bodies—his uniform crisp and clean, as if he were just out of his training. No, we think, as the man draws closer.

His eyes are of emeralds, his lungs of copper, his heart of steel. "Come," the mech-man says, holding out to us a gleaming hand. "Your place isn't here."

We remember a war we never fought; deaths we could never have prevented; but this, we know, has never happened.

This is a vision, not memories

It cannot be real.

"Come," the mech-man whispers—and suddenly he towers over us, his mouth yawning wide enough to engulf us all, his voice the roar of thunder. "Come!"

We wake up, metal hearts hammering in our chests.

*

Nezahual has shut himself in his workshop. He's making a new bird, he's said, moments before closing the door and leaving us out in the courtyard. But his hands were shaking badly—and we cannot quell the treacherous thought that this time, the pain will be too strong, that he will reach out for the bottle of *octli* on the back of shelves, hidden behind the vials of blood-magic.

The youngest and most agile among us, the newest parrot—who brought memories of the blood-soaked rout at Izpatlan when he joined us—is perched on the window-sill, his head cocked towards the inside of the workshop.

We hear no noise. Just the swelling silence—a dreadful noise, like the battlefield after the dirigibles fell, like the hospital tent after the gods took their due of the wounded and the sick.

"Nezahual," we call out. But there is no answer. "Nezahual."

154

Footsteps echo, in the courtyard; but they do not belong to our maker. The second hummingbird takes off in a whirr of metal wings and hovers above the gate—to watch the newcomer.

It's Acamapixtli again, now dressed in full warrior regalia—the finely wrought cloak of feathers, the steel helmet in the shape of a Jaguar's maw. "Hello there," he calls up to us.

We tense—all of us, wherever we perch. None of Nezahual's visitors has ever attempted to speak to us.

"I know you can speak," Acamapixtli says. "I've heard you, remember?" He lays his steel helmet on the ground, at the foot of the tree. His face is that of an untried youth. We wonder how old he really is.

"We can speak," we say, reluctantly. The quetzal flies down from the tree, perches on the warmth of the helmet. "But we seldom wish to."

Acamapixtli's smile is unexpected. "Would that most people were as wise. Do you have a name?"

"Centzontli," we tell him.

"'Myriad'," Acamapixtli says. "Well-chosen."

"Why are you here?" we ask—uncomfortable with this smalltalk.

Acamapixtli doesn't answer. He runs a hand, slowly, on the parrot—we let him do so, more amused than angry. "Fascinating," he says. "What powers you? Steam? Electricity?" He shakes his head. "You don't look as you have batteries."

We don't. In every one of our chests is a vial of silver sealed with wax, containing twenty drops of Nezahual's blood. It's that blood that makes a heartbeat echo in our wires and in our plates, in our gears and in our memories. "Why are you here?" we ask, again.

Acamapixtli withdraws his hand from the parrot. "Why? For Nezahual, of course." He shrugs—trying to appear unconcerned, but it will not work. His heartbeat has quickened. "We—got off to a wrong start, I feel."

"Does your speech matter so much?" we ask. And, because we cannot help feeling sorry for him: "You know what he will say, even if he comes."

"I'm not a fool, Centzontli," Acamapixtli says. "I know what he'll say. But I'm not here for what you think. I don't want Nezahual to teach the recruits about courage, or about the value of laying down one's life."

"Then—"

Acamapixtli's voice is low, angry. "I want him to teach them caution. They're eager enough to die—but a dead warrior is of no use." His eyes are distant, ageless. "We spend our youth and our blood on conquest, but we have more than enough land now, more blood-soaked earth than we can possibly harvest. It's time for this to cease."

Do you truly think so? a voice asks; and, with a shock, we recognise that of the metal man.

The sun above the courtyard is high—pulsing like a living heart. *Do you truly think so?*

155

What in the Fifth World is happening to us? Our nights: bleeding into our days? Our memories—Nezahual's memories—released by our minds to stain the present?

This is not meant to be.

Acamapixtli hasn't heard anything. He goes on, speaking of what the warriors who survive can build—of steamships and machines that will do the work of ten men, of buildings rising higher than the Great Pyramid of Tenochtitlan, and of a golden age of prosperity. Gradually, his voice drowns out that of the metal man—until once more we are alone in the courtyard.

But we have not forgotten. Something is wrong.

Nezahual doesn't come out, no matter how hard we wish that he would. At length, Acamapixtli grows weary of waiting for him, and takes his leave from us.

The sun sets, and still Nezahual hasn't come out. The hummingbirds and the quetzal beat against the window panes, trying to force their way in, but the workshop is silent—and our large spectrum sight is blocked by the stone walls.

We perch in the pine tree, watching Metzli the Moon rise in the sky, when we feel the shift: the gradual widening of the world, so strong we have to close our eyes.

When we open them again, we have a new point of view—a hummingbird's, cradled between Nezahual's bleeding hands—carrying the memories of the fording of Mahuacan, of going side by side with Atl listening for enemy voices in the marsh.

"You're hurt," we say, and the hummingbird's voice echoes in the silence of the workshop.

Nezahual waves a hand, curtly. "It's nothing. What do you think?"

He opens his hands. Tentatively, we reach out, and the hummingbird starts flapping its wings—accelerating to a blur of copper and steel.

"Beautiful," we say, though we are more worried than we will admit. "Acamapixtli came back."

"I know," Nezahual says. He walks to the entrance-curtain of the workshop, pulls it away. "Come in—all of you."

We perch where we can: the shelves are crammed with blood-magic vials, alembics, and syringes, and the table littered with spare metal parts.

Nezahual is cleaning his hands under the water of the sink; he barely looks up. "I knew he would come back. He's a stubborn man. But so am I."

"It's not what you think," we say, and explain, as best as we can, the vision Acamapixtli has for the future. We can hear, all the while, the metal man laughing in the room—but we do not listen.

Nezahual wipes his hand with a cloth of cactus-fibres. "I see." His voice is stiff, careful—as if he were afraid to break something. "Do you think he will come back?"

We are certain he will. Acamapixtli is a driven man. Much, in fact, like

Nezahual must once have been—before war and the drive for bloodshed reduced him to, to this.

No. We must not think about it.

*

This is what we remember: in the silence after the battle, we wander through the mangled field of battle. We see—bullet-torn limbs, sprayed across the blood-stained mud; eyes, wide open and staring at the smoke in the sky—pain and death everywhere, and we can heal none of it.

Near the dirigible's carcass, we find Chimalli, his steel shield and his rifle lying by his side. We kneel, listen for the voice of his heart—but we know, deep inside, that his soul has fled, that he is with the Sun God now, fighting the endless war against the darkness.

And we feel it, rising in us: the burning shame of having survived when so many have given their lives.

"Now you know," a voice hisses.

We turn, slowly. The metal man is standing near us, wearing the face of a younger, eager Nezahual. It jars us, more deeply than it should—to see our maker rendered in soulless metal, his face smooth and untouched by the war. "You don't belong here."

"We don't understand," we say.

He points a clawed hand towards us—and our chests burn as if heated by fire. "Don't you?" he whispers, and sunlight, red and hungry, flickers around him. "I won't be deprived of what belongs to me."

"We took nothing..." we say, slowly, but we know it's not about us. "Nezahual..."

Malice has invaded the metal man's voice. "He was a coward. He didn't die. That was his punishment—to survive when others had not. And I will not have him and that fool Acamapixtli frighten my warriors out of dying."

"Who are you?" we whisper.

"Don't you know?" the metal man asks. He straightens up—and his head is the clouds and the stars, and his hands encompass the whole of the battlefield, and his voice is the moans of the dying. "Don't you know my name, Centzontli?"

Tonatiuh. The Sun God. He who watches over the Heavens. He who drinks the warriors' blood.

This cannot be truly be him.

The metal man laughs. "Oh, but I am here," he says. "Here and alive, just as you are."

We are alive. Not flesh and blood, like Nezahual or Acamapixtli—sprints and wires, copper and steel—but alive enough.

And to this god, who is not our own, we have no blood to offer. "What do you want?" we ask.

The metal man extends a huge hand towards us. "Come," he says. "Leave him."

"We do not worship you."

"You must. For, if you do not, I will tumble from the sky, and the world will come to its last ending," the metal man says—and his voice is the thunder of the storm, and the vast echo of rockfall in the mountains. "Is that what you truly wish for? I cannot be denied forever."

We wake up in the silence of the workshop and stare at the white eye of the moon, wondering what Tonatiuh wants of us.

*

Acamapixtli comes back on the following morning—still in regal uniform. Nezahual is waiting for him in the courtyard, his face impassive, and his heartbeat almost frantic.

"I apologise," Nezahual says, stiffly. "It seems we misunderstood each other."

Acamapixtli's face goes as still as carved jade. "We're both responsible."

Nezahual's lips stretch into a quiet smile. "Come," he says. "Let me show you my workshop. We'll talk afterwards."

Nezahual shows Acamapixtli the spare parts lying on the table; the vials of blood-magic and the wires and springs that make us up. He talks about creating life—and all the while we can hear the pain he's not voicing, the memories hovering on the edge of seizing him.

We wish we could take it all away from him, drain him as dry as a warrior sacrificed to Tonatiuh—but we cannot.

They speak of dirigibles made of steel and copper, of machines that will reap the corn from the fields—and we think of the metal man, filling his hands with the harvest of battle.

We hear his voice within us: *I will not be mocked.*

And we know that Acamapixtli's dream will have a terrible price.

*

This is what we remember: the silence of the infirmary, broken only by the moans of the wounded. We sit on our bed—trying to feel something, anything to as-suage the pain within.

We are not hurt. Blood from the battlefield covers us—but it's not ours, it has never been ours.

Beside us, an Eagle Knight with a crushed lung is dying; his breath rattling in his chest, a horrible sound like bone teeth chattering against one another.

We try to rise, to help him, to silence him—we no longer know. We try to move; but our hands are limp, our fingers will not respond.

We watch—even our eyes cannot close—as the man's face becomes slack; and by the bed is Tonatiuh, his steel hands reaching for the dying man, enfolding

158

him close, as a mother will hold a child.

He looks up—and smiles with golden, bloody teeth. "So he will make his speech, won't he?" He shakes his head. "Does he not know what happens to those who defy me?"

In a single, fluid gesture, he rises from the man's bed and reaches out towards us, his hands extending into steel claws, pricking the flesh of our metal skin.

We watch. We cannot move.

*

The morning of the speech grows bright and clear. For the first time, we wake up after Nezahual, our blood-vials beating madly against our copper chests. We still feel the steel fingers reaching for our chests—to tear out our hearts.

Nezahual is sitting in the workshop, his head between his hands, dressed in his best clothes: an embroidered cotton suit, with a quetzal-feather headdress. He is shaking; and we can't tell if it's from fear or from anticipation.

We hop to the table and perch by his side—the quetzal cocking its head, making a soft cooing sound.

Nezahual forces a smile. "It will be all right, Centzontli."

We fear it won't. But before we can speak, a tinkle of bells announces the arrival of Acamapixtli—still in full Jaguar regalia, his steel helmet tucked under one arm.

"Ready?" His smile is eager, infectious.

Nezahual runs a hand in his hair, grimacing. "As ready as I will ever be. Let's go."

He is walking towards the door of the workshop—halfway to the courtyard—when we feel the air turn to tar, and hear the laughter from our dreams.

No.

Did you think I could be cheated, Nezahual? Tonatiuh's voice echoes in the workshop.

We rise, in a desperate whirr of wings, and in our fear our minds scatter, becoming that of five hummingbirds, of one quetzal, of two parrots, struggling to hold themselves together.

I, I, I—

We—

We have to—

Nezahual has stopped, one hand going to his sword, his face contorted in pain. "No," he says. "I didn't think I could cheat you. But nevertheless—"

Tonatiuh laughs and laughs. You are nothing, he whispers. Worth nothing. You will not make this speech, Nezahual. You will not make anything more.

Behind us, the table shakes; the metal scraps rise, spinning in the air like a cloud of steel butterflies, all sharp, cutting edges, as eager to shed blood as any warrior.

Nezahual stands, mesmerised, watching them coalesce into the air, watching them as they start to spin towards him.

We watch. We cannot move—as we could not move in the vision.

Acamapixtli has dropped his helmet and is reaching for his sword; but he will be too late. Nezahual's knees are already flexing, welcoming the death he's courted for so long.

The thought is enough to make us snap together again: our minds melding together, narrowing to an arrow's point.

"Nezahual!" we scream, throwing ourselves in the path of the whirling storm.

It enfolds us. Metal strikes against metal; copper grinds against the wires that keep us together, all with a sickening noise like a dying man's scream.

I have warned you not to interfere, Tonatiuh whispers. The sunlight, filtered through the entrance curtain, is red and angry. *You are a fool, Centzontli.*

Something pricks our chests—the claws from the visions, probing into our flesh.

We have no flesh, we think, desperately; but the claws do not stop, they reach into our chests. They close with a crunch.

Within us, glass tinkles, and shatters into a thousand pieces. Our blood-vials. Our hearts, we think, distantly, as the world spins and spins around us...

Blood leaks out, drop by drop—and darkness engulfs us, grinning with a death's head.

*

This is what we remember: before the battle—before the smoke and the spattered blood, before the deaths—Atl and Chimalli sit by the camplight, playing patolli on a board old enough to have seen the War of Independence. They're arguing about the score: Atl is accusing Chimalli of cheating, and Chimalli says nothing, only laughs and laughs without being able to stop. Atl takes everything much too seriously, and Chimalli enjoys making him lose his calm.

They're young and carefree, so innocent it hurts us—to think of Atl, falling under the red light of the rising sun; of Chimalli, pierced by an enemy's bayonet; of the corpses aligned in the morgue like so much flesh for barter.

But we remember: our curse, our gift, our blessing; our only reason for existing.

*

Our eyes are open—staring at the ceiling of Nezahual's workshop. Our chests ache, burning like a thousand suns.

We are not dead.

Slowly, one by one, we rise—and the quetzal dislodges a pair of bleeding hands resting over its chest.

Nezahual. You're hurt, we think—but it's more than that.

It's not only his hands that bleed—and no matter how hard we look, we cannot see a heartbeat anywhere. His chest does not rise; his veins do not pulse in his body. Metal parts are embedded everywhere in his flesh: the remnants of the storm that he could not weather.

We are covered in blood—blood which cannot be our own. We still live—a thing which cannot be.

"Come," whispers Tonatiuh.

He stands in the doorway of the workshop, limned by the rising sun: metal lungs and metal hands, and a pulsing metal heart. "There is nothing left. Come." His hands are wide open—the clawed hands which broke us open, which tore our hearts from our chest.

"Why should we?"

"There is nothing left," Tonatiuh whispers.

"Acamapixtli—" He is lying on the ground, just behind Tonatiuh, we see: his heart still beats, albeit weakly. We struggle against an onslaught of memory; against images of warriors laughing at each other, sounds of bullets shattering flesh, the strong animal smell of blood pooling into the dark earth.

"Do you truly think he will make a difference?" Tonatiuh asks. "There will always be dreamers, even among the warriors. But nothing can change. The world must go on. Come."

There is nothing left.

But we know one thing: Nezahual died, and it was not for nothing. If Acamapixtli could not make a difference, somehow Nezahual could. Somehow...

"It wasn't Acamapixtli," we whisper, staring at the god's outstretched hands. "It was never Acamapixtli—it was what Nezahual made in his workshop."

Tonatiuh doesn't answer. His perfect, flawless face is devoid of expression. But his heart—his heart of steel and wires—beats faster than it should.

Mech-birds. Beings of metal and copper, kept alive by heart's blood—and, even after the blood was gone, kept alive by the remnants of the ritual that gave us birth, by the memories that crowd within us—the spirits of the dead keening in our mind like a mourning lament.

"You fear us," we whisper, rising in the air.

"I am the sun," Tonatiuh says, arrogantly. "Why should I fear birds that have no hearts?"

"You fear us," we whisper, coming closer to him, stained with Nezahual's dying blood.

His claws prick us, plunge deep into our chests.

But there is nothing there. No vial, nothing that can be grasped or broken anymore. "You are right," we say. "We have no hearts."

"Will you defy me?" Tonatiuh asks, gesturing with his metal hands.

Visions rise—of bodies, rotting in the heat of the marshes—of torn-out limbs and charred dirigibles—of Atl, endlessly falling into death.

But we have seen them. We have fought them, night after night.

We are not Nezahual. War does not own us; and neither does blood; neither do the gods.

We do not stop.

"I am the sun," Tonatiuh whispers. "You cannot touch me."

"No," we say. "But you cannot touch us, either."

We fly out, into the brightness of the courtyard—straight through Tonatiuh, who makes a strangled gasp before vanishing into a hundred sparkles—the sunlight, playing on the stone rim; the fountain whispering once more its endless song.

Oh, Nezahual.

We would weep—if we had hearts, if we had blood. But we have neither, and the world refuses to fold itself away from us, and grief refuses itself to us.

A shuffling sound, from behind—Acamapixtli drags himself out of the workshop on tottering legs, bleeding from a thousand cuts—staring at us as if we held the answers. "Nezahual..."

"He's gone," we say, and his bloodied hands clench. We wish for tears, for anger, for anything to alleviate the growing emptiness in our chests.

Acamapixtli smiles, bitterly. "All for nothing. I should have known. You can't cheat the gods."

We say nothing. We stand, unmoving, in the courtyard—watching the sunlight sparkle and dissolve in the water of the fountain until everything blurs out of focus.

*

This is what we see: a flock of copper birds speaking to the assembled crowd—of machines, of arched bridges and trains over steel tracks, of the dream that should have been Nezahual's.

This is what we see: a city where buildings rise from the bloodless earth, high enough to pierce the heavens; a city where, once a year, a procession of grave people in cotton clothes walks through the marketplaces and the plazas of bronze. We see them make their slow way to the old war cemeteries and lay offerings of grass on the graves of long-dead warriors; we see an entire nation mourning its slaughtered children under the warm light of the silenced sun.

This is what we wished for.

Empire of Glass

Tanith Lee

One day the Prince decided he must choose a wife. The prospect filled him neither with interest or pleasure. There was no shortage of appealing women available when he was in the mood for them, and his daily life, he felt, went on perfectly well without irrevocably attaching a female to it. Generally he preferred hunting, and liked the company of horses, strong and spirited, bloodhounds, swift and acutely-nosed (five of them being coal-fired clock-work), and quantities of other animals freshly killed and ready to be cooked.

The Prince's princedom, lying south-east in Europe, and landlocked but for a single seagoing river, was one of those Ruritanian ones. For the sake of convenience it will, therefore, be known in this account as Turitrania. In some respects it was an idyllic place, especially for the Prince. However, as the century drew to its close, he has found himself increasingly worried by those events which swept the outer world—revolutions, wars, the rise to eminence of commoners, and establishment of empires. There was, too, the fast progress of science, which had already accessed the military potential of the hot-air balloon and the stream-driven flycycle. Not to mention awful rumours of enclosed ships that might travel *below* the waters, and so pass, unseen and crammed with invaders, into any harbour.

The Prince's marriage plan was accordingly based on the idea of a very rich wife, having extremely powerful connections. In return she would gain status, for his line was historically ancient and noble; plus the prize of himself. He was, in his looks, not so bad as princes went, and reasonably amiable as they went, too.

A ball was arranged. It was to be magnificent, and invitations were sent far and wide. Late summer decorated the forests of Turitrania in silk foliage, and elaborately velvety flowers, and the mountains, visible from all the terraces of the palace, gilded themselves obligingly early in crests of silver snow.

Similarly overdressed, the Prince pulled the ears of his favourite bloodhound, the non-mechanical, flesh-and-muscle dog, Snouter, one last pre-betrothal time. Then he strode manfully to the ballroom.

*

Between the hours of eight and ten-thirty, an evening passed which was both glamorous and loud. A huge orchestra, complete with steam-organ, bellowed dance music, dancing feet pranced, champagne fountains erupted and crystal goblets fragilely clinked. Young women flung themselves, or were flung by eager sponsors, upon the Prince. He greeted them, danced with them, (as princes also went, he was not too bad a dancer) and questioned them intently. Many were rich, several absurdly so, most had connections, some even powerful ones. Some chattered, some were deliberately enigmatic, some were tongued-tied. *Some* were even beautiful—but the Prince tended to prefer prettiness to beauty, and besides, looks were not the prime objective.

By a quarter to eleven, accurately displayed on the Eternal Clock, he was feeling rather tired. He yearned to leave the ball, have a swig of brandy and go to bed—alone. To make a decision was, he began to think, beyond him. He could no longer see the *wife* for the *women*, as it were. As for their credentials—none of them had, he found, quite what he had hoped for: some whiff of true difference—the means whereby to make Turitrania omniscient, the foundation not only of security, but an empire of the Prince's very own.

The Eternal Clock struck eleven.

Exactly then, through the vast doors, came stalking a tall female figure in a beaded white gown.

There was at that moment a brief interval without music, and so the exclamations of the crowd became particularly notable. The Prince peered down the length of the room at the bold young woman. What had excited everybody so? An aide presently informed him. The newcomer was not only uninvited, she was quite unknown. And she had arrived, it seemed, in an extraordinary vehicle—a coach of glass. "But *I* have a glass coach," replied the Prince. *Ah,* hers was not the same. The Prince's coach, a relic which had been in the royal family for a hundred years, only had large glass windows, and these were cracked. (Its steam-powered horse had long since grown rusty with disuse.) The young woman's coach, however, was entirely *formed* of glass. It was quite transparent, and sound as a bell. Nothing at all pulled it.

Just then she reached the Prince, and addressed him directly. "Perhaps you should ask me to dance," she said. "You'll note, I have put on my dancing shoes." She was not unattractive, if rather tall and slender for the Prince's personal taste, but when he looked at her feet, he heart bolted into a mad gallop. Without a word, he held out his arm. The orchestra struck up a waltz, and they took the floor.

"You dance well," said the Prince. "How is that feasible, in those?"

"They're perfectly comfortable," said the young woman, and whirled him round—she had already taken the lead—so his head echoed.

"Where did you come by them then?" the Prince asked, when he had regained his bearings.

"My godmother. The same as the coach. She makes things, you see."

Evidently both the godmother and her charge were cast in a modern mode.

The waltz, itself a modern dance that no one was quite yet used to, ended. The Prince and the woman in white stood alone on the floor, while everyone else stared from the sidelines, with their mouths open like those of horses after a stiff ride.

"But suppose," said the Prince, attempting to be jocular and casual, "if you were to dance really *quickly*, or, say—jump about somewhat—they might...break?"

"Of course not" snapped the young woman. "I'll show you." And signalling audaciously to the conductor, she shouted, "A tarantella, if you please!"

The Prince understood why, though uninvited, she had been admitted to the ball, and his wildly thudding heart was sinking in inevitable resignation. Such was her aura of command, the orchestra meanwhile did as bidden. And in another second, she was dancing boisterously, spinning around, kicking her heels, leaping and stamping, and all the time the gaseous light of the chandeliers splintered and exploded like white fire, from her high-heeled slippers of transparent glass.

When the tarantella was done, the ballroom applauded to a man (if not always to a woman), the air ringing to screams of *Bravo*! And *Encore*! But the girl only bent and took off her shoes. One she left lying, the other she grasped firmly in her hand. "I shall be going now," she said. "If you should want to look me up, that's for you to see to."

"But I don't even know your name!" cried the Prince.

"Cindy," said the young woman carelessly. And the clock struck midnight. And then—and then a swirling seemed to surround her, her garments vanished and she with them in what appeared to be a fall of glass leaves caught in a tornado; this next dazzling away through the room, the alarmed crowd parting before it. She was gone. And soon after, from far across the regal park, there came a strange tinkling sprinting noise of a speeding coach of glass.

*

"You see," said the Prince to his ministers, "at all costs, she must be mine. Take note," and here he flung the single glass slipper with great force against a marble pillar of the parliament building. The slipper slipped to the ground, immaculate. The marble showed a thin injurious crack. "With such a material," the Prince continued, "Turitrania need fear no aggressor by land, sea, or air. With, also, such affiliated secret weapons as my future wife's device for swirling concealment, we will be the most might power on earth!"

The ministers, pale with savage greed, nodded like puppets. Until at last, one ventured: "But how, sir, seeing the young lady has vanished, and no one knows her, or from whence she came—how is she ever again to be found?"

The Prince uttered a bark of laughter. "How do you think? I've got her *shoe*. Go and fetch me Snouter, my best bloodhound."

Steam Horse

Chris Butler

Grace stood guard over the fox in the debris of the construction site. A cold wind sliced in from the North. She huffed impatiently, plumes of her breath condensing in the air. The ground rumbled.

"It's coming," Peter said. He kept glancing at the needles of his dowsing box, and sniffed at
the earth. He had been calling to the mole for a while now, some arcane ritual designed to bring the beast up from the deep.

Grace was a big brute of a horse and did not think much of this new age hippy fox from the
royal court. She tolerated him only because she had her orders. She flicked her tail at an annoying watch-bug; its copper back glistened in the sun as it spun, till it stopped where she could see the time on its face. "Running a little late," she said.

"It's here," the fox said, and skulked away to crouch beside a broken wall.

The dirt and rubble seemed to bubble up, like froth on milk when you blow steam into it, and at the centre of the gurgling mud there came a dull iron shell. It rose up above the surface and set down pneumatic feet. Two rectangular panels shuttered open and closed again, suggesting eyes blinking in unfamiliar daylight.

"Who wakes me up?" the mole said. Its voice boomed from somewhere inside its iron hide.

"I do," Grace said.

A burst of steam erupted from the mole's head. "What do you want to go and do that for?" it moaned. "I was snoozing."

"It's like this," Grace said. "It's getting crowded up here. No space for horses to run in London any more. So our Queen Victoria, God bless her, has given us an authorisation."

Peter rifled through a set of papers, ran over and held up a document bearing the royal signature.

The mole's rectangular panels shuttered open and closed again. "What kind of an authorisation is it?"

"Permission to expand underground," Grace said. She had not told anyone that she would

soon be a dam. It was for her foals that she wanted this, more than for her own sake. "Permission to build a tunnel, good and long, so a horse can run without having to leave the city."

"Underground? But that's where I live," the mole said, "me and my kind."

"Yes, yes," Grace sighed.

Peter said, "It's a royal decree. Consider yourself conscripted."

The mole looked up at Grace. "Conscripted? What does he mean?"

"He means that you're to do our digging for us," Grace said. Another burst of steam shot out from the mole. "Oh surely it's no inconvenience," she continued, "you're going to be down there digging in any case. Just head east for us, steer straight and dig us a nice long run."

The mole shook himself and sank partway back into the ground. "I suppose it won't be too bad, if you just want the one tunnel," he said, "but there's no steam holes heading east from here, so I'll need to dig some of them, too. I don't likes it too humid."

"Dig as many steam holes as you like," Grace said. "And the tunnel."

"For Queen and country," Peter said, his voice rising above its normal timidity.

The mole shuddered and vanished back under the ground.

Grace looked at the hole. "We'll have to build something here. A station of some kind."

*

The mole charged through the earth, its eye-plates closed tight, doing what a mole does best. He had misgivings, though.

"Give 'em an inch and they'll take a mile," he grumbled. "Give 'em an inch and they'll take a mile."

When the air grew thin he dug a shaft back to the surface, but he did not like it there. The city had become far too crowded, as Grace had said. Even the air was filled with mechanical contraptions of all kinds. And the smog, it blotted out the sun.

The humans were the worst. Whenever he saw one it seemed to frown at him and make sputtering sounds. He was only digging holes. By royal decree, no less.

"What's your problem?" he'd say, and burrow back into the lovely soil.

*

Grace kept a watchful eye on the mole's progress in the months that followed. She inspected the beginnings of the tunnel. When her duties kept her above ground she liked to sniff at the air coming out of the steam holes. Though the gases were foul she accepted it as the new way of things, and thought nothing of it when her once bright coat darkened to a dull charcoal.

"It won't do," Peter said.

Grace had not expected a visit from the fox. "What won't do?"

The fox had momentarily become distracted by a watch-bug fluttering nearby. Grace stamped a hoof to reclaim his attention, and learned that a member of the royal court had complained because the mole had surfaced in the street where he lived. It was a very well-to-do street, and the blemish was unacceptable.

"What can I do about it?" Grace asked.

They built a façade to hide the steam shaft, a fake house-front with nothing behind it. It was costly but it kept the peace. To Grace's eyes there were blemishes everywhere. London sprawled and expanded with relentless energy.

Work continued in the tunnel, the mole deligently carrying out the Queen's orders. When at last the tunnel was completed, Grace ran its length from Bishop's Road to Farringdon Street. She felt ecstatic. Her foals were born soon after, in the tunnel, under the earth in the steam and the dark.

"We want more tunnels," Grace told the mole. Her foals needed more space to run. They knew nothing of the surface world, and Grace herself had no further use for it.

"More?" the mole moaned. "I'm not sure that's a good idea." He mumbled something else, which she did not quite catch, perhaps the words "inch" and "mile".

The two of them stood before each other, huffing steam at each other, deep in the underground.

"You guard this territory too jealously," Grace said. "You can relinquish a little more."

"When all this started," the mole observed, "you were a thing of flesh, but now I see your coat is made of metal, much like mine."

"What of it?" Grace replied, her voice deep and slow.

Her iron children came and stood with her.

The mole backed away. "As you command," it said.

170

*

The mole went southwards from Farringdon, then circled back to the beginning of the line. When that was done, he was despatched again, to a district further south.

As soon as a tunnel was completed it would be filled with horses stampeding through. Not just the horses. The humans came with their constant chattering, to each other and to their infernal devices. The dogs, and the rats came. The mechanical bugs that watched and kept time. Even the foxes, who could dig for themselves perfectly well but were too lazy to bother.

The network of tunnels soon stretched far and wide beneath the city of London. The metal horses ran the tunnels, carrying the other animals where they wanted to go.

The mole could feel them always, thundering at his pneumatic heels.

*

Grace no longer troubled herself with any thought of the surface world. She was free to run all day long.

Free.

The word rumbled through her as she pulled into a station. Plumes of steam billowed around her as her doors slid open. Out on the platform a board displayed schedules that had to be followed. Watch-bugs were everywhere, keeping time, monitoring performance.

"Do you even remember me?" Peter asked one day, as Grace carried him towards Westminster.

She remembered the fox well enough. He had learned how to live with the modern while still remaining true to his own nature, and she respected him for that. And yet, the fox was a timid creature and always would be, while she was now more powerful than ever.

Peter brushed his paw forward along the polished brass armrest of his seat. "You are still very lovely in your own way," he said, "and I cannot bring myself to be sorry for all that has happened."

Her wheels clattered and her carriage shook. She powered through the dark tunnel. Fire burned in her heart, steam driving her pistons, sparks flying from the tracks.

Though she was changed, she possessed the thing she had always wanted most of all. Even if she did have to follow the dictates of the watch-bugs, still she could run all day long.

She gave no further thought to the fox. After all, they had never really liked each other anyway.

*

There was no room for the mole beneath the streets of London any more. The steam horses had taken over every mile of it, shallow and deep. So the mole that had dug their first tunnels moved away, and it supposed that no one particularly noticed or cared.

It surfaced many miles distant, in a froth of mud. The sun blazed in the sky. It shuttered its rectangular eye-plates almost closed, and took in the green of the hills and the fragrance of wild flowers.

On the far horizon, a pall of dark smoke could be seen clogging the sky above its former home.

With a shudder the mole vanished back into the earth.

It sleeps when it wants to, and often loses itself in digging, purely for its own sake.

Professor Fluvius's Palace of Many Waters

Paul Di Filippo

I awoke in a soft, damp bed, atop the covers, not knowing my name.

A standing man hovered solicitously over me. His genial face, with wine-dark eyes, reminded me of someone I thought I should know. Thick white wavy locks cascaded to his shoulders. A Van Dyke beard of equal snowiness did little to conceal his jovial, ebullient expression. Yet despite this arctic peltage, his unlined face and clean limbs radiated a youthful vitality.

"Ah, Charlene, you're with us now! Splendid! We have much to do."

My name was Charlene then. That seemed right.

The man announced, "I am Profesor Fluvius. Can you stand?"

"I think so…." Professor Fluvius placed a hand on my shoulder, and a sudden access of galvanic spirits coursed through me. "Why, certainly, I can stand!"

In one fluid movement I came to my bare feet on the warm wooden floorboards. I was wearing an unadorned white samite smock, the hem of which hung to just below my knees. A balmy wind blowing in through an open window, past lazily twitching gauzy curtains, stirred my robe and conveyed to me certain bodily sensations indicating that undergarments of any sort appeared to be lacking in my wardrobe. But the clement summer atmosphere certainly did not require such.

Professor Fluvius, I noted now, was dressed entirely in aquamarine blue, from long-tailed coat to spats. He took my hand as a favourite uncle might, and again I felt a surge of vigor through my cells.

"Let me introduce you to the other ladies first."

We stepped forward toward the door leading from the single room, which appeared to be a guest bedchamber of a quality sort.

Looking back at the bed where I had awakened to myself for the first time, I saw a long slim twisting tendril of bright green water weed adorning the damp duvet.

The carpeted corridor beyond that room hosted a dozen other doors, each bearing a brass number. Professor Fluvius and I crossed diagonally to Number 205.

"You rejoined us in my own modest quarters, Charlene. All quite proper, I assure you. But just across the corridor here, I have chartered an entire suite for you and your peers."

Professor Fluvius knocked, then cracked the door of 205 wide without awaiting a response.

Inside, draped languorously across an assortment of well-upholstered chairs and divans, six smiling women calmly awaited our arrival; plainly, they had been expecting us. Exhibiting a variety of beautiful physiognomies of mixed ethnicities, they all wore simple shifts identical to mine, and remained similarly unshod.

I caught my own reflection then in a canted cheval glass, and was perhaps immoderately pleased to find myself wholly a match to my sisters in terms of mortal beauty.

"Charlene, allow me to introduce your comrades to you. Callie, Lara, Minnie, Lila, Praxie and Sally. Ladies, this is Charlene."

The six women trilled a tuneful assortment of greetings, several of them playfully abbreviating my name to "Charl" or "Charlie," and I responded in kind. Once they sensed somehow my ability to blend into their pre-established harmony, they were up off their perches and clustering around me, indicating by various endearments and mild sororal caresses how happy they were to have me among their number.

Professor Fluvius watched us beneficently for a short while, but then cut short our mutual admiration society.

"Ladies, have you forgotten? We have an important appointment to keep. Let us be on our way now!"

So saying, and recovering his ocean-blue topper from a hat-tree, the Professor led the way out of the suite, and we all obediently followed.

A staircase at the end of the corridor debouched after a long single arcing flight into a splendid lobby, and I received confirmation, if needed, that this establishment was a commercial hotel. The large pillared space was thronged with people—all of them, male and female alike, dressed with considerably more formality than I and my sisters. Nor did I see any man sporting anything like the beryl suit worn by the Professor. It was unsurprising, then, that our passage across the lobby toward the street entrance should attract stares and semi-decorous exclamations. And this attention was not minimized by the Professor's unprompted yet effervescent lecture to us, his charges.

"Witness the glories of the Tremont House, ladies. The first hotel ever to incorporate running water, and thus a fit establishment to temporarily host Professor Fluvius and his Naiads during the early portion of our Boston stay!"

The Professor seemed intent on advertising himself and us, and it was at this juncture that I began to apprehend that I had become, willy-nilly, part of a commercial venture of some sort.

We exited the hotel through its grand colonnaded entrance on Tremont Street and crossed a miry sidewalk and concourse, nimbly dodging carriages and carts.

Amazingly, I found myself stepping unerringly on an irregular trail of clean patches amidst the offal and manure, thus succeeding in keeping my bare feet unsullied. I noticed that my sisters trod a similar random series of sterile steppingstones.

Or was it that the uniformly dirty pavement spontaneously developed virginal patches beneath our feet?

As we seven attractive women and pavonine man hiked determinedly through the streets of Boston, we began to attract a crowd of followers, picaroons and mudlarks mostly, whose unsolicited comments veered more toward gibes and lewd offerings of unwanted intimate services than had those of the Tremont House crowd. But I and my dignified sisters ignored the verbal affronts from the swelling ranks of our entourage, and Professor Fluvius seemed actually to relish their attentions.

"That's it, lads, that's it! Roll up, roll up! Follow us for the most exciting news of the decade!"

Almost immediately after leaving the hotel, we found ourselves in a park full of greenery, and were able to indulge our bare feet on grass. But this respite was short-lived, as we soon exited the Public Gardens and proceeded uptown on a street labelled Boylston.

My eye was drawn to a posted bill advertising a new play—*The Children of Oceanus*, by Eleuthera Stayrook—at the Everett Hall Theatre, and bearing the commencement date of July 12th, 1877.

And so it was that I had my first inkling of what year it was in which I had awakened—assuming the poster to be of recent vintage, an assumption which its unweathered appearance supported.

Reaching a cross-street named Clarendon, we turned and encountered a construction site. Here, a vast project sprawling across several blocks was in its obvious end stages.

The building at the centre of the site was a church of soaring magnificence. Not as large as a cathedral, the brown-hued sanctuary nonetheless radiated a deep gravitas counterbalanced by an exuberant sense of joy.

Workmen swarmed around the nearly complete structure, taking down scaffolding, entering the interior with loads of fine materials, sweeping up debris. One man seemed in charge of the general organized hubbub, and it was toward him that Professor Fluvius made a beeline.

At my side, the woman introduced to me as Plaxie now spoke in a stage-whisper, leaning her pert-nosed, black-ringleted head close to my own auburn locks. Her breath smelled mildly of fish.

"If you think you've seen the Prof put on a show so far, just wait till he gets to work on this mark!"

We now—my comrades, and the raggle-taggle flock that had attached itself to us—came to a stop around the overseer. He was a plump gent with a thick chestnut beard, hair parted down the middle, and an intelligently playful twinkle to his eyes that offset his otherwise stern demeanour. He wore an expensive brown suit.

Professor Fluvius hailed him in a loud voice more suited to the baseball outfield than face-to-face conversation, and I could tell he was playing to the crowd.

"You, good sir, are Henry Hobson Richardson, the veritable visionary architect of this grand dream in rough stone we see before us!"

Richardson seemed more amused than perturbed. "Yes, sir, I am. And may I enquire your name and purpose?"

"I am Professor Nodens Fluvius, and I am here to give you your next commission!"

"Indeed? And what might that be?"

"A public bath house!"

Loud guffaws and taunts arose from the spectators, but Fluvius remained unperturbed, and Richardson continued to express some unfeigned interest at this odd commission.

"A public bath house, Professor Fluvius? I assume you are thinking along the lines of the municipal facilities found on the Continent. But are you unaware of the spectacular failure of the Mott Street Bath House in New York City, some twenty years ago? Since then, no private investor nor any municipality in our great nation has deemed such an enterprise feasible. Nor has the public clamoured for such facilities."

"Ah, but that is because all businessmen and politicos have lacked my farsighted conception of what such an establishment could offer. And as for the public—they know not what they want till it is presented to them."

At this point, the Professor encompassed us seven maidens with a sweep of his arm, as if to indicate that we would appear uppermost on his bill of fare. Some of my sisters lowered their glances demurely, but I maintained a bold gaze directed at the hoi polloi, even when raucous huzzahs went up from the crowd. For a moment, I wondered with alarm if we were meant to be courtesans in this hypothetical establishment. But then I recalled the clean organic thrill of the liquid energies that had flowed from the Professor's touch, and felt reassured of his honest intentions toward us.

"Moreover," continued the Professor, "no prior entrepreneur has held a doctorate in hydrostatics from La Sapienza University in Rome, as do I. Surely you know of the marvellous accomplishments of the ancient Romans in this sphere...? Well, the ultra-modern technics of boilers, valves, conduits, gravity-fed reservoirs and suchlike that I intend to install will make the Baths of Caracalla look like a roadside ditch!"

At the mention of a technological challenge, the architect Richardson developed an even keener expression. "Speak on, Professor."

"I have conceived of a palatial public bathhouse that will employ the latest in hydropathic techniques to promote robust health and enervation in all its patrons. Combining methodologies I learned at first hand from Vincenz Priessnitz himself at Grafenburg with subtle refinements of my own devising, I can guarantee to reform drunkards, cure the halt and lame, invigorate the intellect of scholars and schoolboys alike, and induce passion in sterile marriages—all for mere pennies a visit!"

This last boast raised further hoots and japes from the crowd, who nonetheless, I sensed, evinced real interest on some deep level at the Professor's pitch. Richardson, meanwhile, seemed to be cogitating seriously on the proposal as well, unconsciously rubbing his sizable vest-swathed tummy as an aid to cogitation.

Grinning, Professor Fluvius awaited the architect's response—which finally came in the form of a question.

"How is this ambitious project to be funded, Professor? I do not work in anticipation of a portion of future profits."

"All is assured, Mister Richardson. I assume pure alluvial gold would be deemed legal tender...?"

The Professor removed a cowhide poke from a suit pocket. Uncinching the poke's neck, he grabbed Richardson's hand and poured a mound of glittering golden grit into his cupped palm. Richardson's eyes expanded to their full diameter. Professor Fluvius dropped the poke atop the mound and said, "Consider this your retainer, I pray, good sir."

Very carefully, Richardson poured the gold back into the poke and deposited the pouch in his own suit. "Professor Fluvius, you have your architect."

A roar of acclaim went up from the crowd. I realized that their massed attention had been part of the Professor's sly plan to add public pressure to compel Richardson's assent. Surely by tomorrow this commission would be spread across all the newspapers of Boston.

The two men shook hands. Professor Fluvius said, "I am staying at the Tremont House, Mister Richardson. I anticipate your dining there tonight with me, so that we may refine our plans. And oh, yes, one last matter. I shall need the establishment finished and ready to open its doors in three months' time."

"Three months' time! For an edifice of any sizable scale? Impossible!"

Professor Fluvius removed two more plump pokes from his pocket and handed them over to Richardson, saying, "That, Mister Architect, is a word we shall not allow to trouble us again."

*

I approached the Palace of Many Waters across the modest plaza of varicoloured granite from Barre, Vermont, that fronted its façade. A warm November day, its sunshine still only half exhausted, had left the stones comfortable to my bare feet. But I imagined that neither I nor my sisters would be discommoded even by the arrival of winter.

At my elbow strode the visitor I had met at the train station: Dr. Simon Baruch. Of medium height and trim physique, dressed in a respectable checked suit, he boasted a full head of dark hair and neatly trimmed thin moustache and chin spinach. He walked with a dignified bearing that reflected his past military service, as a surgeon during the War Between the States.

I had met the doctor at the terminus of the Boston and Providence railroad line, adjacent to the Public Gardens. From thence we walked a few blocks riverward, until we came to Beacon, that avenue which bordered the Charles River. We turned left and proceeded a few more blocks to the intersection of Beacon and Dartmouth, where the Palace reared its mighty battlements.

Perched on the banks of the River Charles (one single-story wing housing the Professor's offices and private quarters in fact extended out on stilts above the flood), the Palace was a fantasy of minarets and oriel windows, gables and slate slopes, copper flashing and painted gingerbread. Like some Yankee version of the famous Turkish Baths of Manchester, England, the Palace seemed a *hamam* fit for *ifrits*—to adopt a Muslim perspective.

After demolition of a few inconvenient pre-existing structures, construction of the Palace had been accomplished in a mere ten weeks, without stinting materials or design, thanks to an army of labourers working round the clock; the ceaseless management and encouragement of Mr. Richardson; and a steady decanting of alluvial gold from the seemingly inexhaustible coffers of our dear Professor. (And how marvellously I had matured myself in those weeks, almost as if a new personality had been established upon my own nascent foundations in synchrony with the Palace's construction.)

Our doors had opened in mid-October, just three weeks ago, and in that time the Palace had been perpetually busy. We were open for business seven days a week, twenty-four hours a day, and there were very few stretches when the influx into the Palace was not a copious stream.

Now Dr. Baruch and I stopped hard by the large, impressive main entrance so that he could marvel for a moment at the parade of patrons:

mothers with children, horny-handed labourers, clerks and costermongers, urchins and pedlars, soldiers and savants from Harvard and the Society of Natural History. I noted every type of man, woman and child, from the most humble and ragged to the most refined and eminent members of the *bon ton*, all desirous of becoming clean in a democratic fashion. True, their entrance fees differed, and they would be diverted into different grades of facilities once inside. But all had to enter by the same gate—a gate above which was graven the Palace's motto:

KEEP CLEAN, BE AS FRUIT, EARN LIFE, AND WATCH, TILL THE WHITE-WING'D REAPERS COME.

—HENRY VAUGHAN, THE SEED GROWING SECRETLY

I noted Dr. Baruch's gaze alighting upon the motto, and, after taking a moment to apprehend it, he turned to me and said, "An apt phrase from the Silurist, and not without a metaphysical complement to its ostensible carnal focus. Were you aware that the poet's twin brother, Thomas, was an alchemist?"

"I fear I am uneducated in such literary matters, Dr. Baruch. Our Professor, however, is a man of much learning, and is highly desirous of your conversation."

Dr. Baruch laughed. "I can tell when I am being politely hustled along. Let us go visit your employer."

We circumvented the Bailey's Baffle Gates through which the paying customers had to pass and found ourselves in the Palace's lofty atrium.

Like most of the interior spaces of the Palace, the lofty, vaulted atrium was tiled with gorgeously glazed ceramic creations, representing both abstract and pictorial designs, the latter of a predominantly marine bent. The hard surfaces granted an echoic resonance to the gabble of voices and footfalls. High stained glass windows rained down tinted light upon the hustling masses as they filed in orderly lines towards the towel-dispensing stations and thence to the disrobing rooms. Naturally, the sexes were separated at this point—save for mothers shepherding children under a certain age—as they would be in the baths.

I guided Dr. Baruch behind the scenes, until we reached the door to Professor Fluvius's private offices. I knocked and received acknowledgement to enter.

Professor Fluvius's unique maple desk, a product of the Herter Brothers firm of New York, was shaped like a titanic conch shell. Behind this cyclopean design sat the man whose face was the first visage I had seen upon attaining consciousness. His ivory tresses, longer even than before, fell past the shoulders of his cerulean suit.

Behind him, a window looked out upon the sail-dotted Charles, toward the Cambridge shore. It was cracked a few inches to allow the heady scents of the river inside.

Professor Fluvius ceased fussing with a ledger when we entered, slapping its boards shut decisively, then rose to his feet with a broad smile and came out from behind the desk, hand outstretched.

"Dr. Baruch! A genuine pleasure, sir! Thanks you so much for responding to my humble invitation. I hope to present you with a professional challenge worthy of your talents…"

I hung back near the door, hoping to hear the Professor's proposal, as I was intrigued by Dr. Baruch's character, insofar as it had been vouchsafed to me in our short acquaintance, and his potential role in our enterprise.

But Professor Fluvius would have none of my impertinent curiosity. Pulling a turnip watch from his pocket, he examined it and then addressed me.

"Charlene, don't you have an appointment soon with one of your special clients?"

I knew full well who awaited me upon the hour, but dissembled. "Oh, Professor, I had forgotten. Pardon me."

"No offense needing pardon, my dear. But you'd best be streaming onward now."

I had perforce to leave their presence then.

But I was not to be stymied from my eavesdropping.

What a change in my nature from the humble, timid deference shown to the Professor upon my first foray into consciousness! It was not that I honoured him any the less, nor did my desires deviate significantly from his—insofar as I plumbed either his motives or my own. But I had developed a stubborn sense of my own desires, and a reluctance to be thwarted.

Outside in the hall, I did not head immediately back toward the main bulk of the thronging Palace, but instead approached a nearby window, lowered of course against the November chill. I opened it and peered out.

Some twelve feet below me, the happy waters of the Charles burbled past on their way to the sea, chuckling among the freshly tarred pilings supporting this wing. It would have been a straight, uninterrupted drop to that wet embrace, had it not been for one feature: a kind of catwalk or boat-bumper about halfway down, installed against accidental collisions.

I slipped over the window sill and lowered myself down till my toes met the rough planks. Then I made my way stealthily to a position just below the window of the Professor's study.

"—but inside," boomed Fluvius's voice, "inside, Dr. Baruch, I think you will agree with me that they are as dirty as ever. The waters beneath the skin. You can clean the outer man—and that's a fine start—but the inner man is another matter entirely. A much-neglected matter."

"I confess," responded Baruch, "that I have often considered the possibility of tinkering with the interior flora of the human body, with an eye toward remedying several inherent bodily ills. Many are the moments, mired in the bloody tent of a field hospital or the sputum-flecked ward of a slum asylum, when I fantasized about bolstering the body's natural defences with a dose of some beneficial live culture."

"Yes, yes, I knew of your researches, Dr. Baruch! Just why I summoned you out of all your peers. And my dreams tally precisely with yours! I believe I have formulated a potent nostrum that will benefit mankind in just such a fashion as you envision. My potion will not only re-order the patient's defensive constitution, but also contribute to a more orderly patterning of nerve impulses in the brain, promoting more cogent and disciplined thought forms."

Baruch was silent for a moment, before responding: "If that's the case, Professor Fluvius, then what need do you have of me and my skills?"

Fluvius sounded slightly embarrassed, for the first time in my memory. "My trials of this patent medicine of mine have been not wholly successful. Certain of my subjects did not sustain a full recovery. Admittedly, I was working with gravely ill specimens to begin with, but still—I had hoped for better results. But I realized after such setbacks that I lacked the precise anatomical knowledge of a trained physician such as yourself. It is this expertise that I desire you to contribute to the cause. As for salary, I know you are above such plebeian considerations. But let me assure you, your monetary compensation will be far above any salary you could earn elsewhere. Will you join me in this quest to improve the lot of our fellow man, Dr.?"

Crouching below the window as the sun continued to sink and a brisk breeze blew up my gown, I eagerly awaited Dr. Baruch's response. But my concentration was shattered upon the instant by the sensation of a cold and clammy hand encircling my ankle!

Only with supreme willpower did I stifle all but the most muted involuntary shriek that would have betrayed me to those inside. Luckily, a gull screamed at that very moment to further cover my inadvertent alarm.

Heart pounding, I whipped my head down and around to see who could possibly have grabbed me under such unlikely circumstances.

The shaggy head and leering ugly countenance of Usk greeted my gaze. He stood apelike on the crossbeams of the pilings, evidently pleased as Punch to have caught me in this compromising situation.

Just prior the Palace's opening three weeks ago, a contingent of the Swamp Angels had visited Professor Fluvius as he was giving us Naiads a lecture on our duties. We watched with some trepidation and unease as these hoodlums swaggered into our sanctuary. They boldly demanded a weekly stipend as "protection money," in order to ensure that the Palace remained unmolested in its operations. Professor Fluvius seemed to agree, and they went their way.

But then he summoned Usk.

As if out of the woodwork, the gnomish gnarled fellow, dressed in rough working-man's garb, appeared. None of us had ever seen him before. But he seemed on intimate terms with the Professor.

"Usk, would you see to it that those churlish fellows do not disturb us ever again?"

Usk laughed, and shivers went down my spine, and likewise along my sisters', I sensed sympathetically.

"Righto, Prof! I'll learn them a lesson they won't soon forget."

As mysteriously as he had appeared, Usk vanished.

The Swamp Angels had not troubled the Palace since. And I had heard that, after some enigmatic cataclysm among their ranks, the wounded remnants of their forces had been absorbed by the Gophers and the Ducky Boys.

Since that incident, Usk had surfaced occasionally to carry out the Professor's bidding. But none of us knew where he lived, or how he passed his idle hours.

Now I was face to face with him—in a manner of speaking, since actually he had a more prominent view of my bare nether parts than of my countenance. I resolved not to let him know how much he had affrighted me.

In a whisper, I demanded, "What do you want of me?"

Usk husked out his own words. "Prof'd be a tad peeved, if'n he found out you was key- holing him."

I adopted my most winsome ways. "Must you tell him?"

"Not if'n I don't choose to."

"And what could possibly induce you to choose such a merciful course?"

"Let's say if'n I were to receive certain favours from a certain lady—favours which I'd be more than happy to make explicit to you. Tonight, for instance, after your work's all done."

Usk's grip tightened on my ankle—the rough skin of his palm feeling like scales—and I quailed interiorly. But he had me in a bind. I certainly did not wish to appear a sneak and gossip in the eyes of Professor Fluvius. No, I had to submit.

"Where should we meet?"

"I dwell in the lowest cellar, by the boilers. Southwest corner. That's where you'll find my doss."

"I—I'll be there."

Leering once more, Usk released my ankle, prior to slipping away under the floorboards and among the pilings, sinuous as a fish.

Refocusing my attentions on the study window, I heard only the clink of glasses and an exchange of pleasantries. I had to assume the deal had been sealed, and that Dr. Baruch would be staying with us.

And now I needed to keep my appointment.

*

I pattered barefoot swiftly past the gaudy marble entrances to the enormous, rococo common rooms, big as ropewalks, where the masses of men and women bathed in segregated manner. The sounds of gay and enthusiastic splashy ablutions echoed outward from these natatoria. I could picture the water jetting from the bronze heads of dolphins, the flickering gas lights reflected off the pools, the cakes of fragrant soaps embossed with the Palace's trademark conch shell, the long-handled brushes and plump sponges, the naked human bodies in all their equally agreeable shades of flesh and states of leanness and corpulence. The imagined scene delighted me. The conception of so many happy people sporting like otters or seals in a pristine liquid environment seemed utterly Edenic to me. I was more convinced than ever that Professor Fluvius's Palace of Many Waters was a force for beauty and goodness in this often shabby and cruel world.

Once beyond this area open to the general public—the hubbub abating and I having circumvented with a smile and a nod one of the Palace's liveried guardians stationed so as to limit deeper ingress solely to the elite—I had access to an Otis Safety Elevator. I stepped aboard along with a man I recognized as the Mayor of Boston, a Mr. Prince: grey hair low across his brow, walrus moustache. He nodded politely to me, and sized me up with the same look a chef might bestow on a prize tomato.

"You're the one they call Charlie, aren't you?"

"Yes, sir."

"Well, I'm slated to see your sister Praxie today. But perhaps next time you'll attend me."

"I'd be delighted, sir."

The rattling mechanism brought us to the second floor of our establishment. I parted from Mayor Prince, and watched him enter the room labelled "Praxithea."

On this level of the Palace were the private rooms for our more privileged clientele, where bathing occurred in elegant tubs accommodating from two to several bathers. Included on this level were the seven special suites assigned to us Naiads. In these chambers, the waters themselves were perfumed and salted, and certain luxurious individual attentions could be paid to the selected patrons.

I did not enter directly the suite whose brass plate proclaimed it "Charlene," but instead stepped through an innocuous unmarked door and into a connecting changing room. There I doffed my gown and donned a bandeau top across my full bosom and a loin cloth around my broad hips, leaving most of my honey-coloured skin bare. I let down my long chestnut hair, and stepped through to where my client awaited.

Paul Di Filippo

Frederick Law Olmstead had accumulated fifty-five years of life at this date. The famed architect, known to the nation primarily for his magnificent design of New York's Central Park, boasted a large head bald across the crown, a wild crop of facial hair, and a penetrating expression betokening a certain wisdom and insight into the ways of the world, as well as hinting at burning creative instincts. His supervisory work in the field had kept him moderately fit, although he had not entirely escaped a certain paunchiness of middle-age.

Now he sat, naked and waist-deep in a capacious ceramic footed trough steaming with soapy, jasmine-scented water, puffing on a cigar and looking already well advanced on the road to relaxation and forgetful of his vocational cares, even before my ministrations.

Olmstead had been my client since the Palace opened, and we were on familiar terms. He evidently found me a congenial bath partner, and I had to confess that I had become more than professionally enamoured of him. He had always treated me with kindness and respect and a liberal generosity.

"Ah, Charlie, you're a sight for weary eyes! Join me, dear. I need to disburden myself of the day's headaches."

I slipped gracefully into the tub, sliding up all slippery into his embrace, and Olmstead began to soliloquize me. I kept mum yet receptive.

"This newest project of mine is a bugger, Charlie. Turning a swamp into a park! Sheer insanity. The Fens were never meant to be other than a flood plain or tidal estuary. And yet somehow the city wants me to convert them to made lands, a pleasure pavilion for the masses, part of what they're already calling my 'Emerald Necklace.' Can you fathom what's involved in such a project? Not only do I have to contend with the waters of the Charles, but also those of Muddy River and Stony Brook, which likewise feed into that acreage. I'm going to have to erect dams and pumps, then drain and grade, before layering in an entire maze of culverts and sewers. Truck in gravel and soil, landscape the whole shebang— So much of this city is made land already, hundreds of acres reclaimed from a primeval bog. The civic fathers imagine they can wrest any parcel they desire from the aboriginal waters. Mayor Prince and his whole Vault cabal are dead set on this project. But this time their reach exceeds their grasp. It's a mad folly, I tell you!"

Olmstead paused, puffing on his cigar, then said with altered tone, "Yet if it could be done—what a triumph!"

I felt proud of Olmstead's ambition and fervour. Intuiting that he had expended his verbal anxiety, I said, "If anyone is capable of accomplishing such a feat, Frederick, it's you. But you must return to the project tomorrow with a relaxed mind and body. Enough speech. Allow me to do my job now."

Willingly, Olmstead stubbed out his cigar in a wrought-iron tub-side appliance. I secured a cake of lanolin-rich lilac soap and began thickly to lather up my own form with graceful motions, all the while allowing the

185

ends of my wet hair to drape sensuously about Olmstead like enticing tendrils.

When I had attained a sufficient soapy slickness, I commenced to apply my rich body as an active wash-cloth across his whole frame.

I understand that in far-off Nippon there is a class of women known as *geishas*, whose professional practices resemble what we Naiads at the Palace deliver. But how Professor Fluvius ever came to know of them, in order to use as models for his business, I cannot say.

*

Because the business of the Palace continued round the clock, and some of us must perforce tend the evening shift, the third-floor communal sleeping suite for us Naiads held only four of us at midnight: myself, Lara, Minnie and Lila. It were best to picture us, lounging drowsily on our respective feather mattresses, as four Graces, hued in the sequence above-named: honey, olive, alabaster and tea.

We chattered for a while of gossipy inconsequentials, as any women will, before Lila said, "I see that our newest employee has already been assigned a laboratory."

How quickly news travelled in this aqueous environment, like scent to a shark!

"Do you mean Dr. Baruch?" asked Lara, batting her thick eyelashes. "I wouldn't mind being his assistant. It would make a nice change from the soap-and-slither routine with the high muck-a-mucks."

Minnie asked, "What's the nature of his work?"

"Rumour has it he's crafting some kind of purgative for the rubes," responded Lila.

Lara pulled a face. "I shouldn't care to help in that case, lest he need a subject for his trials."

I did not add any details from my own stock of overheard information. The thoughts of the payment I owed Usk in return for that data were too discouraging.

Pretty soon after this, my sisters fell asleep, allowing me to slip out without needing to respond to any inquiries about my late-night errands.

The same elevator that had delivered me from street-level to the second-floor now took me from third to lowest cellar. Here I entered a phantasmagorical, almost inhuman world.

The sub-basement held all the apparatus that allowed the Palace to function. I felt much like an animalcule venturing into a human's guts.

Congeries of brass pipes of all dimensions, from pencil-thin to barrel-thick, threaded the space, producing a veritable labyrinth. Some pipes leaked steam; some were frosted with condensation. Valves and dials and taps proliferated. The pipes led into and out of huge rivet-studded reservoirs, from which escaped various floral and mineral scents.

Beyond this initial impression of tubular matrices loomed the many boilers, giant radiant Molochs, each one fed and stoked by its own patented "automatic fireman" apparatus, which fed coal in from vast bins at a steady clip, obviating the need for human tenders.

Indeed, Professor Fluvius's early boast—to render the Baths of Caracalla insignificant—appeared fulfilled.

I began to perspire. Vertigo assailed me. I felt incredibly distant from all the sources of my strength, amidst this controlled industrial chaos. Usk had said the southwest corner was his lair. But which direction was which?

I wandered for what seemed like ages, meeting no one in this sterile factory, before glimpsing, beneath a large, wall-mounted mechanical message-board affair, a tumbled heap of bedclothes. As I approached, I noted that the message-board was of the type found in Newport mansions, by means of which masters could communicate with distant servants through the medium of dropped or rotated printed discs. This must be how Profesor Fluvius summoned Usk at need.

The musty midden of bedclothes stirred and out of the stained regalia rose Usk. To my horror and disgust, he was utterly naked, his powerful, hirsute twisted limbs such a contrast to the well-formed appearance of Olmstead or my other clients.

Usk conferred a look of randy appreciation on me, a favour which I could easily have foregone.

"Ah, beauty steps down into the gutter. I am glad you made it unnecessary for me to communicate with the Professor. He's got too many pressing matters on his mind. Big doings, big doings. If you only knew..."

Usk seemed to want to disclose some secret to me, but I did not pursue his bait, for fear of a hook within. So he continued.

"It's a kindness to spare ol' Fluvius any knowledge of your trifling indiscretions. Howsoever, you are not here for us to discuss our mutual master. Sit down, sit down, join me on my humble pallet!"

I sat, and of course, to no one's surprise, Usk immediately began to paw me without any charade of seduction, his hands roaming at will under my gown.

I would like to say that his touch left me cold. But the truth was otherwise. To my chagrin, I sensed in Usk's blunt and callous gropings a portion of the same galvanic power that had thrilled me when the Professor first touched me in the Tremont Hotel, so many months ago. It was almost as if Usk, the Professor, and I were all related, sharing the same sympathies and humours I felt with my fellow Naiads.

No merit resides in delving into the sordid details of the next two hours. Usk had his lusty way with me, not once or twice but thrice, and deposited his thick spunk in several unconventional places.

At last, though, he seemed sated. Sated, yet still demanding.

"You'll be back tomorrow night, my dear. Or the Professor and I will have that unwelcome conversation about your goosey-goosey-gander-where-do-you-wander ways."

I sighed dramatically in a put-upon fashion, yet not without some falsity of emotion. Truly, after tonight's tumble, future encounters with Usk would not be such an unknown burden. "I suppose I have no choice...."

Suddenly, as if my words had pleased him or opened up some further bond between us, he reached beneath his pallet and pulled out—a book!

"Would you—would you read this to me? Please? I—I can't..."

I took the volume. The title page proclaimed it to be *The Water-Babies*, by Charles Kingsley.

" 'Once upon a time,' " I began, " 'there was a little chimney-sweep, and his name was Tom....' "

*

The next several weeks sped by in a busy round of work, sleep, intercourse and two-person Chautauqua between Usk and myself, with the text of our studies moving on, after *Water-Babies*, to Mr. MacDonald's *At the Back of the North Wind*. I could not honestly say I found this regimen imposed by Usk without its thrills and rewards, and on the whole, what with work and all, each of my days passed in a pleasant whirl of activity.

Several times the Professor took all seven of us girls out with him on various expeditions across Massachusetts and nearby New England. Ostensibly, these were gay recreational outings to reward us for our diligent services. But in reality, I suspected that they were calculated to serve at least as much as advertisements for the Palace.

Late in December, on a mild day, we went to Rocky Point Amusement Park in Rhode Island. The place had been much in the news, since President Hayes had recently visited and become the first sitting President of this forward-looking nation to utilize a newfangled telephonic device located on the premises. (He had placed a call to Providence, purpose unreported.)

Even this late in the season, the Shore Dinner Hall was still serving its traditional quahog chowder and clam-cakes fare, and we all ate to repletion, amidst much laughter and chatter.

At one point, without warning, the skies darkened and the waters of Narragansett Bay became troubled. It seemed as if our little excursion would be dampened. I looked up from my half-eaten tenth greasy clam-cake and noted that, across the hall, Professor Fluvius was arguing with the manager of the establishment, about what I could not say. Several park employees intervened, and both men calmed down. At the same time, the sun returned and the sea grew still, and so all was well.

During this period, I spent whatever minutes were not otherwise occupied with Dr. Baruch in his laboratory, which was located in the same wing that housed the Professor's quarters and office. I had taken a shine to the humble physician, and was in awe of his learning. His cosmopolitan air spoke to me of the larger world, a venue I hoped one day to experience firsthand. I was resolved not to spend all my days in the Palace of Many Waters, despite whatever debt I owed to Professor Fluvius for first awaking me. I wanted to travel, to broaden my horizons.

Dr. Baruch was careful not to divulge the nature of his researches to me—a secret he was unaware I already knew—but accepted me as a mascot of sorts to his scientific endeavours, a pleasant female ornament to his glassware-filled, aqua-regia-redolent workspace.

It was in this manner that I became privy to his ultimate success, and arranged to be at my secret listening post when he rushed into the Professor's office to deliver his good news.

"Professor Fluvius, I am happy to report that your generous faith in my talents has been rewarded. Administration of the biotic infusion of your devising is perfected at last. Delivered as a lavage to the lower intestines, the colony becomes well-established and active. Although I forecast that frequent infusions will be necessary to maintain its presence against the body's innate capacity for driving out foreign invaders."

"Excellent, Dr., excellent! I can now begin improving the material condition of the community. And the best way to do that is to start with the health of the men at the very top. With a public servant such as the Mayor, perhaps. If you would be so good as to prepare a dosage for Mr. Prince, and stand ready to offer your testimonial as to its efficacy…"

Perched not uncomfortably on the frigid catwalk, listening to the formation of ice crystals in the burbling water around the pilings below, I received this news as a sop to my curiosity, but did not regard it as any item of significance.

How little I witted or foresaw.

A few days later, Olmstead and I were reclining in our tub prior to my sudsing us up. He looked ill at ease for some reason I could not immediately fathom. His wetted bedraggled beard resembled a nanny goat's. My heart went out to him, and I resolved to exert all my charms to get him to relax. But most uncommonly, I could not. Finally he disclosed what was troubling him.

"You know my project to reclaim the Fens? It's cancelled. Funding's been suddenly withdrawn. The Mayor and his tribe have had a change of heart. They're full of talk about making an end to 'trespassing on the natural order.' Claim the city is big enough as it is. It's as if they've all gone Transcendentalist on me! Progress be damned!"

I ached for his disappointment. "Why, Frederick, that's simply awful! You had your heart set on accomplishing this!"

"I know, I know. But what can I do? My mind's so disordered at this development. Perhaps I should take one of those new treatments the

Professor is offering. It seems to have perked up the Mayor and his crowd. Fostered a strange implacable resolve in them."

I could not offer a solution to Olmstead's worries, and so concentrated instead on delivering the most agreeable whole-body massage I could to this client whom, to my surprise, I had become so very fond of.

The hour after midnight that same evening found me once more down in the depths of the Palace with Usk. After our robust hinky-jinky and a chapter or two of Mr. Ruskin's *The King of the Golden River*, I made to leave. But Usk detained me with a teasing query.

"You picked out your dress yet for the Prof's coronation ball down in Washington?"

I halted in my tracks. "Whatever do you mean?"

"He's got the Mayor and his cronies in his pocket now. Only a matter of time till the whole country's his to command."

"How so?" I demanded.

"That bum-wash what he and the doc cooked up. Makes any man the Prof's slave. Saps their native will and substitutes the Prof's."

"I don't believe you! The Professor is a noble intellect! He'd never stoop to such a thing!"

Usk shrugged. "Believe as you will, makes no never mind to me."

I stormed out, all in a dithery confusion. Should I confide this news to my sisters, and ask their advice? Confront the Professor directly? Or do nothing at all?

I resolved to seek Olmstead's guidance first.

The hours till our next appointment dragged their feet, but at last we were fragrantly en-tubbed together.

Before I could venture my request for guidance, Olmstead burst forth with plentiful yet somewhat inane zest.

"Lord above, I've never felt better nor been more peaceful of mind! All those troubles I was blathering about to you—vanished like the snows of yesteryear! Who cares if the Fens ever get transformed? Not me! And to think I owe it all to high-colonic hydrotherapy!"

*

Rain in great sheets and buckets; rain in Niagara torrents; rain in Biblical proportions.

The skies had poured down their burden unceasingly for the past twenty-four hours, ever since I had left Olmstead, as if in synchrony with my foul, black mood. Nor did they seem disposed to stop.

Just beyond the walls of the Palace, the throbbing, gushing waters of the Charles were rising, rising, rising. I could feel them, even out of sight. It even seemed possible they would soon threaten to lap at the catwalk where I had eavesdropped, high as it was.

All the talk among the patrons of the Palace centred about roads swamped, bridges washed away, dams upriver that were bulging at their seams.

Something had to be done. About my anger, about the Professor, about the subversion of poor Olmstead. But what?

The Professor had been like a father to me and my sisters. We owed him our work, our maintenance, our purpose in life.

But didn't he in turn owe us something? Honesty, if nothing else?

Finally, when I had worked myself into a right tizzy, I stamped my way to Professor Fluvius's office, and barged in without knocking.

He was there, seated behind his big seashell desk, idle, back to me, looking out the window at the incessant precipitation with what I immediately sensed was a melancholy ruminativeness. I stood, quivering and silent, till at last he wheeled to face me. His long tresses, white as sea spume, framed a sad and sober visage.

"Ah, Charlene, my most local and potent child. I should have known it would be you who might tumble to my schemes. I hope you'll allow me to explain."

"What is there to explain! You're bent on accumulating a greedy power over your fellow men!"

The Professor chuckled wryly. "These men are not my fellows. But yes, I need to pull their strings for a while."

"To glorify yourself!"

Professor Fluvius arose and hastened toward me. I took a step or two backwards.

"No, Charlene! Not at all. Or rather, yes. I seek to glorify what I represent. The natural state of all creation. This city—It's an emblem of all that's wrong with mankind. That's why I established my Palace here, on the front lines of the battle. Can't you see what they're doing? Tearing down their hills and dumping them into the waters! It's an assault. Yes, an assault on creation. If they succeed here, they'll go on without compunction, dumping whatever they wish into the seven seas, into rivers and canyons. Before too long, the whole of nature will be naught but a soiled toilet! I had to stop them, here and now and hence forever. You must see that!"

The words of my master tugged at my loyalty and heart. But counterposed against them was my affection for Olmstead, and my own sense of thwarted individual destiny.

"No!" I yelled. "I won't let you! I'll stop you! Stop you now!"

And so saying, I slammed my small fists into his blue-vested chest.

The Professor's face assumed a wrathful mien I had never before witnessed. That blow seemed to unleash greater cataracts from the sky. The noise of the rain threatened to flood my ears. But I could still hear his words.

"You belong to me! You are naught but a tributary! You flow into my vastness! You shall not rebel!"

He gripped me fiercely by my upper arms. Instantly I felt tethers of strange energies enwrap us, coursing into and out of us both. For his part, Fluvius seemed to be drawing on some vast but distant reservoir, while my own forces were smaller, but closer to hand.

Immobile as statues, we struggled mightily in this invisible fashion, while the rain cascaded down.

And then somehow I felt the presence of my sister Naiads at my back, offering support and sustenance. I seemed to hear them speak with a single voice:

"Bold and deep-souled Nodens oversteps himself. He distrusts and hates all men. But we, we who wind our courses gently among them, fertilizing their fields, ferrying their goods, supplying their recreation—we do not. We must give them a chance to be their best selves. End this now, sister."

And I did, with their help.

Out the window that looked upriver, I could see the wall of dirty, debris-laden water barrelling down, high as the steeple of the Old North Church, aimed to sweep the shoreline clean, and take the Palace down.

Professor Nodens Fluvius saw too, and in the final moment before it hit us, I thought to detect a trace of pride and even approval in his expression.

*

When that liquid avalanche struck the Palace, tearing it off its foundations, drowning its boilers, I too dissolved, along with Fluvius and my sisters and even Usk. (Of the poor unfortunate mortals caught therein, I speak not.) I dissolved back to what I had been before I awoke on that damp coverlet, not knowing my name, back to an existence of endless flow, never the same from moment to moment, yet eternal, owning a mouth that pressed wetly against my old master, yet this time retaining my name.

Charlene, or Charlie, or Charles.

Contributors

Jacques Barcia is a weird fiction writer from Brazil. His stories have appeared in American, Brazilian and Romanian markets, such as *Everyday Weirdness, Electric Velocipede* and *Clarkesworld*, to name a few. When he is not writing, Jacques acts as lead singer for the Brazilian grindcore band *Rabujos*. The story "The Siege of Dr Vikare Bissett as Reported by Detective Carlos Werke" appears here for the first time.

Anatoly Belilovsky was born in Lvov, Ukraine, in time to watch tanks roll into Czechoslovakia in '68. He left it in 1975 as a teenager and, after a brief stint as a gas station attendant in Rome, Italy, came to the US in 1976, spent the summer learning English from *Star Trek* reruns, beginning Brooklyn Technical High School (Fred Pohl's alma mater) in the fall. A bachelor's degree from Princeton and an MD from the University of Connecticut completed this rather roundabout path to his current career as a paediatrician in Brooklyn, NY. The story "Kulturkampf" appears here for the first time.

Chris Butler has had stories published in *Asimov's, Interzone*, the anthology *The West Pier Gazette and Other Stories* (Three-Legged Fox Books, 2008) and other outlets. His novel, *Any Time Now*, was published by Cosmos Books in 2001. His story, "Have Guitar, Will Travel," appeared in *The Immersion Book of SF* (Immersion Press, 2010). He lives on the south coast of England and has just completed a new novel. The story "Steam Horse" appears here for the first time.

Elizabeth Counihan is from a writing family. Her father was a BBC journalist and her grandfather a novelist. Elizabeth was a family doctor in the National Health Service for many years. Her stories have appeared in *Asimov's, Realms of Fantasy, Nature Futures* and several other magazines and anthologies. She edited the British fantasy magazine *Scheherazade* and is currently working on a complicated fantasy novel. The story "Electrium" appears here for the first time.

Aliette de Bodard is a Campbell award finalist and a winner of the Writers of the Future award. She lives and works in Paris. Her work has appeared in *Interzone, Black Static, Realms of Fantasy, Beneath Ceaseless Skies*, and other venues. Her novels, *Servant of the Underworld*, and *Harbinger of the Storm* are available from Angry Robot. Her story, "Father's Last Ride," appeared in *The Immersion Book of SF* (2010). The story, "Memories in Bronze, Feathers, and Blood" was originally published in *Beneath Ceaseless Skies* (2010) and is reprinted here by permission.

Paul Di Filippo is the author of hundreds of short stories and several novels. A major influence in the field of speculative fiction, he has been a finalist for the Philip K Dick, BSFA, Hugo, Nebula and World Fantasy awards. He is also a reviewer for *Asimovs, The Magazine of Fantasy and Science Fiction, Interzone, Nova Express, The New York Review of Science Fiction, Science Fiction Eye* and *Science Fiction Weekly*. The story "Professor Fluvius's Palace of Many Waters" originally appeared in *Postscripts, No. 15* (2008) and appears here by arrangement with the author.

G.D. Falksen is the author of the serials "An Unfortunate Engagement" and "The Mask of Tezcatlipoca" which appear in *Steampunk Tales*. His work has also appeared in the *Footprints* anthology (Hadley Rille Books, 2009), as well as Tor.com and *Steampunk Reloaded* (Tachyon, 2010). The story "Cinema U" appears here for the first time.

Toby Frost studied law and was called to the Bar in 2001. Since then, he has worked as a private tutor, a court clerk and a legal advisor to the motor industry. Unable to become Great Britain's foremost space explorer, he is content just to write about space exploration instead. He has also produced film reviews for the book *The DVD Stack* and articles for *Solander* magazine. *Space Captain Smith* is his first novel. The story "Rogue Mail" appears here for the first time.

Tanith Lee is a preeminent master of the field. Over the years, her stories have seen publication in venues too numerous to list and her work has been anthologized multiple times. Tanith is the author of at least fifty-four novels—at last count, anyway—including the *Paradys Cycle* of books and the *Wolf Tower Sequence*. She has won or been nominated for the Nebula and the World Fantasy award several times over. Her story, "Tan," appeared in The Immersion Book of SF (Immersion Press, 2010). The story "Empire of Glass" appears here for the first time.

Gareth Owens has had stories published in *Nature, Mallorn: The Journal of the Tolkien Society, Ruins: Terra (anthology, Hadley Rille Books, 2007), The West Pier Gazette and Other Stories* (anthology, Three Legged Fox Books, 2007), and others. He is a writer resident on the south coast of England. His story, "Mango Dictionary and the Dragon Queen of Contract Evolution," has appeared in his collection *Fun With Rainbows* (Immersion Press, 2010) and The Immersion Book of SF (Immersion Press, 2010). The story "Follow That Cathedral!" appears here for the first time.

Gord Sellar is an American ex-patriot living in South Korea. His stories have appeared in such places as *Subterranean, Asimov's, Fantasy Magazine, Clarkesworld, Apex Digest* and others. He has been given an honorable mention on more than one occasion in *The Years Best Science Fiction*, edited by Gardner Dozois. His story, "The Broken Pathway," appeared in *The Immersion Book of SF* (Immersion Press, 2010). The story "The Clockworks of Hanyang" appears here for the first time.

James Targett has had stories published in *Hub, Andromeda Spaceways Inflight Magazine, Nanobison,* and the anthology *Under the Rose (Norilana Books, 2009)* among others. The story "The Machines of the Nephilim" appears here for the first time.

Lavie Tidhar is an eclectic writer who calls the world his home. His life spent on a kibbutz in Israel, time spent in South Africa, the UK, Asia and remote islands in the south Pacific have clearly shaped his worldview and his fiction. His work has appeared in *Interzone, Apex Digest, Fantasy Magazine, Clarkesworld, Strange Horizons* and selected anthologies. His books include *An Occupation of Angels, Hebrewpunk, Osama, Cloud Permutations, Gorel and the Pot-Bellied God,* as well as the trilogy *The Bookman, Camera Obscura, The Great Game* (forthcoming). His story, "Lode Stars," appeared in *The Immersion Book of SF* (Immersion Press, 2010). The story, "Leaves of Glass" was originally published by Pendragon Press (2006) and is reprinted here by permission.

Lightning Source UK Ltd.
Milton Keynes UK
UKOW050650191011

180570UK00001B/179/P